A BIG ELEPHANT HAS BEEN KILLED

A Big Elephant Has Been Killed

a novel

Yaw O. Agyeman

iUniverse, Inc.
New York Lincoln Shanghai

A Big Elephant Has Been Killed
a novel

iUniverse, Inc.

For information address:
iUniverse, Inc.
2021 Pine Lake Road, Suite 100
Lincoln, NE 68512
www.iuniverse.com

ISBN: 0-595-27128-6

Printed in the United States of America

For

Supi Kofi Nyan, my grandfather,
In loving memory,

And for
Terry, Claude-Salomon, Michael and Matthew Parker

By now it is a fabled story—of the quiet and wistful sort—spun often in casual detachment from the burden of its consequences, like so many stories of its kind. No teller bothers to remind the hearer anymore what the underlying depravity of the story has contributed to the continued dissolution of Sub-Saharan Africa's dignity, or to the needless waste of lives.

It is the story of the idealistic young auditor in post-independence Ghana, who was naïve enough to believe that the wealth of the newly independent nation was intended to benefit the entire nation, and on that belief, took the irregularities he noticed in the course of his work to his superior for corrective action. He had expected praise, but his superior is said to have responded with deep sadness in his eyes at the enormity of the young man's naivete.

"My dear young man," he'd said, "don't you know that Nkrumah, our president, has just killed an elephant? Why do you bother with all these accounting irregularities? There's enough for all of us to eat."

CHAPTER 1

*I*t occurred to Kofi Mensah—in the very few seconds before Chris Agyekum panicked and abandoned his cover—that he had forgotten to tell them that the elephant was definitely going to stop. To an extent this was not critical. The elephant was going to stop anyway, and they would pounce exactly according to the plan laid out: force the driver and the guard next to him out of the car and use them to convince the guards traveling in the back to surrender.

Perhaps it was even better that he had forgotten to tell them, for then they might have become slaves to the script, conjuring a particular set of expectations for precisely how it was all supposed to happen, and possibly panicking at the first sign of deviation from the script. Absent the certainty that the elephant would stop, he would not have allowed Akosua, right up to the final minute, to lie down in the middle of the road. He had asked her if she was fine with a ten to fifteen-minute wait—for the elephant was one of the few things that was ever on time in this land, and they knew when it was due. If she wasn't comfortable with the wait—any wait at all—they could hold off for another five minutes or so.

Akosua had shaken her head and said she was fine. Besides, she'd noted with the wriest of smiles, it wouldn't do for her to be spotted rushing to the middle of the road to lie down, would it? She had smiled say-

ing that, but Kofi was too conflicted to find any trace of humor in the moment.

He had taken her in his arms. "Don't worry, it will be alright, and soon over."

The message was in his eyes as well, but he did not specifically inform any of them that he had it on very good authority that the elephant would stop. It wasn't supposed to matter. They had left Akosua in the middle of the road and moved away to take shelter. For a while after they'd taken cover, Akosua stood there in the middle of the road, looking about her. Something about her motions disturbed him. She stood extremely still at first, then seemed to take in her surroundings with exaggerated longing, the way a traveler leaving for a long, long journey might look upon her children before the first step. He should have known.

As they watched her, she spread out her arms and began to circle around in the middle of the road, across from the shade of the imposing baobab tree. Almost as if she were absorbing all the natural beauty around her, she twirled at the spot—her eyes closed—and began to laugh. It was a perfectly serene sound, by far the happiest sound any of them had heard from her in at least five years. At the end of her laugh she went down gently to her knees and took some more time to absorb her surroundings. Then she sought Kofi out from where he had taken cover. He should have known—the secret was always there in her eyes.

But this was supposed to be the surest thing. Even allowing for the possibility of small deviations from the plot, it was impossible to see how the operation could go wrong. He did the best he could to offer her a final visual reassurance, and she smiled as if she had received the proffered comfort in his gaze. Then she lay down on her side, straddling the road, with her back to the direction from which the elephant would come.

A heavy surge of sadness swept over Kofi Mensah as he watched her lie down. Leading up to the moment, his emotions over the improbability of their intended act were at once over stimulated and dulled in a jarring state of mind underpinned by fear. It had been impossible to think straight while traveling a crooked path carved so willfully away from the light. And the fear was numbing, and all the more perplexing because there was no need to fear failure. So what did he have to fear from success? Kofi had kept his outward calm, and fought a desperate battle behind the veneer. The question was its own pain. He was afraid of the success of the mission because, in fact, the success of the mission would be the final blow to the essence of who he thought he was—the last, twisted mutilation of his moral character. But now, watching Akosua take her sacrificial position, Kofi's will just about gave, and the wave of sadness that rolled over him was so potent his first tears streamed down several minutes ahead of any awareness on his part. For a quick moment he was touched by the beginnings of understanding, a sort of a quick peek into the possible meaning of the mystery unfolding before them.

There was Akosua, the best soul among them, in her sacrificial position: Africa on the highway of progress. Dear God, if that were so—if Akosua were indeed the embodiment of Africa, drained of all creativity in managing her affairs to the point of willfully sacrificing her very life, what did that make him, the progenitor of this plot? Why were all the important women in his life dying in such sad, painful ways?

Kofi Mensah turned away from the question and fled deeper within. But he was gone for only a brief while before the prone figure of Akosua pulled him back. He was thankful for that. At the very least, he was honest enough to acknowledge that he had long moved past finding any inspiration from within, so he did well to stay away from himself, especially in a moment such as this, when the self was so full of reproach. Besides, why was his perspective so single-mindedly gloom and doom all the time?

So Akosua in her sacrificial position invoked a hapless Africa. But tweak the perspective just a little, and maybe this supposedly undignified act was in fact bravery at its most daring. The much ballyhooed highway of progress—what has it all been about anyway? Importing the values of the West, throwing aside African values, and to what end? So money can be made, siphoned away to the few, and grand economic theories raised on baffling assumptions to support that end. Even slavery had its rationalizations—heck some still defend it to this day. And through it all black people suffer. Well maybe Akosua was the first small cog in the money-making machine draining Africa of her soul. Kofi Mensah could feel his mood rise dramatically. This was so much better than the gloom and doom thoughts that were tormenting him shortly ago.

He took in the sight of Akosua again. The road had disappeared this time. She was still on her side, just as she lay now, but in a comfortable bed, looking at him as he massaged her hands. Years had passed since they lay siege to the elephant, and he had been able to provide Akosua with small comforts as she prepared for her final journey. She was smiling a relaxed, peaceful smile at him, and he could tell that she was about to depart.

"Is there anything else?" he asked.

She squeezed his hand, smiled and shook her head. Then, after some time had passed, she asked the same question back, "Is there anything else?"

"Tell Efuwa I'm sorry. I could have—I should have done so much better."

Again, she smiled. "Don't worry, she knows."

It was exactly for these memories yet to come, that any of this was justified. A more comfortable and dignified ending for Akosua might even cleanse his soul of the painful way his wife Efuwa had died. And beyond these small, personal joys, entire communities stood to reap the rewards of their exploit. When Kofi looked again, the image of Akosua in her sacrificial position had become beautiful, and he was visited by a teasing hint of calm. It was probably transient, but he savored it all the same. In the end, no matter the torment within, he simply needed to keep himself on an even keel until the operation was over.

In spite of the temporary emotional calm, he noticed that the tension in his body had grown so taut he was beginning to feel the rise of the dreaded pain in his nether regions—"Easter pain" he called it. He would have to fight past even that.

❋　　　❋　　　❋

It came to him for the very first time many Easters ago. He was long a jaded man already, and in the end this pain came to compound the multiple of pains defining his life. But as with all experiences it was most memorable the very first time.

He had woken up ahead of his wife, an event that almost never happened anymore, and realized why he was the first to rise when he felt the tingling pain down below. Initially it registered as a dull, numbing pain, of the sort one might get from a full bladder too long held. But he quickly realized that he had no inclination to urinate, so the prickly erection holding his groins in taut tension was not on account of a full bladder. Under most other circumstances this should have been a rather happy event. An erection this hard was not a commonplace occurrence these days, when he walked about under the overwhelming sense of heavy impotence.

But then this was an erection, so the easy fall into happiness had to make way first for the more familiar emotion of guilt. Even for one who no longer went to church except on Easter and Christmas Sundays, the one certainty about his early Catholic upbringing was the robust terror of guilt over any sensations associated with sex. He had lived a lifetime without being able to successfully shake the association. It would have been nice if, with so many more important things to worry about, he could count on something as simple as a healthy sense of his own sexuality. But such are the ironies of life, that at forty-five, and with so much weighing on him constantly, he would find himself riddled first with guilt on any reminder of sex—the legacy of childhood indoctrination. Still all this was for a moment, for right past the obligatory ode of conscience to guilt, the small, dull pain took on an edge. It was as if his own body had been toying with him, teasing him out of sleep on the lesser pain the better to teach him about real pain.

He would describe the pain to his friend Kwame thus: "It felt like someone took a blade and used it to slice my penis open right down the length."

The pain had doubled him over, throwing him off the bed, and the guttural groan that issued involuntarily out of him woke his wife. Efuwa, for that was his wife's name, had taken a moment to get her bearings. By then the pain that had doubled him over had, just as quickly fled his body, leaving him sprawled out on his back on the floor, with his erection still straining through his pants. The pain, which had lasted for all of a couple of minutes, had drenched him with perspiration. Efuwa had frowned with puzzlement.

Strangely embarrassed, Kofi had said, "I fell off the bed."

Efuwa had said nothing, but her eyes drifted with great reluctance to the erection he was not covering, and the sight, he could swear, made her wince.

"Oh, I guess I need to go," he'd said, gathering himself.

That was the first Easter pain. It had been exceptional enough that he had to incur the cost of a visit to a doctor, but he was told after the check up that there was nothing the matter with him, at least not physically. He'd been grateful for that. But if this was all psychosomatic, it was an amazing leap for an imagination that had always been modest, at best. The second time the same pain doubled him over, he was stunned by the realization that it was again Easter Sunday. Thus was born "Easter pain". The source of it came to him with time. It was simply the coming together of too many sources of stress, fleshed out in this perplexing reminder of his social impotence. Mostly the occasion of Easter terrified him, and made him ever so ashamed of where he was in life. It terrified him because this was precisely the occasion when expectations from loved ones for obligatory gifts peaked, right along with his felt irrelevance for his inability to meet them.

Around the time of the first Easter pain, he was sitting once at the usual spot he occupied with his friends in front of the *Lonely Hearts* bar. Directly across the street from the bar stood the home of Nti, proprietor of *Lonely Hearts*, who had bought the land and built on it not long after the open market that used to stand there had lost its legs. Nti was one of the very few who had his home sited right by the main drag through town, alongside the small shops that lined the street up and down this straight, two-and-a-half mile stretch. Although much of his house was not painted, Nti had taken pains to paint his bar the red, gold and green of the national flag—each color covering a third of the building in startlingly inexact horizontal strips—with a black star painted right above the front entrance. Clients to the bar hardly sat inside however, so each late afternoon, when Nti opened his bar, he would bring out half his chairs and tables and set them right outside. The bar's colors made it far and away the gaudiest sight down the length of the road.

Since this was the main road through town, a gutter ran alongside it. The gutter, which was open, was only about two feet wide, and two deep. It ran right with the road, serving as the only conduit for liquid waste from the homes and shops lined up and down past *Lonely Hearts*, and was constantly getting clogged with debris. Each time it clogged up, folks would simply throw their waste liquid right into the street—on occasion Kofi had been drenched this way with laundry waste—until some miracle unclogged the debris in the gutter and prompted renewed usage. Time was, this was the only paved road in town, but it hadn't been maintained, and so the buildings on the road, which used to be the only reasonably clean ones aside from the rich peoples homes up the hill, were now soaked in dust like every other house.

The friends were sitting at their usual spot in front of the bar around the time of Kofi's first Easter pain when they saw a hawk come swooping down for a chick that had wandered away from its mother hen—a common enough adventure around here. As it turned out, the mother hen, somewhat belatedly, had noticed the attack and was racing in at full tilt to protect her young. Trying to be of some help, Kofi had succeeded only in worsening matters. He picked a stick to swing at the hawk, but managed to interfere with the mother hen, scaring it off its course, and next thing, the elephant rolled by and smashed the hen.

Ewura Ekuwa, to whom the hen belonged, blamed Kofi. She cried about losing the only hen in her pen that could lay eggs, helping her supplement her income, and compelled Kofi to compensate her. That unanticipated expenditure was significant because shortly thereafter, Kofi's daughter developed some toothache and needed a procedure that cost him so much he was not able to buy his son a new uniform for the school year, forcing the kid to wear the same uniform from the previous school year. And for that his son would later be heard saying that he had "…lost most of my respect for my father."

A couple of weeks after that, the little girl Ruth Amoah came to him while he sat drinking with his friends. She said her uncle, David Amoah, wanted Kofi to pay him back immediately the money he had borrowed from him. Kofi sent the messenger back.

"Go tell your uncle I don't owe him any money. He must be delusional."

The girl Ruth returned a while later. "My uncle says you would do well not to insult your lenders. He says you borrowed some money from him the other day when your made-in-Ghana slippers came undone and you needed some money to have it fixed and he was kind enough to lend you some. He says if you had integrity you would have paid him back before he ever asked. And now you are calling him delusional for being kind to you."

"You told him I said he was delusional?"

The messenger shrugged. "That's what you said."

"It was not intended to be repeated to him."

The young girl simply shrugged. In the uneasy silence, his friends had looked on with puzzlement, but Kofi had demurred.

"I am truly shocked. That was several months ago, when I borrowed the money. I have given that man money on several occasions in the past without ever asking for any of it back. Go tell him I don't have the money. I'll pay him later."

The messenger returned yet again, a while later. "My uncle says that you always say you don't have the money."

Kofi had found himself, incredibly, arguing with the little girl. "What is he talking about? This is the first time he's asked me about this money."

"I'm only a messenger. He says that you always say you don't have the money, but you sit here all the time drinking with your friends. And what you drink is not even the cheaper, local *akpeteshie*, but the more expensive imported beer."

Akosua offered to pay, but Kofi had declined the offer. "Go to my wife and tell her I sent you to collect the money."

When he got home later on, his wife Efuwa was not talking to him, and he understood not to force the issue. For reasons big and small, her patience appeared to be dwindling all the time. And failing her was the absolutely worst part of the shame he felt within. He had taken on this responsibility to provide and protect, some twenty years ago, brimming with a livelier sense of his manhood, and beyond merely failing at the task, he'd missed the boat altogether. His wife worked alongside him with undeterred patience, finding inventive ways to stretch the income he brought home, and in most months, earning even more than he did through her trading enterprises. He knew this, even though she did her level best to protect his ego by never letting him know exactly how much her personal endeavors were contributing to the family pot. She never did anything to make him feel this hopelessly worthless. She'd been nothing in their years of marriage if not completely supportive, open and generous—gifts he had done little to give back in equal measure. So his general antipathy had little to do with the actions of his wife. But over a lifetime of finding no validation, self-loathing becomes as natural as it is potent.

"I detect spite in her eyes sometimes," he'd confided once to Kwame in a moment of stupendous honesty.

Kwame had smiled, lightly, without agreeing. "You're taking marital paranoia to new lows."

And in the dour mood holding his heart captive over so many years of failure in obtaining a firm grasp of his place in the world, he'd said, "I think…actually I fear that perhaps it's inevitable."

"What's inevitable?"

"The hatred that develops between man and wife."

Somewhat alarmed, Kwame had said, "That's ridiculously cynical."

"What do you think your wife's done with all her pent up frustrations from year after God-forsaken year of living this hard life without much reprieve despite all your exploits?"

"Speak for yourself. My wife does not have pent-up frustrations."

"You believe your wife Agnes is a happy woman?"

Kwame had changed the subject, and Kofi was certain his friend had done so to avoid coming to fisticuffs with him. You don't ask a man if his wife is happy on cynical presumptions of the unhappiness of all married women. Important body parts have been lost on much less cynical presumptions. Still Kofi came out of that conversation feeling justified in his self-inflicted sense of impotence. So perhaps this was the reasonable secret evolution had decreed married men from ever sharing with those yet to marry—that eventually their blissful union, weighing on the woman who must do so much to keep anything functioning, sours her to a state of silent seething.

Certainly Efuwa had every reason to feel deceived, even if she could appreciate, in her better moments, that the deception had not been deliberate. But she had been deceived by the circumstances that conspired to reduce the man in whom there had been so much promise to a groveling, empty shelf of a man, increasing her work all the more, in the absence of ameliorating opportunities. Is it possible for anything but the most bitter feeling of deception, fueled further by the daily witnessing of the imperfections of the betrayer, to boil in the heart of a loved one so betrayed? Why didn't Efuwa complain more about her disappointments? Why did she choose to bear so much dashed hopes in noble silence?

It was around the time of the first Easter pain that Nii-Odartey, the squat elder, died of short stature. Actually he had not been an elder. Nii-Odartey had only been thirty-eight when he died, but the rigors of living had squeezed so much life out of him he looked like he was an elder. People pegged him at sixty-five. He died trying to get to a set of keys that he'd thrown over the top of a trunk, which sat on a standing cupboard a full feet taller than he was. In a big rush to leave the house, Nii-Odartey failed to build a sturdy ladder to get him to the top of his trunk, on top of the standing cupboard.

The stool he lifted was in good condition, but he set it on a chair with a weak leg. He must have known that the leg of the chair was weak, as it was the only chair in the room. But possibly Nii had gotten away a few times propping the chair, gimpy leg and all, as a ladder, so he was acting on a known, acceptable risk. As soon as he straightened his gait on top of the stool, Nii-Odartey fell. His fall, though sudden, should have been benign, good for a bruised ego, nothing more. But somehow Nii-Odartey caught his bedpost awkwardly with his neck on the way down, and died.

People said he was meant to go; that God used Nii's short stature as the means. Indeed, unless God wanted him to go that way, wouldn't *he* have given Nii-Odartey enough natural height to allow him to reach the keys without need for the makeshift ladder? So in a way God had set all this up from the get-go. *He* was going to take

Nii-Odartey on this occasion so *he* gave the man short stature and in his own motions of life, Nii acquired this chair that would develop the gimpy leg. He spends a few occasions successfully using the chair as a ladder, gimpy leg and all, until one morning, in a rush to his destiny, he climbs atop the chair and *crunch*! Just like that. Rest in peace. At the hospital, the nurse on duty wrote down what his relatives said, that Nii-Odartey had died of short stature. She laughed when they told her the story.

"So it was an accident that killed him."

One of the relatives, disturbed that the nurse would find the story funny at all, had said, "How could it have been an accident if the Supreme Being had it all planned out to occur just as it did?"

The nurse, wiping the smile off her face, had nodded understanding. "I guess God does work in mysterious ways."

Years later, some bright medical student interning at the hospital saw the cause of death as he browsed through old files for research ideas, and wondered if the nurse had meant that the man had died of dwarfism. He asked this of the doctor running the hospital at the time. What he really wanted to know was whether, assuming the nurse had meant dwarfism, the doctor thought dwarfism was associated with a higher risk of mortality. The doctor and intern actually pondered the possibility of making careers on studying dwarfs; there were so many possible questions to ask. Did dwarfs have the same intelligence as non-dwarfs? Did they have the same sex drive, or was it proportionately smaller? Were they pathologically envious of non-dwarfs? There appeared to be a great bit of fertile ground on which to build a career, but then they found that there weren't that many dwarfs in Ghana on whom to build a career, and, moreover, that dwarfs were not really great biological anomalies.

It was Nii-Odartey who, in the five years before he died, played the Ghana lotto every week. He had told Kofi that it was not the winning alone that raised the spirits; that in fact, there was just as much joy in the fantasies that came to life in the time from the purchase of the ticket to the draw, when the mind could still afford to lie to itself about what it would do with all that anticipated wealth.

"And as you know," he would say, "the mind must keep dreaming if we are to survive each day. Spend a minute in the company of those who have lost the ability to dream. You have never seen death in colder form."

Kofi was in agreement. "It's understandable, won't you say?" he had noted to his friend Kwame on a different day. "Each time I look at the man, I see someone who absolutely needs to dream just to survive."

Kwame had refused the banter. "Beware, my friend. That might be how others see you."

Kofi had not been thrilled. He began to wonder whether, as Kwame had intimated, his view of Nii was more or less the view others had of him—a miserable man who needed to keep dreaming of the long odds of a lotto win if he was to survive, and hold on to whittling sanity while he was at it. To his utter dismay, he joined the lottery crusade for a while, but did so in secret, fearing that he was being judged already in the scornful eyes of society.

But it was not so simple. Nii-Odartey was never married, and never had any children. For him this was a privilege. Kofi, however, could not claim the same privilege. Too often for Kofi what mattered wasn't even the dream between the time of the purchase of a ticket to the draw. Too frequently he couldn't afford a ticket at all, after he had given the wife her appropriate due for the upkeep of the family, and what remained needed to be kept in pocket for some beer. For no matter how sweet the dream, no sane person should ever waste beer money chasing after it—you just don't do that.

Kofi's dream then, was for a day, or more precisely for a month, when he could afford lottery tickets without taking away from his beer money. Then at least he could buy the tickets, which would allow him to fantasize about winning, which would in turn allow him to move on to the sweeter fantasies about all the things he could do with the win. But at least there was some hope then.

❧   ❧   ❧

Perhaps, too, Kofi had been grasping back then onto the puzzling hope that the world did turn on some mysterious justice, when all was said and done. And if it did, then men of integrity—even self-anointed men of integrity such as himself—who went about their lives on the flailing wings of social responsibility, hedging their bets on morality and fair play, would live up to age sixty and be prosperous, and die happy, timely deaths, leaving behind wonderful children and a loving partner, and multitudes of caring friends to miss them and say, "truly, truly, this was a great soul that walked among us." And at the other side, spirits eager to share in their great dignity would welcome them.

The lucky ones seemed to live this funny fantasy. Even Agyei Bimpong, who lived in that big house of his down the street, seemed to be enjoying just such a life. And Agyei was nobody's saint. Heaven knows, Agyei hardly ever bet on morality. But Agyei was blessed, of God and man. He was a man of great wealth in a place and time where even the God of Christians seemed giddily partial to the wealthy. It didn't seem to matter much that Agyei had some thirty-five children with some twelve women, or that nobody knew exactly what business this businessman did. The only thing that seemed to matter was that he reaped considerable wealth from whatever he did, and waved a penis that was suddenly immensely attractive to so many women they did not mind where his insatiable probing took him.

There was a story told, first heard by Kofi when he sat with his four friends at the same spot they occupied routinely in the late afternoon of working days—in front of *Lonely Hearts*—about Agyei showing up at one of his rented flats and asking for the usual, from the young girl he had there.

"The usual?"

Edom, the storyteller, had not appeared particularly excited by the recounting. Then again, since his time at the asylum, Edom had never shed the perpetual stupor in his eyes—that certain look of one who was there without ever being there. He took a tiny sip of his beer, licking the lip of the bottle, and set the bottle back on the table, in the liquid ring of its own sweat.

He'd said, "Agyei had the girl cook him a meal and serve it to him naked. They say he loves to have his girls serve him his food completely naked. Then while he sat to eat, she administered to him under the table."

"Administered?"

"Lip service. It gets better. He has these special glass tables in the apartment that allow him to see what is being done to him while he eats."

Chris Agyekum, one of the friends in their close group of five, squeezed his face in utter confusion.

Kofi Mensah had said, "That's his usual?"

Edom had leaned back in his seat, and sat quietly poised, newly engrossed by the adventurous meddling of one particular fly. His left hand reached out gently and slowly to cradle his beer bottle, and the muscles in his right hand visibly tightened, ever so ominously. He waited, bidding his time, watching. The fly of his sudden interest, presumably oblivious, returned closer to the lip of the bottle, circled it, separated, and finally returned to land right on the lip of the bottle. Edom held for a moment longer. Then he shot out his right hand, palm open, and swiped at the space a few inches above the lip of the bottle, closing his palm in the same fast motion. The fly was gone. Edom shook his closed palm to ascertain that the fly was trapped in there.

Kofi squirmed in his seat, his face contorting with untamed disgust. "You know, Edom, that's a totally disgusting habit. Stop behaving like a stupid little child."

Edom had released the fly immediately. A look of despair seized his face, and Kofi had felt guilty for his outburst. Habits from the asylum—that was all it was. There was never any reason to make Edom feel worse for his unfortunate fate.

Kofi had said, "I'm sorry. But it's a terrible habit. Really, you must stop playing with flies."

❦   ❦   ❦

He was still a young boy when it first dawned on Kofi that the presumed piety of the poor is hardly automatic. It was a revelation. The poor went to church every Sunday, and seemed so eager to invoke the great compassion and mercy of God at every turn. The few wealthy folks about town rarely made it to church, and they were not ones to acknowledge the hand of God in much that happened to or around them. It all made sense, this easy confirmation of the difficulty the rich were supposed to have getting to heaven. In those youthful years Kofi felt sorry for the rich: the easy indulgence of this cycle seemed like such pittance for an eternity of burning. Maybe that was why the poor felt comfortable in their poverty.

His first anxiety came when one of his cousins—it must have been Lamptey—came home from his very first term in secondary school and refused to go to church anymore. He wasn't the first to return home after an absence and claim to have found the sort of enlightenment that precluded the need to attend church, but he was the first person Kofi personally approached for an explanation. Lamptey, with a comment that rattled Kofi's brain, had said that religion was a drug to keep the poor passive and poor.

"Ganja of the masses," he'd said, between a deep inhalation on a roll of marijuana. Then, thinking it over, he'd said, "I mean, hashish of the masses. That's what religion is. No, I mean opium; opium of the masses. Man, this is some powerful stuff!" The last comment was on what he was smoking. "Anyway, that's all religion is. And I tell you, opium is not something you want to mess with."

The comment shook the young Kofi from his comfortable acceptance of his earlier lessons into a state of permanent unease, for which he did not forgive Lamptey for a long, long time. He began to pay closer attention, and came to realize something even more interesting. The prayers of the poor were overwhelmingly for wealth, and not wealth of the spiritual variety either. How could this be? How could those supposedly on the inner track to God be praying all the time for a chance to join those on the outside?

Kwame had taken the question when Kofi asked it of him, and pondered it for a short while. "It's possible the wish of the poor isn't quite literally for wealth, but for a little comfort from the harshness of life. Its main purpose might be psychological."

"There is something twisted about it, don't you think?"

"What do you mean?"

Kofi had said, "I am thinking of Nii-Odartey. Difficult life, would you agree?"

Kwame shrugged. "He tried his best, I suppose."

"He carved his happiness on a pipe dream built on the blessing of mathematical inadequacy."

"Come again?"

"His whole happiness was based on playing the lotto, and praying for a win."

"Well, not entirely. I think it allowed him to dream a better life. He worked hard all the same."

"Why didn't he pick up a weapon and steal, since his dream was merely for wealth?"

Kwame chuckled with some unease. "Why don't we all?"

"You dream of wealth, too?"

"Oh come on, Kofi. Who doesn't?"

"I must be the biggest fool of them all, Kwame. I know we all dream of what we don't have. But I don't particularly crave wealth."

Kwame had turned a quizzical look on him. "What do you dream of, then?"

Kofi said, after a moment, "Validation, I suppose. And understanding."

"Ah, Kofi. Are you absolutely sure that's the full dream? This wish of Solomon brought him great wealth and prestige, too. Is that part of your dream for understanding?"

"Show me a little bit of respect, Kwame."

"Then you truly are the worst fool, Kofi."

"Chris tells me that's exactly what Edom says about me behind my back."

Kwame laughed. "I'm sure there's a lot Edom says behind all our backs."

Kofi had given him a moment of indulgence. "If your dream is for wealth, why don't you pick up a weapon and take what you have coming to you?"

"Now who is showing whom disrespect? I am not a thief, Kofi."

"But does that matter? Do you believe that the wealth of, say, Agyei, is honestly earned?"

Kwame was silent for a moment. "How am I to know?"

"He says he's a businessman. Isn't that a euphemism here for a crook?"

"Well, I think the idea is that you're a crook only if you're caught."

"Exactly. I'm willing to contend that none of us honest, hard workers are ever going to get as wealthy as he is. So the man must be doing something crooked."

"And supposing he is?"

"I come back to my point about Nii-Odartey. Are the poor praying to God for the mettle to become crooked? Or at the end of the day, is poverty the worst sin of them all?"

Kwame had chuckled with some unease. "You're being silly. But I see your point. There might be some hypocrisy there. In some limited way, the poor might want it both ways—fortune on earth and paradise hereafter. But so do the rich—I mean, who doesn't? The poor, in their defense, have limited choices. I fear that you place too much blame on a group with little choice."

CHAPTER 2

*L*ike the calm before a storm, Akosua's first thoughts after she took her position were gentle. Tears had gathered in her eyes while she laughed her serene laugh before she went down to her knees. By the time she took her prone position, and closed her eyes, the tears had begun to flow, but she wasn't actually sad just then.

All that was a necessary ambivalence, perhaps, but as soon as her eyes closed, she saw the figure of the child. At first the child was lying down, and she was walking towards it. Somehow, the child's bed suddenly disappeared, and the child was lying bare in a forest. It began to cry, prompting Akosua, with a rising heartbeat, to quicken her pace to the rescue. But as she neared the child, an incredible pain in her back pulled her legs from underneath her, and suddenly she was the one lying down, in exactly her sacrificial position, and the child, quickly maturing, was taking its early steps towards her. The pace of the child was agonizingly slow, but just before Akosua might have run out of patience, the child stood at arm's length from her. When she reached out to touch the child, whose face was somehow shielded from her, the child stepped away from her.

"Who are you?"

The child stepped out of the obscurity, still always beyond her reach, and snatched her breath away. Akosua was looking at herself. The child stood there with innocence so pure, and hope so large she cast a radiant *glow about her. She stood there devoid of cynicism, unafraid and unaffected. Akosua closed her eyes for a moment and looked into her own heart. It was a struggle initially, but she mustered the necessary determination to fight past the initial fear of what lay within.*

As if on cue, the child started to laugh, although not exactly in a mocking tone. "There isn't enough time for you to find me within yourself."

The child drew closer. Akosua wanted nothing more than to reach out for a touch, but the child's proximity was weakening her. The child walked to within a breath of her and stopped. Now Akosua saw that the child was not the same child. Her looks were intact in the child, but it was a young boy looking at her now. Akosua went through a succession of quick connections, trying desperately to understand, and felt an inkling of irritation. The apparition of the young boy promised none of the understanding she craved.

"Are you my unborn child?"

The child, perfectly radiant, simply stood and studied her. His eyes were the eyes of her father, every bit as seasoned and just as kind.

"I don't feel less of a woman for not having had you."

"Then why did you summon me here?"

She took a moment. "You are every child," she said. "I feel for your generation."

"I see."

"What is your name?"

"I am every child. So you said."

The child reached out to touch her, but before he could, he was pulled away. Akosua, with great irritation, followed the hands lifting the child. She wanted to protest, but her voice had suddenly abandoned her. Through the fog, the child reappeared in the arms of Efuwa. The sight of her sent a chill down Akosua's spine, but the fear was short-lived, for the gentle demeanor on Efuwa's face, coupled with her very kind smile, overwhelmed all fear. Akosua tried to rise, but the weakness in her body was complete now; she could barely move a muscle. Efuwa came to her, sat down with the child and took her hand, bathing her in a warm glow and opening her heart to the child she had failed to find within herself a short while ago. She finally could touch the child, without moving a muscle. The three of them sat in silence for what seemed like forever, until Akosua could feel the deeper peace brought by the two.

Finally, Efuwa said, "You remember the saying?"

She must have planted it even as she asked the question, because the words came quite automatically to Akosua, "Every generation must, out of relative obscurity, find its destiny, and having found it, fulfill it, or betray it."

Efuwa nodded. "There is truth in that. Do not despair on behalf of the generation yet to come. They have their own searching to do."

"Even when we've betrayed them?"

"Leave all judgment to the judge. Here and now you are responsible only for your own life."

Akosua swallowed. She had so many questions, and no time at all. "Did I fulfill my destiny?"

Efuwa smiled. "I can't tell you that. Did you not hear the voice of God?"

"When?"

"It will come to you. Stay attentive."

Another moment passed.

"It gets difficult before the light," said Efuwa. "Sometimes we forget about the light. Don't let the pain blind you."

In that very moment, Akosua heard the roar of the engine, and Efuwa and the child disappeared in a fast twinkle. The intrusion of the sound was so jolting she thought it was right upon her, but in fact the elephant had just rounded the corner, and was still a little over a mile away from her. Through a dangerous ambush of potholes, she heard the armored car sink and jump, rattling sturdy metal parts into the space of the quiet surrounding, and begin to pick up speed.

❦   ❦   ❦

When they first decided on the location, Kofi had wanted them to lay the siege all the way at the very end of the ambush stretch, in the direction away from where the elephant would arrive. That would have meant that the elephant would have to cover the full two-mile stretch of the ambush site before it got to Akosua. The obvious drawback to the idea, pointed out by Edom, was that setting the ambush too close to the opposite end of the elephant's entry increased the likelihood that a car coming from that end would completely surprise them. And they obviously needed no witnesses. This was the main flaw in their choice of location. But it was a minor flaw, and all things considered, an inconsequential one, since there was really no better place to lay siege to the elephant.

It was odd, the location, in that it almost invited thoughts of an ambush. What was interesting about the location was that although it was just one isolated stretch on the long, bumpy, pothole-riddled road that passed through Mankraso and wound its way like a burrowing creature through the forgotten towns scattered about the region, here the road suddenly straightened out, and narrowed inexorably to the point where it was impossible to see how two cars could share it.

The first time Kofi encountered the stretch as a young boy traveling to Kumasi for the very first time, he thought he was going to die, along with every passenger in the tro-tro. They were eating up the potholes at an amazing speed, approaching a small roadside hill that hid all view of the road beyond. Right at the hill, the road suddenly disappeared before them, twisting away on a sharp, nearly perpendicular angle. If the driver had encountered this sharp curve before, his driving said nothing of it, because he threw the van on the effort to stay the course. Miraculously, the van kept its balance.

But even more spectacularly, the road beyond the hill had suddenly narrowed to something that could, at best, accommodate one car, if barely. And there was another car already on the road, barreling towards them with the same speed they were barreling towards it. Kofi remembered that his initial fear had been so sudden and intense that he barely had any time to register a reaction. Someone had called on Christ of Nazareth to save them all. But their driver had not seemed the least bit perturbed. He had actually been smiling in reaction to the fear of the passengers, and as if to mock them, he picked up speed. The other driver, apparently possessed of the same addiction for danger, shot his passenger van at them. The two drivers had been smiling at each other.

Just before the two cars could collide, both drivers shifted half the weight of their vehicles off the road, then regained it as soon as they were past each other. Sighs of relief flew out of open mouths, and the passengers angrily told the driver to slow down before he got everyone killed. It didn't take very long for them to cover the two-mile stretch. There was a giant baobab tree to the left of the road if you were traveling from Mankraso. It sat just past the halfway mark of the stretch, a bit out of place, like African heads of state at a meeting of world governing bodies, although the tree was far more imposing in this surrounding. Another roadside hill stood at the opposite end, blocking view of the road beyond, and again they were thrown when the driver took the sharp curve away from the stretch.

Past the stretch between the two hills, the secondary forest, which seemed to be embracing the road over the stretch, opened up again, losing the intimacy. Then the journey became uneventful the rest of the way, even after the road met the bigger freeway—some forty miles northeast of Mankraso—that connected much of these places to the bastions of Ghanaian civilization, Kumasi being the closest of those bastions.

The stretch between the two hills sat twenty miles from the town of Mankraso, and another five or so miles from Yensu, the closest town through which the trains made a stop. If you wanted to plot a crude killing of the elephant, with some thought to using the train as an initial getaway means, this was not a bad choice for an ambush.

There was, however, another important potential flaw about the ambush site, which Kwame raised. "The element of surprise would be all-important in this undertaking, yes?"

Kofi nodded.

"What would justify our presence around the area? What I mean is, what would prevent the driver of the elephant from being suspicious at the first sight of a pedestrian around there, and stepping on the gas?"

"There are some farm lands nearby," had said Kofi. "We could be farmers."

     ❧   ❧   ❧

On the very last day before they were to lay siege to the elephant, Edom walked into *Lonely Hearts* with the biggest smile anyone had ever seen on him since he was a little boy.

"I am walking on water, people!" he announced. "I am walking on air!"

He had always had a quaint swagger in his walk—for back in the day Edom was one of the best footballers of his generation—but on this day the swagger had emerged into the limelight from the forced humility of years gone by. He was practically sauntering. He burst into *Lonely Hearts* with beads of happy sweat trickling down his forehead, and looked expectantly about the bar. He had hoped it would be packed, but there was hardly any guests there—just Amponsah, Konadu and Anan the barber. Amponsah and Konadu were sitting together over a game of checkers, and Anan, who was sitting at the bar, was watching their game and holding some idle banter with Nti, the proprietor of the bar.

"Isn't it just a beautiful day, my friends?"

Eyebrows went up in collective curiosity. This was an amazing bit of happy energy from the usually dour Edom. The group of four awaited the follow-up.

"One round of drinks on the house!"

The eyes of Nti, the proprietor, narrowed. "Are you out of your mind?"

Edom corrected himself. "I mean on me! One round of drinks for everyone in the house, on me. And I don't mean one round of the local stuff either. I mean one round of imported beer. Put it on my credit. And Egya Nti, I'd like to take this moment to confess that I've always had strong feelings for your daughter Grace. I know people say she is not so good looking, but I think she's beautiful, full of generosity and kindness. In fact, I intend to ask you for her hand very soon, after I've had some fun. Isn't this just a beautiful day, people?"

He stretched out his arms where he stood, and inhaled with furious intensity, as though he was devouring the intake into his lungs. For a moment he walked towards them as if he intended to hug each one of them, but Amponsah, who would have been the first to be hugged, looked mystified and frightened, and Edom thought better of it. Instead he twirled where he stood, with such energy that he lost his balance, and went staggering into some of the furniture, knocking his head against the back of a chair before he regained his balance and avoided further injury. The close call did nothing to dampen his spirits.

"I see the furniture is old. We'll have to do an upgrade. We can put nicer tiles on the floor and bring in more comfortable chairs for the clients. Oh it's a beautiful day, friends. It's a beautiful day in a beautiful world. I love you all so much! No, really, I mean what I said: I love you all!"

He said this as he danced out of the bar, leaving a baffled audience in his wake.

❦   ❦   ❦

Before any thoughts of the moment they were about to face could disturb his mind, Edom walked to his position with a smile on his face. He was recalling the surprised looks on the faces of the four men in the bar, and how heartwarming it felt to be alive again. He felt that Egya Nti, owner of the bar, was a lucky man. Somehow, by a strange stroke of luck, the man had fathered the beautiful Grace, whom Edom intended to marry—and now Egya Nti stood to benefit from Edom's generosity when they became in-laws. He would ask the hand of his daughter soon, even though he did not intend to get married right away. Asking Grace's hand from her father would ensure that no one else's proposal would be considered. But having secured that assurance, he didn't really intend to marry her right away.

There was so much living to do before that. When he thought of the sweet life awaiting him—the sweet life people like Agyei lived—his heart fluttered with warm anticipation.

❦   ❦   ❦

Imagine, for instance, this story he heard about Agyei some years back. On the day he related the story to his friends, he'd paused somewhere near the start to catch a fly, and Kofi had annoyed him greatly with his insensitive comment about fly-catching being a disgusting habit. He might have said something back, but for the fact that Kofi had been buying him his drinks that day, as he did most of the time.

The story he had heard was about Agyei going to one of his flats and having one of his young girls cook him a meal, serve it to him naked and administer him lip service while he sat to eat. Edom told the story exactly as his sister, who had heard it at the market place, told it to him.

"So the young woman is catering to Agyei while he eats. Agyei had coached her on how he liked it."

This lip service thing, from what Edom understood, had become Agyei's favorite thing since somebody did it to him in England or something.

His sister had said, "As this is going on, someone comes barging in into the flat before they can cover up. The intruder turns out to be another of Agyei's girls. He had invited her there on the wrong day, and since all his girls have keys to his flats, the girl just let herself in. Not only that, she had met the rector from the church on her way and made the trip with him. The priest was paying one of those unannounced visits to see about getting some donations from the rich man, and found him sitting at his dining table having a meal, while a naked girl gave him lip service. You know what happens?"

Sheepishly, Edom shook his head.

"Well, the girlfriend who just arrived is extremely hurt, as you can imagine. She begins to scream obscenities at the man and goes after the naked girl who was doing Agyei's bidding. And all the while, the priest is standing there making excuses for Agyei, saying that the Lord Jesus Christ has great compassion for the upright man fighting valiantly against his weakness."

When Edom relayed the story to his friends, this part had been so fascinating to him he could barely control himself long enough to describe it.

"The priest called him an upright man, people, I kid you not. He referred to Agyei as an upright man, and chastised the girls for being burdensome temptations. He is said to have told the girls that they should beware because, as the Lord had said, temptation must come, but woe onto them through whom temptation comes."

Edom had been particularly interested to see the reaction of Kofi, Kwame and Akosua to the story, but it was Chris Agyekum, clearly the most confused person at the table, who actually reacted first.

He'd said, "When you say lip service, do you mean that the girl kneels in front of the man as he eats and sings his praises?"

Edom had found himself in uncontrollable peals of laughter in spite of himself. "I guess you could say she does that, if her mouth wasn't full."

"Oh. So she's eating while kneeling in front of him?"

"No, Chris."

"Then what is her mouth full with?"

"Him, of course."

Chris had sat in silence for yet a while longer, still perplexed.

Edom, somewhat impatiently, rolled his eyes, then clarified, "They take his thing in their mouth."

But his clarification only seemed to confuse Chris further. "So you are saying that the man likes to have girls put his thing in their mouth?"

"Yes, that's what I just said."

"Why?"

"It's pleasurable, I guess," was Edom's uneducated supposition.

"Eyi! My ears have heard some amazing things! But you know, I still don't understand. What do they do, exactly? Do they chew on it?"

"God no!" It was Kofi who offered the answer. "That would be painful. They lick on it."

"What are they licking?"

"Just the skin. You should have somebody do it to you some time. It feels very good."

"You've had this done to you before?"

"I hear it feels very good," Kofi had clarified in face of Chris' horrified reaction.

"And they do this sort of thing in England? Are you sure it is not just a myth?"

"Well, it can't be a myth if it's happening right here."

Chris remained in a trance. "That is just amazing to me. Imagine a woman being forced to lick on Agyei's thing. If that's the sort of thing people learn from going to England, I don't ever want to go there."

Edom had rolled his eyes again, but he did not respond to the wicked urge to mention that Chris was not in any danger of traveling anywhere beyond the shores of Ghana. "From what I hear the men also do it to the women."

Chris gasped upon hearing that, and for a while seemed on the brink of fainting. He looked at what was left of his beer as though he wasn't sure he could ever enjoy beer again. "My God." He couldn't stop his head from shaking. "If a man puts his face down there, where does his nose go?"

Akosua started laughing so hard she almost fell off her chair.

Kofi Mensah, for his part, smiled sadly and shook his head. "You've never heard of this sort of thing before, huh?"

"I tell you, never! But now I understand. With this sort of thing going on here in Ghana, no wonder we are going nowhere."

By then Edom had given up hope of getting the sort of spontaneous reaction he would have liked to see from the other three. He recalled that a young girl came by hawking watermelons, sliced to generate some profit, and that shortly after she was past them, Kofi asked if Edom knew who the girl was.

"Which girl?"

"The one rumored to have been servicing Agyei."

He had not given his answer with any measure of joy. About the only thing Edom had been most fascinated by, then as now, was the idea of possessing the power to be able to do such a thing—to keep young girls, have them cook you meals and serve it to you naked, and then administer you lip service while you ate. He wasn't too sure that he'd personally want this sort of lip service performed on him, but that was a dispensable detail, and setting it aside did nothing to diminish the fierce, sweet intensity of Agyei's power. And that was just one of the stories about Agyei's exploits—barely a tip of the iceberg of the pleasures sweet wealth can bring. There was so much living to be done, dear God.

          🍁   🍁   🍁

The same story about Agyei's exploits had had a much different, almost nauseating effect on Kofi. Everything about it had been overly excessive. To Kofi it confirmed an important point his grandfather used to make—that contrary to what the new values proclaimed, man is actually content with enough, just as long as a life is validated and loved. That Agyei would resort to so much excess proved the point. He was clearly possessed of a great emptiness within him—a spiritual void so vast he required the virtual enslavement of the people around him to distract him from so much unhappiness.

And therein lay the irony. His wealth had clearly failed to give him the happiness he craved, for why would a man satisfied within himself abide such dehumanization of his fellow man? And yet the young girls who would themselves abide such indignities were doing so precisely because they craved some of this same wealth as a means to their happiness. About the time Edom was done telling that particular lurid tale, a young girl, no older than thirteen, had come walking by. On top of her head, she carried a large flat tray, on which sat several rows of finely-cut watermelons, swarmed by flies that she occasionally tried to intimidate away by swatting into the empty space above her head with a straw fan.

"Water milo-oooo-water-milo!" she hawked between the vain attempts to disperse the flies. As she walked by, she looked hopefully towards the four men and the woman sitting together in front of the bar. They looked back, but none of them offered to buy, and the girl, distracted by her hopeful anticipation, made to cross the street and almost walked into the path of the elephant, before the sudden roar of the engines forced her back. Kofi watched her cross the street and felt a sinking feeling turn his stomach. Here was a young girl taking her first steps in the direction of self-sufficiency—a hopeful sign. But in this social order, where even people such as themselves, grown men and a capable woman of differing abilities, sat about bemoaning the impotence of not being able to draw on the dignity of providing sufficiently for their loved ones, what great opportunities lurked for the young girls? The watermelon seller was a good-looking young girl. So at some point would she, too, on account of her looks, become the plaything of another Agyei Bimpong, just to survive?

Kofi recalled that Chris, not over being perplexed by the story just heard, had said, "I think they should ban this sort of thing in Ghana. And put people like Agyei in prison just for that alone."

But everyone seemed momentarily distracted by their own thoughts. A solemn silence had taken seat. Chris kept looking at his beer, but his appetite for the drink was clearly gone, as he visibly struggled to come to terms with the idea of lip service he'd just learned. Kofi's eyes continued to dwell on the girl with the watermelons, seemingly absorbed completely by a new thought in no way related to the story Edom had just told. Kwame Bonsu simply sat, expressionless, as though he had too many grievances than he knew how to handle, and Akosua went back to reading the newspaper.

Finally, Kofi had said, "Who was this girl that Agyei had catering to him?"

It was only after the question had been asked, and the answer given, that Kofi bemoaned the damning curiosity that prompted him to ask in the first place. They used to laugh over the old saying, which claimed that perhaps it is best that, in the absence of a remedy, the healer refrain from inquiring about the ailments that afflict people. Perhaps. Perhaps, too, as Kofi himself liked to say in his more bitter moments, it is best that all mothers-in-law kill themselves as a gesture of affection to their children-in-law. Who knows these things?

Edom, his face pained by the moment, had answered his question by saying, "I believe the girl who was administering to Agyei was your sister, Araba."

*   *   *

Was his reaction warranted? Could he have exercised better judgment? Did he advance any facet of humanity with his action? When the family elders summoned him into their presence later on, following his own act of folly, Kofi Mensah actually defended himself long and hard, crying for the desperate need for a restoration of dignity within the family.

His friends did not discuss the matter with him. If they had, he would have maintained that it was still a mistake on all of their parts to pretend that they had to accept the world as it was simply because that was just how it was. But none of them raised the issue, and he knew better than to force the debate and pretend that his motives had been altogether in the service of preserving remnants of decent social mores. He knew better. He had acted out of indignation, true. But he had also acted, in equal parts, on jealousy, and on the rage of feeling so diminished. Agyei was master of everyone's domain, and he had Kofi's own sister as part of his collection, to use in this manner! That was the central source of all of Kofi's rage—the shame of being a helpless actor while another man raided his family and took away the dignity that held them together. It was not enough that he had to seethe in silence at the vulgarity of that man. Now the man had reached out into Kofi's own family with the disease of his ways.

Kofi's reaction was to go over to his parents' home, where his sister still lived. Without greeting he had beaten his sister, slapping her "six humiliating times," she would say of her affliction.

"That's a lie! I only slapped her four times." He actually did say this in his own defense before the family elders. He would later admit that his anger had rendered him downright nonsensical. The elders had been baffled to silence.

Understanding that he was to be punished, Kofi at least persisted in getting one point across. "We have never been wealthy," he'd said, "but we have always been a people of dignity. Now you bring me before you because I sought to preserve that dignity."

"By physically assaulting your own sister?"

The elders never bought it. They acknowledged that it was unbecoming of Araba to become a plaything for Agyei for the sake of some money—and indeed she would need a reprimand for that. But the answer to her mistake was not criminal betrayal of the sort Kofi himself had committed. He was fined for his behavior and made to issue a public apology to his sister before the elders. He tried to plead down the fine, citing his wife and children, to no avail. In the end he needed two paychecks to cover it, and Efuwa spent the four months that he needed to receive the two checks talking a great deal about how their poor children were starving to death, even while the children burped their satisfaction into the melancholic shade of every setting sun. It was of some concern to him that this was the first time in a long while that he remembered Efuwa being very cross with him. And while his immediate reaction was to lash back with his own reactive anger, he'd felt sufficiently besieged that he pulled inside, and kept the damage only as far as it had already reached.

Who would listen to his individual cry in a nation of mourners? What unnatural level of arrogance could seize him to make him want to pour his personal grief about his sense of impotence to a multitude of disabled people, and suggest that it was all about the preservation of the dignity of his people? Even the elders hadn't been particularly animated by his talks about preserving dignity.

Efuwa had put it very simply to him. "I am not saying that I agree with this, necessarily, but people find dignity in being able to afford what they want. It is the way of things, and I'm sure if you asked your sister, you will find that she is stooping to these lows not because she has no sense of dignity but rather because she has no other means to obtain what she wants.

"If she had every opportunity and was fully capable of providing for herself, but she still resorted to this kind of behavior, you might have a point, but you have to realize that your sister is a young woman with needs, and little prospect of meeting them. She is probably in love with someone of her generation, who is entirely incapable of providing for her. It is the same story with most of the young girls around here, and it is more about survival than it is about a lack of dignity.

"Listen, I know you try and provide for her son—your nephew—and no doubt she is appreciative of it, but you can't very well expect her to be happy simply because they are not starving. It's all a bit more complicated than that, and I know you know this. That is partly why I am particularly cross with you for going over and laying your hand on her. It was cowardly of you."

She was right about the cowardice of his act, of course. Yet the whole time she was speaking, all Kofi could think of was whether Efuwa was suggesting—with this convincing argument—that she would herself resort to being someone's plaything if it would bring her closer to her material wants. If so, then his humiliation was complete, for then the love of his wife was an illusion, and morality was simply to the highest bidder. The morality of economics had become so powerful now, trumping all else. Back on the day of the first Easter pain, he remembered gathering himself from the floor filled with dread over the fact that his children were soon to come solicit money for their Easter gifts. And there he sat, full of love for his family, but fully incapable of showing that love with the symbols that were said to show love in its purest form. He had turned his mind over desperately in search of a novel idea on how he was going to turn them down.

For a while he had pondered the possibility of seeking some help from Kwame, but Kwame had borrowed money from him not so long ago and hadn't offered to pay him back; ergo the man was in no position to help him, and there had hardly been any other possibilities. So he'd known that he was going to have to resort to the old trick, where he would find the most improbable excuse to throw a serious tantrum in the early morning, and threaten harm on any of the children who would dare approach him the rest of the day. Silence would engulf the family for the whole day over this transparent ruse of a father incapable of showing true love, forcing his children to abide the shame of having nothing new for Easter.

❧   ❧   ❧

On the Easter Sunday of these poignant recollections, Efuwa had woken up to find Kofi on the floor, sweat dripping off his forehead. She had been surprised—this was something unusual, and for the briefest of moments she was amused, even if she could detect the small inkling in the gaze that suggested sexual intentions.

On this point Efuwa herself was at a loss. Their physical intimacy had been such a thing of wonder in the beginning, despite her fears as a virgin on their wedding night. She could accept that that magical chemistry would taper off with time. But was it inevitable that they would drift apart spiritually as well? Was it inevitable that they would embrace this silence that grew sharper with time, cutting to shreds the strong emotional bond they used to share? She understood what happened to her husband, more than he ever thought she did. Indeed, back when Kofi's family came to see hers' with his intent, she had been completely awestruck. At the time he had only engaged her in a few conversations, when he would come by her father's now defunct chemist store to buy medicine. She remembered that he addressed her with great respect and kindness, but she had not suspected his attraction.

Much like everyone who knew of Kofi, Efuwa had assumed that he would soon be marrying Akosua and moving to Accra, the capital city, where they would become important people. Akosua, of course, was the ultimate prize for any man. She was ridiculously good looking and was smart and full of promise, and even though Efuwa would later learn—from Akosua herself—that such a combination is harrowingly frightening to most men, Kofi certainly was an exception to this rule, if only because they'd been friends forever. It was widely assumed that the two of them would bring great honor to Mankraso. But life is ever so precarious and unpredictable, all the more so in the particular quest for a life mate. That much Efuwa understood, which was why she didn't waste time wondering about why Kofi and Akosua failed to follow everyone's presumed logical path, but still she had thought she would be moving to the capital city with Kofi when they got married.

But then there was a sudden change in government, a *coup d'etat* that shook the nation, and all of Africa with it. By the time the dust had settled from all the pointless *coups* and counter-*coups*, the nation had been ran aground, and the dreams of many aspiring nation-builders long derailed. The toll the derailment took on her husband was shocking. It killed the life in him, and she never thought that was a necessary outcome. So much of his vibrancy went with the missed opportunity occasioned by the very first *coup*.

She had once confessed her frustration to her mother, on what she considered the most difficult aspect of being married. "He wouldn't talk to me," she'd said.

Her mother had nodded agreement. "Men are ruled by a different kind of fear."

"Is that what it is?"

"I think so. Kofi fears that he's a failure, even though he had no control over the events that derailed his dreams. And anyone who lives with the burden of feeling like a failure is bound to have a good measure of self-loathing."

"But that is so stupid. He's still an able provider, when they pay him his salary. He is doing a reasonable good to society as a teacher. We have two wonderful children. If he feels so much pain, why can't he share it with me? I'm his wife, for Christ's sake!"

Efuwa's mother had smiled a sad smile. "Welcome to the club. Frankly I think that that Akosua woman makes matters worse. He probably confides in her. What is it that makes her spend all her time in the company of men anyway? Doesn't she know that people think she's strange?"

On one encounter with her, Efuwa, in a cheeky tone, had asked the question of Akosua herself, and Akosua, in her arrogant way, had said, "Who said I care about what people think of me?"

"It's still a bit strange that all your friends are men. Why is that?"

Her answer had surprised Efuwa. "Women are petty," she'd said. "Like you coming to ask me these petty questions."

In those early years of her marriage, Efuwa still felt a strange mix of respect and insecurity around Akosua. But her feelings towards Akosua had evolved with her own maturation, and by the time her first child arrived, and she found herself doing so much to hold the family together, she had moved past thinking of Akosua as one of the problems in her marriage, or as one to be held in awe. She still admired her, and she certainly respected her, but she actually began to feel sorry for the woman. She wondered if a woman could truly ever feel like a woman without bearing a child—and Akosua was clearly not going to bear one. That surely had to be a source of pain for her, no matter what she claimed. But setting that aside, Efuwa was just happy to eliminate Akosua as the reason for her husband's disengagement.

She was saddened by her husband's refusal to bring her into his tormented world. She could have helped, and gotten help from him in dealing with her own fears. They truly could have been a couple. But her husband was obsessed with the future that had been denied him, as though he could restore the desired trajectory simply by refusing the one he was living. Why, for instance, would a man of his intelligence have such judgment for a single mother who would do whatever it took to ensure the welfare of her children? Her husband had gone and laid a beating on his sister for being Agyei's plaything. And Akosua, while not loudly endorsing the act, was more sympathetic to Kofi's view than she was to his sister's.

"The things Araba was doing for money shames all women," had said Akosua.

Efuwa had nodded. "It must be nice to be well educated and gainfully employed."

Her comment caused Akosua pause, and after a moment she smiled. "I understand reality, Efuwa," she'd said. "But no one gave me what I have. I worked hard for it. And if things had been different, I would have helped a lot more young girls find their way, so we don't have to be playthings for men. All I'm saying is that we can't go on using the excuse of a difficult reality to abandon all our integrity."

Which was Efuwa's exact point. What Akosua preached was "if world" living. If every girl was as smart as she was, and if they all got a chance to go to school, and if they all did well and were then rewarded with gainful employment—that was "if world" living. And it was the reason she felt sorry for Akosua. She and her friends, Kwame and Efuwa's own husband, Kofi, lived the same difficult reality as everyone, without seeming to think they did. In her better moments, Efuwa despaired for them. The world is harsh for the occasional dreamer, more so for the perpetual dreamer. You had to wonder how it would all end—this "if world" living of theirs. And the worse habit of such dreamers is that they frequently forget that all around them others are getting their hands dirty to allow them to dream. She despaired for them because of what they chose to ignore. That was in her better moments. More frequently she simply felt overwhelmed by her husband's silence. It was the only thing she ever demanded of him—a little sharing. His silence killed everything. It even killed his desire for her—why else would he have stopped touching her for months upon months at a time?

By the time the sharp, searing, intermittent pain in her chest arrived, she had herself withdrawn to the point where she did not feel very much that her pain was their pain. She kept the pain to herself, even when, some years on, the pain was almost unbearable in its intensity. She began any number of inventive maneuverings to stretch their income while saving a little bit each month, hoping to accumulate enough to go see a doctor—and what did Kofi do? He hears one silly story about his sister and Agyei and marches right into the home he had built for his parents to beat her.

The fine levied on him as a result of that act had been considerable enough that she had had to dip into the money she was saving for the trip to see a doctor. She could have killed him for that. It was about then that she stopped smiling away that impossible pain in her chest. She no longer cared if he saw her wince when the pain came, but she realized quickly that he was afraid to find out, because he never asked, even when she was sure he had seen her wince. So she was genuinely surprised that Easter Sunday morning, when she woke up to find him in that funny position on the floor. His embarrassed look had been deeply endearing, but he had not tried to meet her initial amusement. If she could have had any wish she wanted, it would have been for them to stay in that space, his guard momentarily down, and make up for so much lost time by finding the roots of their earlier connection and nurturing it the way it should have been.

But no sooner had she come awake than the spell was broken. Kofi had sheepishly offered that he needed to use the bathroom, and welcomed back the silence between them. The sudden rise of the pain in her chest weakened any resolve she might have had of resisting the bane of silence he'd welcomed. She could feel herself falling apart, in her body and soul, right along with everything around them.

"Happy Easter."

"Yes," he'd responded. "Happy Easter."

CHAPTER 3

❀

*B*efore he took his position in the forest, Kwame himself had looked about him with deep longing. It didn't surprise him at all when, a short while after they had taken their positions, Akosua stood and looked about her with similar, deep longing. All through her laugh, and the subtle, initial ritual leading up to her taking her sacrificial position, he thought he understood what she was feeling.

The longing in his heart was for the path they missed, and the time before the sobriety of adulthood stole away the angels of hope from their youthful hearts. He didn't doubt that they would successfully kill the elephant. But in this moment before the dawn of the new life to come, he could hardly help wondering how it might have been.

But how far back was far enough to start over? For those who despair to tears over the present, how far back is far enough to return, so different choices might be made? And is the trajectory really different? Or in the end do all trajectories bring us simply back to who we are? This last question raised so many more questions that after a moment he simply smiled.

Akosua went down to one knee, then the other, almost in supplication. If she prayed, Kwame hoped it was for the deepest healing.

❦   ❦   ❦

To Kwame recollection, everything around them had been constantly falling apart, all the time, at an easy methodical pace that was ever so painful because the inevitability of it all was never once in any real doubt to him. Not since the shattering event of so many years ago, even if he did manage to carry on believing. For him, the obvious manifestation that the dream had begun to disintegrate came around the time they finished their secondary school education.

Despite his impressive results, Kwame was denied admission to the University. Kofi and Akosua got in. Thus they were the ones to carry the torch. It wasn't that Kwame gave up on their collective dream immediately. Far from it—but he needed more than a secondary school education to seriously think of forging his way into affairs of the government. And if he wasn't able to go any further with his own education, then he needed, at the very least, the clout of well-placed friends who shared his vision and would give him the chance he felt he deserved on account of his forceful concern for the plight of the nation alone. Even then, he spun into a deep depression over the rejection that denied him a place at the university, and over the cruel fact that he was back in Mankraso, to be confronted with the beast he thought he'd escaped. It was of some comfort that Kofi and Akosua both shared his distress, as he knew they would, but that comfort was far from enough.

On the day he explored his initial options following his rejection, the two were there with him. It was Kofi who asked, "What would you do now?"

And since part of him needed them to carry on without being too concerned about him, he'd said, "I'll try again to get in. None of us ever thought this was going to be easy. But I'll try again. I hope to join you before long. Meantime I'll just stay here at home, look for work and try to be of some help to the family."

"What work were you thinking of?"

"Teaching, perhaps. I'm sure I can find a position with one of the schools around. Or perhaps law enforcement. I might consider joining the police."

He had fallen into a sullen silence for a while. Then suddenly, and somewhat forcefully, he'd said, "It's all going to hell!"

At the time, Akosua and Kofi had just returned from a trip to Accra to visit the university, and notwithstanding the concern they showed regarding his personal plight, Kwame felt that they were too giddy from the visit. And such giddiness, he thought, would surely augur the beginning of the erosion of ideals if there were no efforts made to reel it in. But what was the sense in trying to tame the youthful exuberance of his friends at what was surely one of the highlights of their young lives? He was aware that this was a thought he should have considered, but his mood simply won't allow it. Neither Kofi nor Akosua had said anything back. It was no time for them to be told that anything was going to hell, never mind *everything*.

Burning with what appeared to be a surprising hint of jealousy, Kwame had said, in the same tone of his outburst, "I went to see my grandmother and the rest of the family." By that he meant he had been to his village.

Kwame was from Kromantse, which sat right next to Nankesedo, from where Akosua and Kofi hailed. The three of them had met in their youth attending the only Catholic elementary school in the area. In the early years following independence, Mankraso, which was the only town nearby, took off on a head-spinning burst of growth. That all of their families took off in search of a better life in Mankraso was all but inevitable. As children they had been afraid initially, when they learned that their respective families were leaving for Mankraso, but it turned out perfectly for them. Their families moved after they were done with grade six, and together they continued their education, enrolling as Form 1 students at Methodist Primary in Mankraso. Every so often, whether in tandem or alone, they went back to visit the extended family.

A trip back to the village for any one of them invariably pulled them into a state of deep depression. That much was a given, so for a time the concern was whether they should go back to visit at all. Was it in their best interest or even in the best interest of those they went to visit, since so much was expected from them on every little visit? They convinced themselves that despite the obvious drawbacks, it was better they continued to link back to the village. Ignoring anguished kin to escape temporary depression did not offer lasting relief from the deeper sense of guilt that plagued them all. Besides, they needed the reminder of where they'd been, if they were to understand fully where they were headed. Accepting that there will be guilt rooted in their helplessness over the poverty of their kin, they could at least be for each other a source of support.

Over a deliberately lengthy pause, Kwame, still fuming, had said, "They still live a life dogs shouldn't live. Don't ever lose sight of why you are going to school. It still is—it will always be, about the poorest of our citizens, relatives and strangers alike, left to burn in a hell they had no hand in creating. It's always about them. The plight of the least among us reflects the humanity of all of us. Don't you ever forget that. On the global stage we are shamed by their shame, and no amount of individual prestige you can attain to will change that."

Surprised, Akosua had said, "What's the matter, Kwame?"

"Is anything I said not true?" Somehow, on this day, each opening of his mouth expounded the problem.

Kofi had said, "You are preaching to us with condescension. Since when did it become all right for you to insult us?"

There was fire in Kwame's eyes. "You went to Accra to visit the wonderful university you will be attending. What did you see?"

Kofi had walked out of Kwame's room right then. Either out of great disappointment, hurt, or anger—or perhaps a powerful fusion of all three, he had clearly lost the fortitude to stomach another moment in the company of Kwame.

Akosua said, "We saw what you would expect to see on a trip to Accra. What did you expect us to see?"

"Did you find a people with clean water to drink, and flush toilets to dispose of their waste?"

Akosua just stared back at him. Her own patience was quickly eroding.

"Did you, Akosua? Did you find a people driving around in fancy cars that we here in Africa still can't seem to manufacture? And were they stupid enough to think there's anything but shame in parading around in things that only betray our own ineptitude? Were they busy making themselves look important because they live in Accra and can get Coca-Cola to drink? Well, in the village, and even here in Mankraso, most do not have clean water to drink. Certainly only the smallest percentage have a decent way of disposing of the waste that comes out of them. And our folks are still walking across two-hour distances to fetch dirty lake water to use, right here in this land of flowing streams. So please, do contain your enthusiasm over your admission to the university. It has done nothing for Africa that you two are headed for the university. Everything is still disintegrating, all the time."

Akosua had walked up to face Kwame and drawn so close he could feel her breath. It was the first time he could recall provoking her anger, and even in his own confused anger, he was surprised to realize how much of a quickening he got from just the wisp of her breath on him. Without warning, she slapped him, and stared him down as their collective temper heaved in threatening fits.

She had said, finally, "Whatever is bothering you, Kwame, we are not your right targets. Neither of us has said that getting to the university is paradise attained. But it is a necessary step to any dreams we might be entertaining for ourselves and for our country. We are supposed to be sharing this dream, Kwame, and all of a sudden you travel to the village and decide that you're the only African who's been to the village? Perhaps you ought to be asking yourself if you're not being blinded by jealousy. Right now I am completely disappointed in you."

Kwame had watched her leave after she'd said that, without responding. He did question himself in the hot midst of his exasperation, after Akosua had walked out, but the emotions he found were eclectic and confusing. He had been equal parts angry and overwhelmed by the weight of his helplessness in face of the poverty he had seen on his visit to the village. His rejection at the university had not helped, to be sure, inasmuch as it set him back that much farther from the path they had dreamt of together. In that regard he felt no small measure of shame for being the weak link in their collective dream to help set their country on the course they felt was right. Sadly enough, he also saw a certain justification to this setback to his dreams. Yet, for all that, he realized that he was most exasperated for reasons that were not immediately selfish. He was angry, he thought, to be part of a society so rotten it tainted every one of its members with humiliating indignity. He was angry, he felt, over the kinship he shared with this particular mass of humanity that silently accepted its status of irrelevance without an outcry. He felt ambushed by values that did nothing to advance his people but still enticed them strongly enough that they were immune to redemptive alternatives.

Even where the motives behind his anger were selfish, he was angry over the expectations the village folks held tightly around his neck. If only things were a little better in the country; if only Ghana's wealth were accruing to Ghanaians, with some modicum of equity. The village folks would not call him savior then—even if, to be sure, he were no more than a castrated savior now. They would not call him savior because enough of them would be doing well for themselves, making it easier to help along those on whom good fortune had failed to smile as generously. Instead he was compelled to play savior, himself a man needing salvation in the worst way. And he hated it all, in a deep, passionate way that begged for an outlet he could not locate. He hated the torment from his personal demon, the impotence it caused him, and the social norms that compelled him to abide it alone. He hated the friends whom he couldn't share his misery with, and most of all, he hated himself for his inability to get past a silly little moment from his past.

That Kwame could recall, everything had been constantly falling apart, all the time, and at some point, they were going to have to find a way to mend the core, or be destroyed.

*　　　*　　　*

Edom did not have any great moment of calm before the storm. From the moment he took his position, he began to burn with anticipation. He had had to walk the longest distance to his spot, at the end of the stretch of the ambush, opposite to where the elephant would be coming from. Akosua was already in her sacrificial position by the time he took his station. Unlike the others, his immediate concern was to ensure, yet again, that his weapon was sound. He had not imagined that holding a killing instrument could feel this intoxicating. The weapon sent warm shivers from the tips of his fingers to cover his whole body, and made him shudder. But this was not an affordable pleasure as yet.

He observed the set scene and was only slightly surprised that they were here in this funny moment, having all lived a lifetime without understanding anything at all. Edom felt happy; there was no need to pretend otherwise: he was happy about the moment. What would happen here in a short while should have happened ages ago, when things first started falling apart. They had waited much too long to decide, not out of any great wisdom on the use of time, but out of sheer cowardice, and everything that was the exact opposite of wisdom on the use of time. He was certain Akosua was going to die. This was not necessarily a happy thought, but he wondered about the alternative and despaired even more on her behalf. She had suffered so much already. For his part the choices were simple: he was either going to kill himself, whether with his own bullet or by standing in the line of fire, or he was going to move on to a spiritually detached, but materially comfortable existence. It would be fine either way, he felt, for at least he would be past the absolute dreariness of living just to breathe, eat and defecate.

Years ago, he had personally caused the death of his cousin, Antobam, and here he was now, part of this conspiracy to kill Akosua. It made perfect sense to him to be here. Life is not a sensible journey; it is merely what the traveler makes of it, along with whatever rationalizations the traveler chooses to decorate the moments lived. That was why he appreciated this moment a little better than his friends did. And in his mind he saw how it would all evolve. Akosua's dying would be different from Antobam's, of course. Antobam had run blindly into the street, chasing after a rolling ball sent by Edom, and when the contact with the car came, he flew through the air and landed with that heavy thud, lifeless. Antobam had not issued a sound—not a cry, not a scream, absolutely nothing at all. And this was perhaps the worst possible scenario, since Edom had to imagine the voice of his cousin in the moment of his death. At least Akosua will not go flying through the air, for what that was worth.

Edom checked his gun again to ensure that it was ready. His hands were steady. His mind was very clear, actually. It was the closest he had been to finding true peace. He still wasn't sure exactly what he was going to do, but he just about knew what would happen to the others. Kofi, he was certain, would freeze in the final hour, trapped by a heavy conscience. Chris would die an unfortunate death because his whole life had been more or less unfortunate. Kwame was more difficult to read. There were times when Edom wasn't sure how much of Kofi's consciousness Kwame truly shared. Depending on how deep their connection run, Kwame would freeze like Kofi himself, or he would seize the moment with decisive action. Either way, Akosua would be crushed.

Returning to himself, the only thing he could fully appreciate was that he felt completely at peace, but was it because he was finally on the cusp of a liberating final chapter in the sweet vice of opulence, or because he was on the cusp of a final chapter of immediate and utter destruction? Even now, he wasn't fully sure of what he was going to do. Perhaps he was being disingenuous, considering the poignancy of his expectations for a comfortable final chapter to his life. Perhaps. He had become so unpredictable, even to himself. Still, this was far and away the most delicious wait he had ever had to endure, and beneath the surface of his outward peacefulness, the anticipation was killing him.

Edom would have agreed with Kwame that things had been falling apart around them all the time. Was there any better proof of this than the saga of his personal life? He had started out with the same promise as any of his friends, and he could remember with painful keenness the early years, when they spoke with the flamboyant idealism of youth about the changes they would bring to their community—even to the country as a whole. After all, they had once been big men in waiting, with national ambitions. Was it all so laughable now because they were too young to have been entertaining such ambitions in the first place? Or was it laughable that they never grew past those memories, and attendant ambitions, filled with hope strong enough to burn his eyes with tears, even after all hope had been scorched to ashes in the withering heat of inertia?

Edom could not remember exactly when the rest of them lost their fire, perhaps because they spent so many years living contradictions. But at some point it came to him, clear as day, that their life trajectories had brought them to the same moral junction. That should have been the time they decided to find ways to enjoy this life. Instead they sat by idly, civil servants of no consequence, watching their lives dissolve into this slow motion of meaningless hours spent drinking beer and marking time in front of *Lonely Hearts*. Unless of course they simply came to the realization that they were ill prepared, and too far short of the mettle to rob society for their own pleasure. But if so, then they should have listened to him.

Maybe Nkrumah was to blame. When they were young and impressionable, this man came along and led the country to independence, and they believed in him. They believed, as the man proclaimed, that the salvation of Africa depended entirely on a union—a pre-emptive acceptance that the nation states left behind by colonialism were never going to deliver Africans from essential, continued slavery. So many times they repeated Nkrumah's twist on the words of Christ with gleeful appreciation: "Seek ye first the political kingdom." The choice before Africa had been so clear, and so simple. On the one hand, unite and enable the possibility of embarking on the sacred mission of restoring the integrity of a people uniquely afflicted. On the other hand, stay divided and rooted in the wretch of the worst form of indignity, forever a charity case on the world stage, occasionally thrust in the limelight to entertain others into some hypocritical state of guilt, shaming those who would claim to help and those who are helped in that quagmire called development. The case had been starkly laid out, that the independence of African states would remain a farce so long the powers of the world were allowed to continue meddling in affairs of the continent. And the powers of the world would meddle so long the nation states stayed divided, thereby lacking proportionate power to counter their exploits.

When children are made to embrace strong ideals, such as they did when they listened to Nkrumah, it can be downright impossible to wrench it from them. They became prisoners of these internalized ideals, and lost their ability to adapt to the realities around them. Over years of fiddling about with ideas of how they would help the cause of unified progress, none of them considered alternatives, even when they all knew that the West, champions of democracy, were reaching out for the throat of Pan-Africanists elected into office by their own peoples. So Nkrumah goes, and the bottom falls out. Disciples are strewn asunder, chained by ideas of what might have been, what ought to be, and riddled with the impotence of inaction in the ongoing reality.

Not that any of this had any real significance for how Edom's own life turned out. Fate chose him for destruction long before any of this could have truly mattered to him. He was a child when his cousin Antobam died that God-awful death during a simple game of football. In those days the asphalt that used to cover the road passing in front of *Lonely Hearts* had finally surrendered to the battering of traveling tires, an expected end since the battering was never accompanied by any effort at maintenance. Back then, when the road first began to disintegrate, *Lonely Hearts* did not exist. The ground it occupied now was nothing but plain clay dust, on which daily games of football sprang to life in the late afternoon, lifting the joyful voices of young boys finding release for the energy of happiness bundled within. And across the street from *Lonely Hearts*, in the spot now occupied by Nti the proprietor's house, used to stand the open market, mostly on the legs of small traders who converged daily from surrounding towns and villages to hawk necessary and sometimes fortuitous goods in barters of all kind. In times of economic hardships the market would lose its legs, to be revived later, when conditions improved. But eventually the loss became permanent—the battered legs of the market could not be revived as traders succumbed to unprofitable inertia.

Antobam had met his end in the middle of the road between where Nti's properties—the bar and his home—now stood. Where he'd met his end, the swirling breeze took on a physical form, lifting dust in gentle, uncoordinated skyward twirls, turning them over and around, and folding dust and debris onto themselves in a gentle reminder of time's stillness in motion. It had all started so gleefully well. Antobam, even at his young age, had already established a reputation for his searing running commentaries during games, including games in which he was a participant. If you were in the opposition, you had to be prepared to be called unflattering names that cut deeper at times than a knife. On that day, right after kick-off, Kofi, a dashing footballer at eleven, cradled the ball with his right foot and spun easily to make a pass.

Antobam was already in form. "Look at 'rhino-face-with-elephantiasis Kofi', trying to pretend he can play. He finds 'mosquito-legs Joe Koomson' on the left flank. Look at him trip and stumble like a girl, but oh look, the ball miraculously rolls to his teammate, 'elephant-ears Kobina Krobo' who tries to fan it down with his ears. Now Krobo moves to his right, accidentally getting by one of our boys. He holds his dribble and surveys the field, but his ears are in the way, so he taps an easy pass to 'giraffe-neck-with-no-legs Akwasi Hagan'. But our supreme defender Edom is there to steal the pass. Watch that impeccable form and deft moves. Edom leaves 'giraffe-neck' sprawled on his bottom, and spins with the graceful balance of the great Pele himself, to give a back pass…"

Edom's back pass left his feet with far more than the calculated velocity he intended.

"It is a fairly tricky play, but I, Antobam the great, will save us from the humiliation of facing a corner kick from these clowns."

Still in commentary, Antobam dove to the ground to cover the ball that was threatening to speed past him. He had the trajectory covered, until the ball, at the very last gasp, hit a small bump and hopped over his twisting attempt. As the ball rolled past him, a collective gasp rose out of the playing boys, for the ball was rolling onto the street, where it could be crushed by drivers who took perverse joy in destroying the playthings of young boys, as if they could replenish the dwindling happiness in their own lives by robbing young boys of theirs'.

Antobam was immediately on his feet and in hot pursuit, bearing the collective concern of the boys over the fate of the football that Kofi had managed to get from the Reverend Father James Fish of the Anglican church. If they caused the destruction of this ball, they would have to go back to the balls they manufactured themselves out of orphan socks stuffed with tightly balled plastic wrappers and papers—truly not an alternative to the beautiful object rolling towards the road. None of them saw the car. Everywhere, it seemed, blindness was taking over. Everywhere the seeing was horrifically narrow, trained on a shiny football so easily crushed by passing tires, taking along the child life that carelessly threw itself in front. The sound of the tragedy had been nothing like what Edom would have imagined.

"*Flata!*"

Antobam's frail body went flying. Was there life in it any longer during that flight? Or did the spirit jump at the surprise, oblivious to the arrival of its own time? There was a screeching of tires, and the flight of nearby chickens, more typical victims in these sorts of misadventures; there was, too, the gasps of young boys, and much later, the first scream from a passerby. The guilt Edom felt shut him down.

🍁   🍁   🍁

There were many attempted comforts. His grandmother, Nana Tsetsewa, told him some reassuring tale of souls whose stay in this cycle is sometimes much shorter than loved ones might desire, and about the easy logic of it all, when the open mind is able to sift through the timeless currents bearing the wings of souls from one cycle to the next. She told Edom many times over that he did not cause Antobam's death. Antobam had died that day because he was meant to die that day. Even with the mind of a child, Edom found himself vexed by the obvious question: was the wandering of souls across time and space without purpose? For if it did have purpose, what had been the purpose of Antobam's short sojourn in this cycle? What possible understanding could there be for the particular concoction of fate that brought Antobam's soul in communion with his', in the form of a cousin, only so he could usher the progression of that soul into the next cycle in such a ghastly way?

"We are saddled by imaginations too limited to understand that purpose can be found in the smallest of breaths. A life lived is not a wasted turn, no matter how brief, simply because you fail to grasp the possible meaning of such a small turn. The whole is so much bigger, and the connections so much more complex."

In Nana Tsetsewa's riddle-infested world, the progression of Antobam's soul served a purpose. But whatever greater purpose it served, Antobam's departure landed Edom in an asylum. He'd spent the first month following the tragedy in absolute silence, refusing food and barely tasting water. Then he'd begun talking to himself, all the time. Worried elders put their heads together, and ordered ritual appeasement to the gods. A goat was brought to the slaughter, fresh blood coated over Edom's skin to repel demons seeking his flesh for a feast. Elaborate ceremony, time tested and true. To cover all bases, he was then taken to the Christian church for more prayers. Edom reacted by expanding the range of his self-absorption. He began to engage in active dialogue with his dead cousin. He would feed Antobam his food and sit amidst the morsels scattered about him laughing at his cousin for almost choking on his food. He would pour Antobam water to drink, and take off on races with him.

His mother tried, but she was helpless, and so against her impassioned plea, he was sent away. She was told that awful spirits had invaded the sanctity of the family, stealing Antobam's life and the sanity of her son. Where Edom was sent, at the asylum, dank floors reeking of urine and feces provided novel ideas for continued conversations with Antobam. He was chained by the ankle of his left leg to an iron rack nailed into the floor, in a long line with hundreds of adults who spent their time harming themselves. And in the absence of any other medicine, herbal liquids were dripped into the noses of the patients to help them sneeze out the devil, with clergymen praying with great passion to help the cause, to no avail. It took the arrival, several months later, of a doctor trained in Western medicine, for him to be released.

Edom found it downright ridiculous that Akosua would intimate, several years on, that in the Ghana she dreamed of, the frontiers of psychological research and treatment would be advanced aggressively, and facilities made available to better care for those with mental health problems. Akosua clearly did not seem to realize how big a facility would be needed, since, as far as Edom was concerned, half the country, including everyone in their circle of friends and families, was suffering from mental health problems. At any rate the thought itself was silly. It was too much of a leap of imagination for her to suggest that a better Ghana would have prevented the inevitable moment of Antobam's death, or that Edom would have turned out differently. He wasn't conceited enough to think that there was anything exceptional about his life. It was the old tale revisited, of wasted lives on this smoldering treadmill to nowhere. A hundred children here, a thousand there, another million yonder, passed right on through the chambers of the forgotten, on their speedy, meaningless passage through this time. There was nothing exceptional about him.

However, this fed right into the source of his greatest outrage. If life was all so barbaric, and civilized people smiled civilized smiles at the plight of the wretched and drank more wine, why did the poor insist on abiding their humility in civilized silence? At what point does the pain of the poor assume militant fervor, spurring action that leads to the acquisition of that which can't be acquired by tricky legal means? To him that time arrived many years back. But no matter how many hints he dropped, his friends, who had been of all this invaluable help along the way, turned out to be civilized cowards. He noticed somewhat belatedly that his friends were not the type of people in whose company dreams came true. They somehow failed to grasp the simple fact that the only thing that matters in life is power, which comes, naturally, from the acquisition of wealth. And for that shortcoming, their company was immeasurably infuriating. Daily they sat and bemoaned a nation gone amok. Daily they pretended that they were doing the world and their children some favor by toiling in this thankless obscurity. If there had been any indication along the way that the nation was in motion towards something wholesome and healing, he might have developed some measure of appreciation for their leanings. But he could not remember when there was ever such a generalized movement to preserve the best of the national character in the pursuit of a more livable community for all, or when a particular leadership, including even the independence leaders, proved itself fully committed to the upholding of law and fairness. And since then, thieves had run the country with blatant impunity.

The elephant was the final word. For as long as anyone could remember, the elephant had been making these runs. Its run dated back to colonial times, back when the wheels were human legs and the cargo they carried from the gold and diamond mines were destined for coffers of robbers from across the oceans—white people plundering to build their empires. Some ten different men had assumed the mantle of leadership since this land proclaimed itself freed. The elephant's journey had never once stopped, although the wheels of sturdy automobiles had replaced the legs of men. If anything the elephants became more numerous, and their destinations increased with the numbers. Everyone knew that the great wealth on the elephant's back eventually wound up in the coffers of thieves ruling this very land. And even greater wealth went to thieves sitting abroad somewhere. Obscure airports had been built at funny locations all around them to facilitate the plunder, and the thievery had attained such sophistication no one quite knew what was being transported where and when. Was it cash? Was it gold? Was it diamonds? No one knew, exactly. But coffers were being filled all those years, and there was no real change in any of the lives of the ordinary people.

So it was infuriating to have friends who insisted on a different wisdom. What would have been so wrong with following everyone's wisdom, and doing whatever it took to get ahead? Wasn't that the only morality? Some day, he hoped,—if the circle of wisdom was not too large—it would pierce their resistance and embrace them. The transition then would be easy: they would agree with him that the elephant had to be killed. He bid his time. It was a long wait. But then, in quick succession, Kofi's mother and wife both took ill and died while Kofi stood helplessly by. And then Akosua caught the plague. And all of a sudden, it was all about money. And with that, the falling apart emerged in startling relief.

CHAPTER 4

*P*ast the visit from Efuwa and the child, Akosua Nyamiah lay there
on the street in a heavy blast of mixed sentiments and awaited her
fate. She kept assuring herself, through the foggy swirl of her clouded
thoughts that she was not going to die this grisly death. It might be a
close call, but she was not really going to die in a manner quite so
undignified. No doubt it was the cocktail of medicines assuring her, but
she needed the assurance, for in a short while, if the armored car did not
stop, she would be crushed to death. For what it was worth, she was glad
that Kofi's assurance had been firm. The elephant would stop, he had
promised. But how could he know for a certainty that this unnatural
act on all their parts was not destined for the most unnatural end for
her?

Strangely, even now she did not find that particular expectation of
death immensely terrifying. What was going through her mind was
understandable, in a way, if somewhat unexpected. She had expected to
be thinking back on her life, trying to savor her most important tri-
umphs, or perhaps accept her failings in a final embrace of her humanity. But what about the understanding that she sought, the great
understanding presumably sought by all souls? At this moment, had she
not earned the promise of clarity that is reserved for those who sit at
death's gate?

Why then, of all things, did the mindless dying of a dog concern her now? Certainly the clarity coming to her could not be that her life had been about as senseless as the wasted one of the dog, could it? Then why was she now being visited by this memory?

❦   ❦   ❦

She was thinking of a dog, in a single memory retrieved from some years ago, before she got sick. Perhaps this was because the dying of the dog had itself caused her to think of life in different ways than she had allowed herself the luxury before.

It was over the stretch when news from around the African continent was dominated by images of Rwandans gleefully massacring one another before the stunned witnessing of the world. Leading up to the massacre, Akosua and her friends were engaged in what turned out to be largely moot debates about whether or not it was the French and the Belgians still fanning the flames of discord between the Hutus and Tutsi's—a sort of modern day, elemental divide and conquer that had carried over from the colonial order of recent history. Then the Rwandans set upon themselves, and Akosua lost all faith in Africa. It was such a shattering wound to everything decent within her, and such a final demolishing of her belief that Africa still harbored some hope yet, that she could have taken her own life on that account alone. The massacre effectively shut them all up. Akosua had been proposing some interesting theory on the truest triumph of European colonization of Africa. She said it was not in the obvious mockeries of self-determination strewn about the continent, but rather in the extent of the African's retarded mental development.

"Every last African believes that our redemption lies in blind imitation of Western styles of governance, Western cultures, Western tastes. The fact that the Hutus and Tutsi's of Rwanda are known to have developed the worst of their deep hatred for one another following the fine efforts of the Europeans in playing one against the other proves my point."

Her friends hadn't been contrary, really, but Kwame had indicated his uneasiness with the facile attribution of all of Africa's woes on colonialism.

"I can't tell you how strongly I reject that school of thought. There is nothing in the ills of Africa that is not directly attributable to our own idiocy, inhumanity, or whatever it is that makes us tolerant of the suffering of our own."

When the Rwandan massacre occurred, the sheer force of it muted all arguments. On the day of the dog's dying, images of the massacre had been splashed on the front pages of *The National Times*. The friends read the report and sat in deep silence, under the long shadow of an appalling force.

Across from where they sat, the stray dog had appeared, seemingly out of nowhere. The look of the dog was immediately disturbing: it was missing its left hind leg, and whatever encounter had caused the loss must have been fairly recent, because the dog was bleeding in persistent drips from the remaining stump. What could have done this to the poor animal? It staggered in utter confusion, tracing a zig-zagging course along the side of the road, some twenty-five meters away from where the five friends sat.

In its lilting disorientation, the dog, clearly not yet adjusted to its present fate of being without a leg, ambled awkwardly and fell into the open gutter that run alongside the road, knocking its jaw on the edge. In the struggle to get out, it drew the attention of some children playing across the street. The children, spotting the anomaly, picked up sticks and began to chase after the dog. One of them—Akosua recognized him as Kwame Sarpong, son of the assistant headmaster at the Methodist elementary school—caught up to the animal and lashed out at it with his stick. The startled animal whipped around, confusion and pain in its eyes, and stumbled on the first effort to flee, as more young boys came after it.

Akosua bolted to her feet. A frightful burst of anger welled up in her throat and choked her. She was so quickly enraged that even without the loss of her voice, she wouldn't have known what to say. Both Edom and Kwame, sharing her alarm, got up to their feet. The tragedy was developing quickly, but slowly enough all the same for all of them, and anybody else paying attention, to anticipate the painful end, and then to hope with bated breaths, that it might be avoided. But there was simply no time to intervene. Akosua wasn't sure whose voice she heard, but one of her friends at the table said, in a near-whisper, "For the love of God!" She also heard a sudden yell from their table, directed at the children, telling them to stop. It was the voice of Kofi, and it went completely unheeded, even though the rumble of the approaching elephant had risen suddenly and grown ominously loud.

What possesses little children to pick up such unnatural acts so easily? Kwame Sarpong, the kid closest to the dog, pounced on the oddity before him once again, with his stick. The confused dog yelped with increasing terror, twisted to flee from the horrible gathering of humanity and lost its balance another time. This time its awkward stumble sent it onto the street, and almost immediately the large tires of the armored car smashed it. The dog's entrails shot out of it from the pressure of the crushing blow, completing the nauseating heap of its lifeless body. The armored car roared on, one of its back tires treading again over the mess in one continuous flow. The armored car always roared on. It did not seem to matter what it left behind. Once, at a meeting of the Council of Elders, the concern was raised by the elder Ama Amponsah, who felt she had seen enough close calls to know that sooner or later, the stupid armored car was going to trample over one of her grandchildren.

"And," she'd said, "I don't even think those drivers would stop if they killed a child. Why exactly do they drive so recklessly?"

"They transport a great deal of wealth," was the answer given.

Ama Amponsah's face knotted into an angry frown. "Whose wealth? And why must our grandchildren's lives be risked for the enrichment of anyone?"

Nothing came of the complaint. The chief's court had agreed to bring Ama Amponsah's concern to the civil authorities, but nothing changed. The director of the municipal council, who was known to be a very hostile man, had said something like, "First of all, you people have to learn to keep your children under control. I have seen your little children with my own two eyes, running around like animals without a leash." Then he'd promised to "see what I can do."

The elephant continued to barrel through town with reckless abandon. Ama Amponsah was said to have made another appearance at the chief's court to find out about the continuing practice. Akosua had asked her about the inquiry, and the grandmother had chuckled as one on the brink of tears.

"They say the authorities told them that the elephant stops for no one."

Akosua did not find that terribly surprising. It's always the same when there is money to be made: there is nothing sacred. Foreigners and kin enslave human beings because there is money to be made. It is possible to say that the structures have changed a bit along the way, shifted here and there, right along with the centers of power. But have the patterns changed? Has today's glorious free market critically altered the essential feature of wealth accruing to the very few on the backs of the many? Here, in a society long rooted in respect for the absolute sanctity of a life, even the children have become expendable, with the council of elders able to withdraw into their conspiracy of silence in the face of flat dismissal from civil authorities on the welfare of the children. Truly, the dog had stood no chance at all. In small ways and in large, soul-wrenching way, the message was much the same: the sanctity of life was no more.

The question for her then was whether, with this superseding act, she had finally decided to cast her vote in favor of this new morality, despite her lifelong protestation against it. And if so, then was she perhaps the worst hypocrite of them all?

Chris Agyekum remembered that dog quite well. The accident had brought him at least three instances of intense nightmares. The nightmares were so intense he wet his bed each time, even though he was a grown man. But he couldn't remember the exact content of the dreams, except that they had something to do with rabid dogs chasing him. He couldn't understand any of it at all, especially why the dogs were chasing after him as though it was he who had been driving the elephant. He couldn't understand it at all, and said as much to Kofi Mensah one afternoon.

He'd said, "I don't understand it at all." But he hadn't told Kofi that he'd been wetting his bed for three nights in a row.

He did remember the occasion of the dog's dying, although the memory, for all its startling impact, had not left the deepest impression on his mind, even with the disturbing dreams. It wasn't that he didn't particularly care for dogs the way he did cats, although it could have been just that. He hadn't actually considered how he felt about dogs—that he could recall—but he certainly did like cats. However, that was not to say that the impact of the accident would have been any greater if the animal had been a cat. But that was not the point here, really. His relative preference for cats was not the reason the occasion of the dog's dying had failed to leave the deepest impression on him—of that he was certain.

He had been under a much bigger cloud at the time. Heaven and hell had fused in his mind to generate the beginnings of a mind-bending ambivalence, and for more than a month surrounding the death of the dog, Chris had been petrified numb, from learning that there was a distinct possibility hell did not exist at all.

In the wake of that monumental appraisal, much of life took on an oppressive air of irrelevance, pulling him fast into the vortex of the most frightening state of imbalance. Against the raging fury of that mental pall, the death of the dog, though disturbingly spectacular, and obviously unnerving, had not left the indelible impression it otherwise might have. Nothing in those harrowing days could penetrate the rigid chaos of his mind to leave a lasting imprint. The battle within, centered on existential issues he had never known to even question before, had been much greater.

🍁   🍁   🍁

Lying here watching the charge of the elephant across the road, Chris was visited, for the first time since that ghastly stretch of some seven years ago, by the same kind of vivid terror that had almost caused his brains to explode back then. The new terror effectively stole the thrust of the old, flooding his senses now with the heaviest weight of opprobrium.

Akosua was going to die!

In this moment, there was suddenly no doubt to be found in any recess of his mind: she would be going straight to hell for this horrendous suicide. And later, when the man in the long dark coat came knocking on their respective doors, each one of them, lying in wait, would pay the ultimate price for this same life that they had conspired to sacrifice. He watched in spellbound stupor as the elephant shot into view and raced down the road, on a straight line towards the prone woman. That was how unnatural the evolution of this whole episode was. Whoever heard of a driver of a sane mind and sober judgment racing down this road in a straight line? What car could ever hope to survive such an ordeal?

Yet the armored car had rounded the sharp corner and was racing with just such madness, its massive tires churning and overwhelming pothole after gaping pothole, blazing a horrific trail towards the prone woman. This was the one woman—his mother aside—that he had ever loved, for as long as he could remember, and he was lying here ready to watch her die a death this painful, this undignified. The prospect of what was to happen threw his stomach, and on the reflex, he thought he was going to give up his lunch.

It came to him, in that moment, that what you feel in the starkest, decisive moment is all the truth that matters. And what he was feeling now was the presence of God, which was terribly nerve-wracking because God was furious! For in this moment, he could not imagine that there could be a sin greater than this willful sacrifice of a loved one, for no better reason than personal enrichment. The throbbing in his head began to peak, and he heard the ringing sound of his inner voice echo into the void of the chamber of sin that was his mind.

"Oh God, oh God! There is a hell! And this is just the beginning of it!"

🍁   🍁   🍁

In his youth, Chris was not like most of his peers. His mother had conceived him in the lean years before she declared herself "born again", which meant that Chris drank a lot of alcohol and was high on weed many times before he ever began his struggle to join those living outside the womb.

From as early as he could recall, people said he looked funny. His left eye protruded farther out of his face than did his right eye. His lips defied alignment, and in their pull against each other, one fled north and eastward, the other south and westward, such that in their conflict they shoved his front teeth out awkwardly to challenge the sun for brightness. People said he walked funny, too. Both legs had a slight, permanent bend, from the outside of the left knee and the inside of the right knee, tilting him sideways, and his feet hooked inwards, almost facing each other. He didn't so much walk as he managed to amble, hoisting one foot over the other in a permanent act of determination. This made him stumble a lot, but he believed he was a good dancer, challenging Kofi on several occasions over the years to "try me, just try me, I'll dance you right off the floor." His left hand held a permanent hook at the elbow and at the wrist, where it curled in.

One memorable day, when he was still in sixth grade, a classmate of his', for no apparent reason that Chris could recall, called him the equivalent of a "fucking retard." Actually, the fellow said specifically, "You're a fucking retard." It would happen a few more times, but that was the first time.

Kwame Bonsu and Kofi Mensah, who had both found Chris and left him behind in sixth grade, stepped up to the bully and shoved him around a few times. Thus began his friendship with them. Chris repeated the sixth grade about four times, in which time he came to appreciate that he had been moved along in the earlier grades because it was felt no harm was being done. But then he came across this thing that the headmaster called "reality check", which prevented him from moving on further. After his fourth year in sixth grade, he tired of school. His mother congratulated him heartily nonetheless, and told him that Jesus was very proud of him, which made Chris begin to seriously like this Jesus fellow, even though he could not recall that they had ever met.

Kwame Bonsu was the one with whom Chris actually developed the closest of kinship, in part because Kofi went on to study for a while beyond secondary school, when Kwame had been forced to abandon his own educational pursuits—something about the university turning him down. Kwame had suggested to Chris that Kofi was very smart. Thereafter Chris always thought Kofi was pretty smart, and burned with impatience to let his friend know of the high esteem in which he held him. Then one day the chance presented, and he told Kofi just how smart he thought he was. He said something like, "I think you're pretty smart."

Kofi had smiled, but not said anything. Chris felt immensely comfortable and validated in the company of the group, although now and then, an event would cause him to wonder a bit about each one of them. He recalled how Kwame Bonsu, his closest confidant, had once, back when they were still young, adamantly denied being his friend in order to be accepted by a group he was impressed by and wanted to join. One of the boys in the group had wanted to know why Kwame spent so much time with "the retard", and Kwame had said he felt sorry for him. Chris, who had overhead that part of the conversation, felt a pain unlike any he had ever felt before, and took himself away to his hiding spot in the mango forest behind Mr. Anthony's bungalow, where he wept bitterly to himself until the pain had subsided.

He recalled the day Akosua, who they knew to be very compassionate, insulted him for complimenting her, and then a week later ruthlessly slapped Kofi Mensah's daughter, Esther, then a child of six. It would come out that Akosua, although she had said no to Kofi's proposal many years before, had gone on to harbor a terrifying space of vindictive jealousy in her heart towards Efuwa, the woman who had said yes to him, releasing some of it in one blind action against her child on a quiet Saturday afternoon in July. Chris could not even remember what the child Esther had done—that's how trivial it was, because Chris usually remembered things pretty well.

On the night his whole brain almost exploded, he had been sitting with Kofi Mensah in the small veranda in front of Kofi's house. Kwame had left to return to his family shortly after dinner, leaving the two of them in the company of a thousand stars, a thin crescent moon and two crickets sparring to out-chirp each other. It was an unusually peaceful night, devoid of the usual noises of the evening, including the habitual cry and laughter of children with too many emotions to shed before sleep time. Even the chirping of the crickets was decidedly subdued.

Kofi had casually remarked that it was rather "mind-boggling, when you come to think of it," that all those tiny stars were massive bodies traveling through space and time, just like this planet of ours, some so many hundreds of thousands of years ago, in an expanding universe. Then, shaking his head in obvious awe and fascination, he'd noted fluidly that it blows the mind to think that our planet itself is a tiny one in a solar system that is a small fraction of a larger galaxy in a complex of galaxies. He went on to say something about some milk in the way somewhere up there. Chris noticed that Kofi seemed faintly bemused, perhaps somewhat awed, but he said all this rather casually. Even the simple act of drinking water could not be more casual than the way Kofi said these things.

"It makes you wonder," he'd said in his final assault on Chris' mental fortitude, "what if we are truly no more than lucky accidents after all."

Chris managed the question, "What do you mean?"

"You know, how we got here, the whole process of evolution."

Chris' obvious confusion seemed to puzzle Kofi at first, but then he appeared to have remembered that Chris could not have possibly known these things. Starting slowly, Kofi tried to explain to Chris what the learned ones of the world say about how we got here. He was patient and thorough, but Chris sat in petrified stupor over the mind-bending idea of this black hole out there somewhere and the explosion—Kofi called it a "big bang"—that occurred and eventually caused life to start. Chris wondered as an afterthought who caused the explosion if there was no life around. Kofi brought up the milk in the way up there again—did he say a milky way or just milk in the way?—the planet earth and her neighbors and their relation to the other galaxies and all the "beautiful mess that is this ever expanding universe."

And Chris, sitting next to him, heard these things for the first time in his life and almost died with fright.

❦   ❦   ❦

Depression descended on him like a burst of flame, swallowing him. For three days after Kofi's version of creation, Chris said very little, even in the company of his friends. It was supposed to be that God created the heavens and the earth. *He* was supposed to be out there somewhere, omnipotent, observing from *his* heavenly home, seeing all. Because of *him*, there was a hell, whose avoidance made life bearable for Chris and his friends, and all people like them—toiling in oblivion into oblivion—and gave them a small measure of silently cherished satisfaction in knowing that the excesses of the rich, fat cats would be duly punished on the day of judgment.

Chris felt a depression so deep he started to lose his appetite by the third day, the same day Agyei Bimpong, the most abominable fat cat, used his big car to splash Chris as he walked by a roadside puddle on his way to join his friends. Up to that point Chris had borne the burden alone, crippled by the inability to describe the depth of his feelings, especially since Kofi Mensah did not appear even remotely depressed by what he had shared with him on that night of countless stars.

On the third day after the staggering news, when he was sullied by the dirty water scattered by Agyei's reckless driving, Chris abandoned the road altogether and took the shortcut that wound behind the gutted building sitting next to the *God is Love* restaurant. The gutted building was formerly the town's branch of the Ghana National Bank. He didn't like using that shortcut because even though it was right by the main street, a spontaneous landfill had sprung up behind the building shortly after a mysterious fire brought the former bank building down a few years back. And if that was not enough, what was left of the building itself had become a nighttime lavatory for some townsfolk, young and old. The first time the stench from the human excrement and the growing dumpsite conspired to address him, Chris was so stunned he actually reacted physically, stumbling backwards.

He recalled the tense occasion when concerned members of the community went to launch a complaint at the municipal council and were collectively brow-beaten by the director of the council, already a very hostile man who had not received a paycheck for quite some time.

He said something like, "First of all, you fucking hypocrites should be ashamed of yourselves, coming to us to ask us to clean the shit you've been shitting in that building. I'm even sure some of you standing here complaining have relieved yourself there on many an occasion. Do I look like I was appointed to this position to come and clean your spontaneous shit? Second of all, how did that landfill behind the burned down building even start? Did God drop the rubbish from the sky? Is he the one letting it grow? You create your rubbish and come to ask the government to wash it off your dirty bodies. And besides, even though we haven't been getting our budget, haven't we been doing our best to reduce the stink?"

It wasn't clear to anyone what his office had done to reduce the stink, but that was not really the point just then. The point, perhaps well taken, was whether God was the one dropping the rubbish from the sky. Most people hated that municipal council director, especially when he told a simple truth like that—and he, in turn, hated most people of the town. Nonetheless Kofi Mensah said the man had a point. Chris was not sure how he felt personally towards the man. What he did know was that every trip through the shortcut depressed him, and on the day Agyei splashed him, his depression only deepened. He just could not believe that there was a distinct possibility that no hell existed for that fat cat to go to when he died; that somehow, they could all be headed to the same nothingness after their walk through this cycle. Truly, what was the point then? You come into this world and suffer so much through no fault of your own and then you die and become bones on a planet hurtling through space because of this big bang that happened spontaneously the other day. What was the point? He joined his friends that day and refused drink and dialogue until Akosua prodded him on what was wrong.

Reluctantly, he'd said, "I'm very depressed."

His friends seemed surprised. Kwame, in point of fact, had looked at him quizzically and said, "That's surprising."

"I've even lost my appetite," Chris had said.

Kofi Mensah's brows had lifted. Like the rest, he did not seem to believe that Chris was truly depressed. To prove his point, Chris had begun fasting. He did not actually fast, except in the presence of his friends, but eventually he began to drift perilously close to actually fasting, since he spent so much time with them. For a week, his friends did not see him drink or eat. Only then did they seem to acknowledge that he was truly depressed. Akosua asked him if there was something wrong. Was he depressed or something? This was slightly annoying to Chris, since he had spent a week trying to prove just that point. But he said yes, he was depressed, and felt some relief from his depression almost immediately, as a result of the long-awaited acknowledgement.

CHAPTER 5

❀

*T*he utterly perplexing thing about finding out that the universe is
so big—besides the sudden depression that springs from the
belief that ignominious fat cats of Agyei's ilk might go unpunished
when all is said and done—is the extent to which the knowledge
completely liquefies everything in the stomach. Although Chris did
not actually fast when he began to lose his appetite, the truth was
that for a while he might as well have. Liquids and solids alike passed
through him as though he were a defective faucet, perpetually dripping. He had questions burning him every which way he turned, and
so inevitably, he took ill. The illness prompted him to summon the
courage, finally, to bring his questions to Kofi Mensah. On the day he
brought his questions to his friend, he was met with the same understanding Kofi always gave him, even at times when Chris was himself
afraid that perhaps his questions were too stupid.

"Does God know this?"

Kofi had smiled, without being condescending. "He must know, if
he created it all, don't you think?"

"But I thought you said he wasn't even there when that explosion
happened."

"Oh, that." Kofi fell into silent contemplation. "What I told you
the other day is based on the best that our human mind has logically
put together. Whether our human mind is the most trustworthy

guide is another matter altogether. The Bible, for example, gives another perspective of the human mind, as inspired by something different. But if you take the Bible, as an example, what it says about how we got here is not meant to be taken literally. And what is understood about the logic of the human mind doesn't necessarily mean that there is no spiritual realm to go with it."

Chris nodded with a sense of renewed hope, feeling a bit better almost immediately. "But does that mean there are many gods, and our god is just one of them?"

"Why do you say?"

"Well, I'm thinking of all these planets that are even bigger than ours. So I figure maybe our god created ours, and other gods created the other ones, you know?"

"Ah." Kofi smiled wanly. "I see your point. But that's not our faith. To have our faith is to believe that God created absolutely all of it."

Chris could sense that Kofi was trying hard to be reassuring, perhaps without too much conviction in the mission. He stayed withdrawn for a moment longer.

"You must hold on to your faith, Chris," he'd said.

"So we are not accidents then? If I hold on to my faith, I must believe we are more than just accidents that went right."

A laugh burst out of Kofi that was perhaps the bitterest laugh Chris had ever heard. And it persisted for too long, until, on a very abrupt turn, he became stern.

"We *are* accidents, my friend," he'd said, finally. "We're all bloody accidents if you ask me. You must not have been paying much attention to the human animal. We are ungodly, beastly accidents destroying everything that's beautiful around and about us."

Chris had shrunk back, completely thrown by Kofi's sudden mood change. In the ensuing silence, he had tried to search Kofi's eyes for some sign of reassurance, and found something empty and frightening. A sullen feeling washed over Chris, and made him feel that perhaps there were some things better left unknown. Frightened by the weight of the unknown, he had dropped the matter for that day.

❦   ❦   ❦

The very next day, he resumed the conversation. "What do you believe in, Kofi? I need your honest opinion."

Kofi spoke without any deliberation. "As children the church made us afraid of God. I think I grew up believing in God because I was afraid of hell. That's a truly terrible reason to believe in anything. But there've been many times in the past when I would look around me, see the evils going on, and say to myself that there is no way an existent God of goodness would allow these sorts of things happen, especially to innocent children. But then I would wonder almost immediately, what if I'm wrong? What if God does exist and there is a hell?"

"I think the same thing. Well, not exactly for myself, but for those who don't believe. I think to myself, boy, would they feel stupid when judgment day comes."

"Right. Fear is a powerful motivator. But as I said, if God is to mean anything to us, it must be for reasons other than that we are afraid of going to hell. It defeats the purpose, I think. We've made God out to be an egomaniac dictator, or an impetuous child, depending on your view—creating things only to destroy them under a funny load of rules no one could hope to ever meet. And churches use this to keel millions of rational beings into irrational cowardice."

"Is that why you don't go to church any more?"

Kofi smiled again, genuinely this time. "That's one reason. I find religions obstacles to true spirituality. It's an important reason why I don't go to church often these days. But it's only one reason."

"What are the other reasons?"

Akosua, rejoining, had said, "He hates the sight of black people worshiping a white Jesus."

A very dramatic silence, teeming with a thousand contentious ghosts, filled the spaces between the friends. Chris felt the uneasy weight of frightening new revelations descend and hover over his head. He felt cornered, and might well have given up on the conversation for yet another day. But the mere thought of the additional wait twisted his heart with a fanciful burn.

"But that is Jesus, isn't it? I saw him with my own two eyes in that film, you know, the one that comes around every year."

Akosua, sensing the rising tension in Chris' body, drew closer and took his right hand in both of hers', but said nothing. He failed to recognize the guilt on their faces from having forgotten to explain that movies are a different kind of reality.

Kofi said, "Jesus was not European. There's a passage in the Bible that suggests he looked very much like you and me."

"It's not supposed to matter," had noted Akosua. "If we believe at all, then we walk by faith, not by sight."

"And yet the Europeans drew that farce of Christ and sent it all over the world for people of color to bow and worship. If it was of no consequence, can you tell me why they couldn't paint a picture of a Black Christ and hang it in their churches?"

Tears had shot into Chris' eyes, but where he normally would have cowered away from his fear, he refused to leave the matter this time. "Who do you see when you close your eyes to pray?" he'd asked Kofi.

The bemused look disappeared from Kofi's face. "I imagine a deep void, all encompassing, in which I myself am only a small part. God is the void itself."

Akosua, with a smile, had said, "I didn't know you ever prayed, Kofi. Anyway, if what you just described works for you, fine. Leave Chris to worship as he sees fit."

Chris had said, "Except I feel I never made the choice, you know? I always see that white man—he's the only God I've ever imagined when I close my eyes to pray. And you want to hear the truth? I wonder sometimes if I can ever be good enough, since I'm a black person and everything, to be accepted into his kingdom. I mean, I feel like I have to try harder than white people, you know?"

Akosua, trying to be helpful, had said, "Try to think of a black man just like yourself. Or, better still, imagine a black woman. I can't think of a better image for God than the image of humankind's first mothers." She'd paused to gauge Chris' reaction, but received none. "It's quite simple, really. If we are each created in God's image, then God looks just like you. That's really the end of that argument."

Chris, newly frazzled by the idea of God as woman, and a black one at that, was silent for a while. "That drawing is not Jesus?" He asked that of no one. "But it's in every church I've ever been to. Why?"

There was no answer. And as he sat in numb isolation, the countless lies of the world rolled over him and diluted his morale in one fast sweep. It was in the midst of these troubling times that the elephant summarily crushed the three-legged dog. Even with the pursuit of rabid dogs in his dreams over the following three nights, the incident had not left the sort of indelible mark it otherwise might have.

What was so monumental, after all, about the accidental death of an accidental dog trying to survive on an accidental planet sprouting from accidental explosions? Accidental man need not worry. His time will be up soon enough.

His final reach for assurance came in the charged silence of the weeks that followed, just before the topic might have lost all its currency. He had been alone with Kofi that day.

"So what do you truly believe in?"

To his utter surprise, tears had shot to Kofi's eyes. "I don't know what I believe in anymore these days," he'd said. "I do wonder why I don't commit myself to seek the greatest advantage if there is no consequence for anything beyond this cycle. Have I just been pro-grammed to fear so deeply?"

For a while Kofi was silent, and Chris' confusion deepened. He didn't think that was an answer to the question he'd posed.

Kofi's voice was mournful after the pause. "I believe we are part of something larger. But I don't think we act like the children of God, because God's children, I imagine, must be necessarily committed to ideals that uplift all of creation.

"I think we Africans shame our Maker. We shame God because we refuse to see the simple truth, that everything happening around us is the work of man. We are all expendable entities while the plunder-ing of our riches go on. What is happening to all of Africa's wealth? It is being stolen as we speak, by powerful people and corporations with no care for any of us. And you know the best that we do, as a people? We sit about, our worthless leaders at the front, beg for a few tokens, and as long as we have that, we will sing and dance all day. That's what Akosua means when she says that the world has gone to the dogs and that we have gladly given it to them.

"And in face of this reality, what do you hear when you go to church? You hear confused prattle from priests who would have you believe that God has willed this indignity on us, causing our children to starve and die needless deaths, our women to toil in vain and die without their suffering even recognized, and us, the men, to idle away without any good cause to justify our lives by. God did not do that to any of us, Kwesi."

Chris flinched. It was never a good sign when Kofi decided to call him by his Akan name, forsaking the European name he had been christened with, which Kofi occasionally expressed open disdain for.

"God did not do that to us and he is not coming to bail us out, not in this life and not in the hereafter. Have you ever wondered how, if we are children of the God with enough wisdom to put together such a complex universe, we can't seem to have the ability to transcend our pettiness and reach for a much better Africa for us all?

"From a long time ago, I've always believed that the kingdom of God that we pray for is a kingdom of justice, a kingdom of true compassion for one another that we can build right here, right now. I believe that Christ came and spent his whole life arguing for the cause of the downtrodden because justice and righteousness are much the same thing. So in fact righteousness, I believe, is about using our lives in the quest for a more just world, so that all of God's creatures can live in dignity. I don't believe that righteousness is about loud yelling about praise Jesus this, praise Jesus that, from a people who would otherwise accept the most undignified station just because they are afraid to confront the very real practitioners of evil who would consign them to their beggarly ways. If there is love at all, it must manifest in our desire to work towards a better world."

He was silent for a while, and his chest heaved as if he had more to say than his confused heart could find articulation for.

Chris had calmed down considerably by then. "Do you feel like a godly person?"

"No. I have done nothing to make this a better world."

Chris, observing Kofi's demeanor in a new light, had felt the deepest sadness. "If God came today, he'd be disappointed in all of us then."

Kofi had walked to the open window and cast his gaze on the empty, blue sky. He didn't need to reply, and indeed he said nothing. Chris finally thought he understood a little bit. He was no longer afraid that God might not exist, but for reasons he couldn't fully explain, tears welled in his eyes and began to flow unfettered. If God was not responsible for the misery he saw around him, then the world was an even sadder place than he had thought.

❧   ❧   ❧

At about three-quarters of a mile from the object in the middle of the road, Sylvester Preko, the guard riding in the passenger seat next to David Ofosu, the driver, picked his rifle up from his lap and wrapped his right hand tightly around the handgrip. Fear cradled him with the love of a mother, in one rush of a sweeping breath. Preko had never encountered a robbery attempt on any ride before. He was new yet, and robbery attempts on the elephant were certainly not commonplace. But the refrain during training had been the same: any attempt to stop the armored car must be treated as an attempted robbery.

His eyes dashed to Ofosu, then to the road, back to Ofosu, and back to the road, as though the rate of repetitiveness by itself could induce some event-altering effect. Preko's trepidation was readily apparent, if not easy to swallow. Since their car stopped for no one, and since the human form sprawled on the narrow road was at such an angle as to obviate the possibility of driving around it, they were going to have to crush her on their merry way. But could they—were they actually going to do this?

In Preko's mind there was always a time when one could break any binding codes for the right reason, just as long as the one wasn't him. He always knew that if someone came along and for the right reasons said let's break this or that code of conduct, he would gladly do it. For instance, back when he was much younger, there was a stretch of years when things had been really bad for his whole village. The harvest was awful, the market was not thriving and every one seemed to be struggling to get by on very little. He used to go starving at the time, and would often sit and think for many hours about stealing some food—any food. Coconuts were particularly easy targets because if you chose your time right and made sure no one was watching, you could climb up one of the trees with a machete between your teeth and cut one open right up there and eat it before you came down. As much as he starved that season, Sylvester Preko could not find the courage to steal by himself. But if any of his friends or cousins came and told him they were going to steal, he boldly joined them.

Ankrah—his favorite cousin—used to tell him that they were doing no wrong. Preko would ask why it wasn't wrong for them to be stealing, *and Ankrah would say, "Because we are stealing food to eat. There's no crime in that."*

Preko wondered how far he could push the limits of that justification. He found out quickly enough when, as a fourteen year old, he stole a gold chain from the saintly Mrs. Ankomah, and swore, upon being caught, that he was only hungry and fully intended to use every dime he would have obtained from the sale of the jewelry for nutritional purposes. People didn't seem to buy that. In fact he was lucky to have escaped with his life that day, when mob justice descended on him with blinding speed and fury. It led to him fleeing his village, and precipitated his enlistment into the military. For all that, he held the conviction that there were times when one did not have to walk the company line. But he was not about to share that sentiment with Ofosu. If however, Ofosu, who was at any rate his superior, were to suggest that they did not have to kill a woman lying prone on the street on the justification that the elephant stops for on one, he knew he would wholeheartedly support the man. And so they drifted towards the prone body.

By his estimation they had bowled their way through the mirage of potholes to within a quarter of a mile of the prone figure lying across the road. The hands of fear, until now surrounding him in an unnerving, gentle cradle, reached out suddenly and grabbed him by the neck, then squeezed. He could see that the figure on the street was that of a woman. There was nothing immediately noticeable about her to suggest that she was in need of any medical attention, which meant, obviously, that this was indeed a mere ruse to get the elephant to stop. The stupidity of her act was astonishing to Preko. Why not set up some elaborate scheme of logs and cement blocks or something? True, the elephant was capable of bowling over most things, but one would think that out here in the middle of nowhere, the would-be thieves could make some ingenuous use of the surrounding secondary forest to try and stop the armored car. They had chosen instead, if he was right, to hedge their bet on the presumed compassion of the driver. This was completely baffling. Didn't everyone from these areas know that the elephant stopped for no one? It was not a matter of human compassion at all. It was simply that when great wealth is being coveted, ant-workers—and he certainly knew enough to know he was one of those—are paid whatever they're paid to deliver the wealth where it is meant to go. Exercising humanity is not an option for an ant-worker.

"What are you going to do?" He was looking eagerly at Ofosu.

"She'll rise." The way Ofosu said that, it was quite obvious he was only expressing a wishful thought.

Preko said, "What if she doesn't? Maybe she truly is in need of some help?"

"Can you see anything about her to suggest that she's in need of medical help?"

"There are so many mysterious things about women. Maybe we just can't see what's bothering her."

The elephant crept dangerously closer as they spoke, and Preko was not entirely certain that there would be enough time left to avert the disaster if they did not begin braking right away. Completely frightened by now, he thought it might be best if he shut his eyes and pretended that none of this was taking place at all. Sylvester Preko was about to shut his eyes when he caught the sudden motion in the bushes through the window on the driver's side. Ofosu caught it, too, almost simultaneously. It was the sight of a man, waving frantically, obviously very alarmed. From this angle, it was hard to discern exactly what was going on with the man. He was concealed waist down by the bush of the secondary forest, further adding to the mystery of his intended action. He looked as if he was doing battle with the forest for his freedom while trying to wave down the armored car, although it was not immediately obvious that he was armed. Then, almost as suddenly as the mysterious man had appeared, a single shot tore into the quiet, empty space of the eerie encounter, its source unknown.

"It's a trap!"

The realization breezed past Preko's lips and seemed to immediately trigger an instinctive response. Leaning back, he aimed his rifle across

David Ofosu's face, in the direction of the man struggling with the forest, with only the slightest acknowledgment of the fact that this was perhaps the worst possible course of action under the circumstances. Although he did not pause to reflect on it, Preko felt a strange sensation crawl down his spine on the frightening premonition that this could well be the end of them all. He cupped his finger over the trigger of his rifle.

Ofosu, the driver of the elephant, clutched tightly at the steering wheel and reached for the clutch, his face a mask of sheer terror and perplexity. But he registered his greatest alarm at the sight of the barrel pointed across his face. His expression seemed to suggest that, notwithstanding the alarming prospect before them, he could not believe the guard's first reaction was to aim his rifle across his face. He was about to say something, it seemed, when the rifle went off.

☙   ☙   ☙

Akosua sat in the waiting room of the district hospital and held on tightly to her black handbag, trying to suppress the shiver within. The effort was in vain. Even her heart shivered and burned relentlessly, as though everything inside of her was doused in flames. Rose, her good friend from elementary school, used to say that the biggest problem with African women was their persistence in suffering in silence. Akosua herself had amended the statement.

"It's not just African women," she'd said. "That's one trait we probably share with most of the women of the world."

"Well it's stupid. It is stupid, stupid, stupid. Why do we have to bear our suffering in silence?"

Akosua had said, "I think it's because men are stupid enough to do just that."

"That's just foolish," had said Rose. "It's foolish, foolish, foolish. All it ever got them is an early ticket to the grave. I refuse to abide any suffering in silence."

Ah, Rose. She'd been such a delight to have around. It was said of her that she was so impatient her mouth spoke ahead of her mind's ability to process what she wanted to say. She died in labor, and true to her word, that woman went screaming so loudly there must not have been a soul in all of Mankraso that did not hear her agonizing departure. She was still remembered for that small act of inconsequential defiance. Akosua, holding her breath under the strain of her own searing pains, wondered whether perhaps there was something to be said for small acts of inconsequential defiance.

There was a knock inside her head. It felt alternatively like the rip of a chainsaw, or the steadfast, regular thumping of a hammer, swinging on a pendulum. It would smack left, generate a searing wave of pain and then ride on the momentum of the pain to the adjacent end, cutting along the way like a hammer adorned with many blades. With each strike, Akosua would grit her teeth and close her eyes, fighting to hold back the tears that were threatening to gush out in heavy flow. And always, she felt terribly alone. Down below, the effort to control her fright was not proving as successful as the effort to hold her tears. Claps of thunder would register somewhere in the region below her rib cage, then rumble with an irrepressible growl down the length of her intestines, slowly, snarling louder every step of the way. She kept her eyes down at her feet, but she could feel the uncomfortable glances stolen at her by the other patients in the waiting area. The glances would cause her to shiver even more, spurring the burning in her heart, just when the hammer of blades would swing against the walls of her skull, triggering further claps of thunder in her rib cage, thus bringing more glances her way. She just sat there, and held very still through the ordeal of having her own body treat her as the most unwelcome guest. It was all she could do.

Directly across from her, on a long bench sitting against the opposite wall, a young child, very lean but with a bloated stomach, lay across its mother's lap, struggling to breathe. The mother had the child lying on its back—from where she sat Akosua could not make the child's gender—so she could massage the child's chest in the effort to ease the asthmatic wheezing. The effort wasn't helping. The child appeared to be dying—so strained its desperate breathing—and the alarmed mother, close to tears, was clearly not interested in hiding her panic. Her eyes moved continuously, from her child to the others in the waiting area, to the nurse who sat in an enclosed cubicle further down the corridor, to the closed door that led to the doctor's office, and back to her child. The white of her eyes seemed to widen a bit more with each inspection of her child. No one was paying attention. Akosua took a moment to cast a searching glance over the rest of the patients waiting with her. A quiet, large crowd had grown from the two she found when she first arrived. The large number temporarily threw her. She was surprised to notice that in her deep fear for herself she had completely lost consciousness of her bearings. Now that she was registering them, she saw a depressing mirage descend over her ever-sinking mental state, dulling the physical pain within and replacing it with something far more threatening.

This was the only district hospital within a thirty-mile radius. Those who took the journey from surrounding villages to come here did so only after they had exhausted every other potential source of relief. That much was common knowledge. But she was only now noticing that she was sitting with just such a crowd because she did not recognize any of those sitting in the waiting area. They were out-of-towners, and every one of them was ailing too much to see the pain next to them. For a moment Akosua was deeply ashamed. After all, for all her mental agonizing, she was not in as bad a physical shape as anyone else in the waiting area, at least on the surface. And it was possible that the paralyzing fear holding her captive was nothing more than a nightmare drawn up by a mind not easily forgiving of itself, for her one moment of terrible indiscretion. Then again, maybe it was not. The one thought that struck her with the coldest reality as she scoured the length of the verandah was that this was not a society that cared for itself.

Once she was chatting with Dr. James Ofori-Quaye, who used to be stationed here, about the state of the population's general health. The doctor had been lamenting bitterly about his felt helplessness—a medical doctor incapable of the simplest healing task because the hospital he ran never had adequate supplies. He told of the several occasions that he took his complaint either to the regional office or the health ministry in Accra, when he could steal the time to make the trip. There was never much to show for his troubles. Colleagues in Accra would chastise him for wasting his talents on poor, insignificant people in the middle of nowhere when he could be using his skills on important people. They were further astounded by the stupidity that would lead him to come banging his head against walls. Ultimately they felt sorry for him. Dr. Ofori-Quaye would return to the hospital in Mankraso and inject the patients with water for their ailments. This was the unspoken rule of all encounters with doctors: an injection had to be administered. The patients simply won't hear otherwise. They felt it was the least they deserved for taking the long journey to come to the hospital. They deserved an injection—some proof that a doctor had been consulted and a painful cure administered, the more painful the better. Mothers would beg for it, for themselves and for their children, oblivious to the greater risk of infection from needles that couldn't always be properly sterilized.

"Do they know it's just water you're pumping them with?" Akosua had asked.

Dr. Ofori-Quaye shook his head.

"But then shouldn't they be disillusioned by now, since they probably do not get well from receiving the water?"

"I think they actually *will* themselves to better health, most of them, just on the belief of the curative power of the injection."

"You can't be serious."

A guilty smiled touched the doctor's face. "I don't help matters. I avoid giving them water injection except for benign conditions. So they almost always get better."

"Why must you give them the false hope?"

"Because it is hope still. What is the alternative?"

"Maybe they shouldn't be coming here at all. It may force them to rely on traditional medicines. Or you could make it your business to organize them in such a way that they can petition for better services from the proper authorities." She smiled when she said that—presumably because here in Ghana such idealism is always laughable—but the doctor did not share her amusement.

"I know some of our traditional medicines work. We could do a better job of using sound research to find out which ones work for what, and tap into that resource. You're right about that. And I know that empowering our people to know how to make the government accountable is not a bad idea. Our traditional systems of rule have favored transparency and accountability anyway, so I don't even understand why we can't seem to integrate those traditions into our politics. So yes, I agree with you on that as well. But look at me. I'm hogtied from dusk till dawn, feeding folks the false hope they need to make it through a day. When am I supposed to find the time to become a social activist?"

Somewhat surprised by his indignation, Akosua tried to massage the silence with a conciliatory gaze into his eyes. But the doctor, in a startling outburst unlike anything she had witnessed from him, had said, "Nobody in this country who could make a difference gives a damn! None of them gives a damn!"

About three years after that conversation, Dr. Ofori-Quaye left for Accra to launch another complaint and never returned. He must have tired of pumping water into his patients. The pain for those who despaired for a better society was massive, and it cut deep. Akosua herself had once, in an irreverent outburst in class during her university years, said that the domestic policy of most African leaders was a not a policy at all but a state of mind.

"They're stuck somewhere at the intersection of deep apathy and unmitigated greed, which is where every domestic policy of theirs appears to spring from. And don't even ask about our foreign policies. It pretty much boils down to perpetual begging. You would never guess that we inherit what is arguably the world's richest continent in natural resources."

In those debates during the university years, she was part of a small faction of the student body that was already issuing an urgent call for the newly-independent nations of Africa to seize their collective destiny by the horns—damn the opinion of outsiders—lest development become a mere ruse for outsiders to continue dominating the affairs of the land. She had made the point again in a letter to Kofi.

"We need to find ways to put a stop, even now, to the erosion of our African essence. Otherwise we are robbed of our purpose, and this can only lead to the continued domination of the continent by Eastern and Western hegemonies. We need to channel our greed toward the pursuit of dignity instead of consumerism. I am worried, Kofi, by our lack of urgency in these matters."

Kofi had responded with a very sympathetic letter. "I see your point," it had said, in part. "The signs are already disturbing. African countries coming into independence are still more interested in their relationship with the former colonizer than with other African nations. I pray that it is not too late already, and that something can come out of the movement for unity. I pray that enough of them give a damn to take a stand for our people, and our heritage."

CHAPTER 6

Of her many frustrations—and Akosua had many—few were as maddening as the constant reminder from men that at forty she still looked as if she was barely breaching thirty, and that her physical attractiveness had dimmed only slightly from when she used to turn every man's eye. So much nonsense made her want to scream. There was simply no end to the sheer idiocy of men. She was supposed to feel a sense of fulfillment from that—from the knowledge, apparently, that she could still be the focus of the wet dreams of a few men. What, dear God, were the women of the world doing allowing such idiots to run things?

But then she would remember her belief in the pettiness of women. Not that she was particularly wed to any of these concerns, but the idea that she was supposed to draw some bizarre pride from her enduring physical attributes invariably triggered the more legitimate concern, related to the legacy she hoped to leave behind. This was a sticking point for her like no other. In a somewhat disingenuous move, she had handpicked one her nieces, Adjoa, to become the embodiment of her own legacy. She had picked Adjoa because the young girl, her sister's second child, had shown great promise from her earliest years. Akosua's idea was to pour as much of her resources as possible behind her niece, and nurture and support her development, so that by the time she matured, Adjoa would be an advanced version of Akosua herself.

Adjoa died of malaria at the age of six, when she was supposed to have escaped the most vulnerable years. She was one of twelve nieces Akosua could recall burying, but her death had been the most difficult for her to take. She died needlessly because of the length of time it took for her mother, Akosua's sister, to get her request for help to her and for Akosua to send the medicine they wanted back to the village. The village of Nankesedo was only fifty-six miles from Mankraso. It took three days for the request to get to Akosua. That fine son of Africa, Nyerere, had put it succinctly when he noted in mocking tone that the White man set out for the moon at about the same time that the African set out for the village. The white man has been to the moon and back, several times, while the African continues to struggle to get to the village.

By the time the medicine reached the village, another three days later, Adjoa was dead. In the numbing aftermath of the tragedy, Akosua, heaping equal blame on herself and on the system that held all of them prisoners, had vowed that heads would roll when she returned to Mankraso from the funeral and went to the district office to voice her complaints. She returned to Mankraso and was very unpleasant to everyone for a full week, telling Chris to shut up and grow up when he complimented her for looking nice. Here she had gone to bury the niece who would have carried her legacy, and again the stupid focus on her looks. For that particular rudeness, Kofi had confronted her. He had done so with some sympathy, actually, noting that he understood her loss, but that there were better ways of grieving.

"To hell with you! You are all the same. You take the life of a woman and reduce the significance of it to whether she featured in your wet dreams. One day I will cut off my breasts and thighs and feed it to your stupid, puny and useless minds."

Kofi, gritting his teeth, refused to indulge her quest for a pro-
tracted conflict. He had said instead, in an immediate, final rebuttal,
"You insulted Chris today. All he did was compliment you for looking nice. No one said that should define your sense of being. Yet for
that you insulted him, and his family with him. You claim to want to
be recognized for the content of your character. If we did, you won't
deserve the friendship of any of us, certainly not on the basis of your
recent manners. I don't think you even know who you are yourself."

A week after Kofi spoke like that to her, Akosua slapped his
daughter Esther, so hard the girl fell to the ground, all because the
young girl had taken too long, in Akosua's estimation, running an
errand she'd sent her on. She had had to endure the fury of Kofi's
wife—Efuwa—on that occasion and it had been scary.

"I don't mind you disciplining my child for just cause," she'd said.
"But the next time you lay your hands on my child like that, I will kill
you. Go have your own kids and beat them up if you want, but don't
ever take your madness out on my children."

It was perhaps the most depressed time of her life, not much
helped by the stupidity of the men all around her. But her world was
spinning out of her control for more substantive reasons. She was
angry and frustrated over so much, beginning with the choices she'd
made in her life. All her ambitions had mostly died unfulfilled, and
there was only minimal comfort to be drawn from knowing that she
had given some good effort. She had tried to build an after-school
academy for young girls, intending to provide them with additional
knowledge and skills, but never could secure the funds for such an
undertaking. She tried to join with some of the churches to offer special lessons to young girls that equated godliness with the fight for
their rights. This would have been a boon for their self-esteem, but
the effort, like the first, collapsed long before it could take form.
None of the churches cared for the idea. In her classroom, she tried
to engage her students to start small, homegrown enterprises, both
as a means to teach the virtues of collective enterprise and to make

their community better. That, too, fell through. There was not much support from the start, except from Kofi and Kwame, who were otherwise engaged, so the germs of ideas died in early infancy. Over fifteen years of trying out these small ideas, she eventually ran out of them altogether, but not before she had turned down Kofi's proposal for marriage.

She actually felt she deserved better at the time, and was soon to leave for Accra, where she would miraculously rise to national prominence. Then what would she do with Kofi for husband, given that Kofi had willfully given up all his ambitions for national leadership? So she turned him down. But whatever she considered better, she never found it, perhaps because sometimes life offers the best it has to offer next door. There was, too, the belated realization from communications with old college mates, that those women who were finding their ways to the chambers of power were resorting to means to get there that Akosua was not ready to consider. Generalizations aside, too many of the women were being forced to lose the best of themselves in order to ascend the ladder of power, at which point it didn't matter that they had made it, since they became the embodiment of the very ill they intended to do away with when they first sought power. What alternatives there might have been were not apparent to her.

In her arrogance she had partly believed that Kofi would wait and ask her again, when he could ascertain that she had outgrown her dreams. Instead Kofi decided to move on with his life, and she was never convinced that he liked the choice he made, although they both knew that once he had made his choice, it was final. It should have never gotten to that point.

❦   ❦   ❦

She would later go to the municipal council director's office. She wasn't exactly sure what she expected a powerless man like a municipal council director to be able to do about her grievance, but there was at least the possibility that she could vent away some of her frustrations. It was in the middle of the afternoon when she paid him that visit, cuddling the recollection that the man was very hostile.

When she stepped in the office and said hello, the man, without even looking at her, kept ruffling through his drawer. She said something about wanting to lodge a complaint. That drew a reaction from the director. He paused his fussing long enough to enjoy a great laugh, and when he was done, he looked at his watch and told her to hurry up with it. Then, and only then, did it hit her that she did not even know what was so specifically infuriating to her. She stood there for a while, and the surprising, and rather simple inquiry came to her almost as an afterthought. "Why?"

"Why what?"

"Why do we live in a country that tolerates such undignified living for its own citizenry? Why do we live in a country that has such little regard for the lives of its own children? I just lost my niece to malaria because it takes nearly a week to get medicine over a distance not more than sixty miles."

Hostility replaced the laughter on the face of the director. "First of all," he had said when she was done, "I'm not going to take the blame for this. What do you want me to do about your niece dying? Everybody has relatives who die of malaria all the time. Last week my own nephew died of malaria. In fact, in the last several months I've lost about three or four relatives through malaria. I don't know why you are coming to me to tell me about your niece's death as if she is so different from everyone else. As for the roads you are complaining about, and the general difficulties with the communication system, you talk as if I am responsible for building the infrastructure from here to Nankesedo. But that is not my responsibility. In fact, road maintenance and communications are not my responsibilities at all." Then, as if a sudden revelation had struck him, he'd said, "Maybe we can go out for a drink tonight and I can fully assess what your problem is and how to make you feel better."

Akosua had walked out without another word. Her next option would have been to go to the district office, assuming she actually thought something would come out of the trip. She knew better. So much for the thought of heads rolling because her niece had died unnecessarily. Years ago, she used to write letters to the editors of some of the national newspapers, decrying the abominable conditions of her community, which, as far as she was concerned, mirrored all but a few of the nation's communities. She thought she could stir up some debate on the miserable state of the environment around them, the exhausting, oppressive poverty, and so doing maybe raise a collective outcry, perhaps even compel the government to develop some small sense of accountability. Her reward: a couple of her letters were printed, and her friends saw it and told her each time that it was a "pretty nice letter." And that was that.

For a very long time now, there had truly not been anything to stay around for. When she made the casual decision to entertain the advances of Francis, the former classmate who had returned from years of traveling abroad and living in Kumasi, it was against her better instinct, and it reflected her near-complete loss of inspiration about the trajectory of her life. She could almost see how, in acting so forcefully against her gut instinct, the condom they used in their one and only sexual encounter broke.

And so it had come to this. Perhaps she did not have to die. But for that to be true she needed to be living for something, and she had exhausted all reasons. Death no longer held for her the kernel of fear, which was why she could lie here in this unconscionable wait and find that her biggest fear was to come out of this alive. Meanwhile the fog around her mind had thickened. It wasn't simply that she found the struggle to carry on unbearable. It was more that everything was so meaningless now, so utterly without purpose there was a genuine curiosity over what lay beyond.

Was the painful, slow death that awaited her a dignified alternative to what she was half hoping for now? Her mind, badly clouded by now, did not offer an answer. She thought she heard the heavy rumbling of tires get very close. A spinning sensation filled her head, and for a moment or two, she felt as if she were levitating, and thought for a moment that she could see herself sitting up, without having any control of the action that brought her upright. Her eyes had grown unnaturally heavy by now. She fought to open them.

❦   ❦   ❦

It was finally her turn to see the doctor. At least she tried to convince herself that it was more or less her turn. In fact there were two patients she had found there upon her arrival, who deserved, in all fairness, to see the doctor ahead of her. Had the nurse kept the schedule it would have been so, but Dr. Nketia had stepped out briefly after attending to the asthmatic child, and seen Akosua. He called her specifically to "come in, Akosua. Come in. Why didn't you tell the nurse who you are?"

"And who am I?" she'd wanted to ask. "Whoever am I?"

More pertinent, she had wanted to say that she was content to wait her turn, but she arose instead and followed the doctor. Experience had taught her that those left behind do not necessarily open their arms with appreciation to welcome those who refuse to join the line of the chosen. Once before, when Ofori-Quaye was still the doctor in town, Akosua had gone to the hospital and been invited by the doctor to jump ahead of those she had found there. She had smiled thankfully and told the doctor that she would wait her turn, thinking those sitting in the waiting area with her would think her decent and just. Instead, throughout the rest of her wait that day, the other patients treated her with open disdain. She got the sense that where they were concerned, she had taken the simple opportunity to distance herself from the ordinary, and shoved it right in their face. The poor are not lesser people, but they do not cherish the fact of being poor, and certainly do not admire the silliness of those who spurn the opportunity for even fleeting privileges away from them. She entered the office and took the seat she was invited to take.

"So, how are you today?"

In that moment she knew. Perhaps it was in the unexpected, cordial offering from the doctor. Nketia had been trying for as long as he had been posted in Mankraso to get into Akosua's pants. He was an incredibly self-assured man, the sort of man in whose hands the art of healing became a weapon of the worst sort. He had no qualms admitting to friends that he could get his way with just about any woman he desired because he often met them at their most vulnerable. The first time he saw Akosua he offered her the world, with a straight face, and said his wife did not have to know. To his credit, he did not single-mindedly pursue her with quite the frightful promise he had given her that he would. He was clearly pre-occupied with too many easier catches to worry over the few who escaped the wide net he cast.

But he was persistent, never missing a chance to renew his pursuit when she showed up at the hospital. The last time she saw him the doctor been surprisingly compassionate. She had told him about the mishap in her only sexual encounter in many years, and noted that, coupled with the discovery she had made about the object of her recent affections, she was afraid the die might have been cast. Doctor Nketia, assuring her that the odds were in her favor, personally took her blood sample and told her that he would make sure the blood got to Accra for the two most reliable tests, but that it would take a while. Then he made a pass at her. Somewhat perplexed, Akosua had asked why he kept on making passes at her when he knew exactly what he was going to hear? He had said, with a light shrug and an easy smile, that it never hurt, and besides one never knows when a woman would change her mind, not even the woman.

She said in response to him presently, "I'm doing fine, thank you. And you?"

"Never better. You are looking very lovely today."

A small grin sprinted across her lips. "Thank you."

For a moment he sat and stared at her quite bluntly.

"So," said Akosua, sighing heavily.

"I don't know if there's any other way of breaking this news to you." A small, lingering silence tried to take seat between the breadth of his delivery, then vanished as the roar of her heartbeat began to ring in her head. "Your test was positive."

The words raced from his lips on a straight trajectory, without hesitation, and slapped her head-on. She had thought that she would burst into tears immediately at the news, but no tears came as yet. Instead her eyes dried up almost completely at the hearing, and stood frozen on her face, looking at the doctor. She saw a mirage. She became, once again, keenly aware of the beat of her heart, a furious pounding that seemed to be the only reasonable expression of the fear gripping her. For a second her head spun, forcing her to clutch the armrest of her chair and shut her eyes. Here in this moment of having her death announced to her, she found that her first thought was to Kofi Mensah. Much as she had tried to ignore this essential truth of her life, there was nothing more important to her than Kofi, a simple fact immensely magnified in this most desperate of times when the love of a single soul was the absolute minimum requirement to carry a shattered self past the early storm. How was she going to share this shame with him? Or was that not the right way to think about this? Was it better to ask how she was going to share this tragedy? Either way, shame or tragedy, what would he think? What would the other friends think? Would they accept her folly and comfort her in her time of greatest need? What possible comfort could they give her? Could she accept her own folly and forgive herself and the man involved?

Rather suddenly, in the wide frame of her mind's eye, a thousand faces began to flow. They glided by gently, like the gentle currents of a gentle river, with an infinite space to explore. A cloud of the whitest shade carried them, as though they were the inheritors of the very essence of vanity, here to remind her of the vanity of her own life. Family and friends, dead and alive, came to wave their immediate smile at her, but she noticed they were not reproachful. These were smiles of comfort, from a collective of kind faces. Even the faces of those towards whom she harbored hostility, not all justified, or who harbored it for her—even they came smiling, but with a look of pity that made her shrink inside. What would the ones living say of her when they heard of her dying? How impossibly small she felt in this moment. How impossibly worthless she felt in this moment. It came to her, in this moment when her time seemed to stop, that there could be no feeling worst than to be burdened by so many regrets over one's life so late along the way. The world had come and sat on her shoulders, and found them wanting, but had shown no pity in perhaps relieving her of the weight of her own conscience. How could her whole life have dissolved into this essential failure?

She had dreamt of saving a nation, for the love of God! She had dreamt of having the courage, the dedication and the luck of the draw to be a player on the national front. Instead here she sat in her pitiful glory, in this God-awful hospital, in this improbable situation, without even the simple comfort of one loving soul to lean on. Then again, perhaps that was the point. Intentions are of some consequence if followed by the right choices. And she was in this lonely state not because her heart had been in the wrong place, but because she never got wise enough to choose well when the moments presented. At least so her heart told her.

The voice across the table drifted to her through a silent drum, "There is no shortage of men you could have had. I just don't understand, Akosua. How could you have made such a poor choice?"

Dr. Nketia was voicing his opinion, as unnecessary as that was in this moment. The sound of his voice caused the dam to break. Her first tear came down in one long thin line, falling off her chin into a void deep down below, where she was sinking, body and soul. She wasn't sure that it was the doctor's question that made her cry. The tears appeared to spring from a much deeper source than anything the question could have provoked. It felt like the beginning of a deeper appreciation of everything about life, even the simple drift of a voice through a silent drum across a table. A soft sigh lifted her chest gently, and released it in a heavy fall. The doctor arose from his chair and came around. She arose too, trying to gather her wits about her, and moved towards the door.

"There are drugs to help you live longer."

Akosua, pausing by the door, smiled a small smile. "Yes, but who has access to them? Besides, I can't afford them, you know that."

The doctor drew closer. There had never been a time that she could recall, when his approach, however brazen, had not been respectful, until now.

"I can help you," he said. He had taken a strong hold of her forearm. His intent staggered her, and for a good stretch her disbelief clouded her face.

Tears returned to her eyes. "I could kill you." She did not intend it as a threat, the first time. She was actually concerned for him.

"That's why there's protection. Heck, I'll use two condoms if I have to, however much I hate those things. But I'll be fine, I assure you. And we can keep you going for much longer."

Her rage raced back into her heart, providing the warmest reminder that she was alive still, and here, however temporarily.

"I could kill you." She meant the statement as a threat the second time, with such cold gentility the doctor shrank back. Akosua opened the door, still in disbelief, and walked out already engulfed by the powerful pull of loneliness. The next transition was surprising. She began to hear her voice almost as soon as she had crossed the threshold of the doctor's office. I'm going to die. I'm going to die, dear God. I'm going to die. It was an echo and a still voice, all at once, penetrating, becoming. I am going to die. They filled the void of her heart, the void of her mind and completely took over her being. I'm going to die, dear God. In short order there was no void within her at all; the fear had taken over completely, filling every void and crevice with the substance of the felt fear. I am going to die, and what have I done with my life?

The door closed behind her. Almost simultaneously, a lump of something mysterious shot up from her heart and clogged her breathing. Her head spun, and she wheezed in a desperate reach for air. The faces of the other patients in the waiting area threw themselves at her, children and their parents, suffering masses of humanity awaiting the administering of water, the prolonging of pain and agony without end. She gasped at the sight of her own hell, heaved and moaned, drowning in the stale air of the hospital, and collapsed in a heavy fall right outside the doctor's office, trying desperately to call for help.

❦   ❦   ❦

Even discarding the possibility of a collective unconscious, the memory of the three-legged dog that was summarily crushed by the elephant years ago was easily the most appropriate memory for the moment. It required such little effort, really.

Like each of the witnesses to the unfolding of this most unnatural event, excepting Edom, Kwame cried within. Time rolled by, keeping its rhythm, and after the accumulation of sorrow had topped the vessel within, what was inside of Kwame eventually gushed out unfettered, flowing freely. He cradled his gun in a firmer grasp. This was too painful, this witnessing of their ultimate destruction of themselves. It was insane, and it was stupid. But he had a part of him that understood somehow that much of this was also inevitable. Their lives had turned into a pointless journey long ago—long back when they sank into a routine of marking time.

If a man would watch his life slide into a routine of meaningless gestures—if a man would, of a good conscience, fail to find an ounce of meaning by which to measure his passage through this cycle, then surely that man is to be likened to a wounded dog that had its life snuffed by the reckless driver of an armored truck in a poignant celebration of all things meaningless.

❦   ❦   ❦

Kwame remembered the dog well. For him, what was even more unforgettable about the dog's dying was the aftermath of its death. For a week or so after the accident, the carcass of the dog lay there, in the middle of the street. Most drivers navigated around it, a few particularly vile ones passed over it again. By the forth or fifth day worms were crawling out of every orifice of the carcass. The dog's eyes and mouth had turned into black holes spewing a million maggots that mingled comfortably with flies in the continuous flow of their own existence. Then the smell began to rise and take over control of the immediate environment.

Some angry community members went to the municipal council to complain to the director. They demanded to know how it was that the office responsible for matters of public good did nothing for the public good. How could a dead dog be left rotting in the street in the middle of town like that? Kwame recalled that particular protest because he had been caught up in it by a determined crowd that was recruiting as it went, and Kwame had acquiesced, keenly curious to hear the popularly hostile director's response to their outcry.

"First of all," had said the director, "you fucking hypocrites should be ashamed of yourselves, coming to me to ask me to wipe that stinking carcass off the street. I'm even sure some of you hypocrites enjoyed the spectacle of the accident and did nothing to stop it. Do I look like I was brought here to wipe the stinking carcass of dogs off the street? Whose stupid dog was that dog anyway? Why don't you ask that person to clean the stinking carcass? Second of all, I hear that your undisciplined children chased the dog into the way of the car. Why don't you let the children wipe the carcass off the street?

That will teach them something about chasing dogs into the street when cars are passing by. As for you parents…"

What happened next had taken everybody, the municipal council director foremost, by total surprise. Right in the middle of his last statement, an empty beer bottle flew through the protesting group, barely missing the forehead of the director, and smashed to pieces against the wall behind him. Faced with the sudden and immediate danger, the municipal council director's eyes widened. Like everyone else present, he was fully cognizant of the weight of the moment. The sudden tension was palpable, for the next moment would determine whether an angry mob incited by the daring act of one of them closed in for the kill, or whether the director managed to save his skin by regaining control of the situation.

"Busumtwi!"

The call came out of the director plaintively, almost as a wail, ending abruptly in a grunt. The municipal council security guard, Busumtwi, stepped in front of his boss and, as Kwame recalled, made some fanciful noise with the gun in his hand to suggest that he was ready to fire it. A sudden, deeper silence bathed over the protesting group. This was something new, this improbable moment of impasse occasioned by the threatened use of force by the municipal council security guard.

Someone had said, "That thing isn't even loaded!"

The eyes of the director widened further. If in fact his bodyguard's gun was not loaded, then the danger to the director's life was not over as yet. Busumtwi responded by firing a single shot into the air. Nobody in the whole town of Mankraso knew that this solemn, always subdued Busumtwi would go to such lengths to keep his job. The gunfire just about froze everyone. An inkling of regained confidence seeped into the director's eyes, dimming the brightness of his fear. Slowly, a wisp of pleasure returned to his face, as relief cleared the cloud over his brow.

Another voice rose out of the crowd. By then the reason for their protest was entirely moot. The new voice had said, "Your zombie security guard can protect you now, but we know where you live!"

But the municipal council director's confidence had returned in full force by then.

"First of all," he began in response, "you fucking hypocrites had better know that I have some vicious dogs behind the walls of my compound." This was quite true, as everyone already knew. "Second of all, Busumtwi stays with me. He will be within his legal rights to shoot anybody who threatens me. I would like to see one of you try it and see for yourself. In fact, after today, I will no longer allow your dirty children to come and pick the fallen mangoes from the trees in my backyard. You fucking hypocrites don't even deserve that. You have no manners, coming here to throw bottles at me because you refuse to remove the carcass of a dead dog from your own street."

He had offered this to the last of the protesters as they began to file away, "That's exactly what's wrong with this town. Everybody says they want things to be better, everybody is always complaining about how our society is moving backwards, but no one ever wants to do anything to make things better. Fucking hypocrites!"

On the day of that protest, while the protesters still milled about in frustrated unrest, Kwame, feeling a sudden surge of depression, had walked away from the gathering. He took the path up the small hill in the direction of the police station, taking care not to step in the infested, green-yellow liquid that trickled from the waste bucket in the house latrine behind the Quainoo home. He continued up the rocky hill behind the Quainoo family house, walking past the abandoned shed that used to be one of the symbols of Master Quainoo's prosperity, now a sore sight that the Quainoo family did not seem to want to do away with. The Quainoo family claimed that the shed marked the limits of their property, relative to the grounds of the police station, even though a short wire-fence separated their property from the police station.

Past the dust-soaked police station, there was a stretch of three canteens, where lunch came cheap, affording the police officers a place to eat on credit from mid-month, about the time they found their monthly salaries exhausted. Kwame had worked here before, in the dusty office he now walked by without emotion. This used to be his window, too. It gave view to nothing but the brief rise of clay ground that lay in total waste, devoid of fertility or promise, reminding all of the waste of human lives around here. The land rose on a gentle slant up the small hill, then stopped its brief ascent and dipped suddenly and sharply down the clay ravine. Wasted lives, land without promise. You had to wonder how the living continued at all, for all the desperate souls swimming against the relentless currents of imported, irrelevant, soul-less modernity, against a morality that was all by itself the greatest obstacle to their welfare.

It was one of the reasons Kwame used to like Master Quainoo—his determination not to succumb to the idiocy of things new just because they were modern. But his protests against the idiocy of accumulation of unnecessary materials just for its sake were mocked. Of course one needed to show a sense of dignity by owning big television sets. Master Quainoo, a flawed man, told the world of its idiocy all the way to his grave. Kwame's liking for the man extended to the fact that he had also been a wonderful headmaster at the Methodist Elementary School. Unlike most other headmasters, Master Quainoo enjoyed teaching as well. His favorite subject was history, "particularly colonial history, but also Ivan the Terrible history," he would say.

Nobody quite understood his obsession with "Ivan the Terrible history." For two generations he taught the same lesson on Ivan the Terrible. For two generations he laid the whip to his pupils for not answering his penultimate question correctly: why was 'Ivan the terrible' a bad ruler?

The answer: Ivan the terrible was a bad ruler because, due to his greed, blood was spilt, lives were lost, and it was terrible.

One particular day Kwame's son came home from school after a history exam, immensely distraught. He had done terribly on the last question of the exam and had been caned for being wrong. Kwame went in to see Master Quainoo the next day. He did so with some trepidation, to be sure. Master Quainoo was too frequently of a sour mood to be ever taken lightly. Word had it one of his own children once called him 'Mister' and was slapped senseless for it. "I am your Master! Master Quainoo. Don't ever call me mister again! I will kill you!"

It wasn't likely that anyone else besides his children was afraid of being slapped senseless by the stout, belligerent headmaster. All the same, no one called him anything other than Master Quainoo. A visit to the Master's office was always an improbable ordeal. He insisted on seeing people by appointment alone, even though there was no telephone at the school. Hence to see the Master, the guest was expected to get himself to the school, just to arrange to come another day. Once in a while Master Quainoo would agree to see a guest on the same day they came in to make an appointment, just as long as the guest had compelling reasons for wanting to meet with the headmaster. Master Quainoo's secretary would ask a series of questions: what do you want to see the good Master about?; did you bring any donations to help with school administration? A positive answer to the second question would usually earn you an appointment, but it wasn't the only condition. Whether or not you got audience with Master Quainoo depended in equal measure on his mood in the hour of your visit. If he was in a good mood, chances were Master Quainoo would send the guest packing without audience—"I don't want anyone to come in and spoil my good mood." On his bad days he freely welcomed all comers, and sent them back "shitting peppers." On the day Kwame went to talk about his son's history exam grade, Master Quainoo freely welcomed him.

"You gave my boy a terrible grade and caned him for his answer to the last question on the history exam." Having thus began his complaint, Kwame sat there, awaiting a response.

Master Quainoo initially just sat with stone-faced silence, clearly seething. Then he began to shake his head, and a small smirk touched his face. "How dare you come into my office to question me about how I run my school?"

Kwame was taken aback, for all his preparedness to deal with the headmaster. "I am not here to question how you run anything. I just came to…"

"Who are you? Who do think you are? Who are you? If I remember well, you didn't even pass your exams to get into the university. Isn't that why you ended up becoming a petty police officer? And even then didn't your morally questionable character cause you to lose that job? Stupid boy, how dare you question me?"

There had been a grinding of molars, but otherwise determined calmness from Kwame, as he continued reminding himself that the man was just this unpleasant, all the time, and he had to fight to get past it. "Your question was why Ivan the terrible was a terrible ruler. It was the last question on the test."

"Yes! And your boy got it wrong. Which does not surprise me at all, since I remember you also got it wrong when you were in Form One. Am I right? Obviously it is a genetic defect." Master Quainoo had laughed heartily at his own keen insight.

Again, a grinding of molars, and this quiet answer, "I looked at my son's answer. He wrote that Ivan the terrible was a fine example of the evil of untamed greed, which resulted in great losses in human and material resources, and ultimately proved a destabilizing force for his country."

"Yes, I remember. It sounded like the same wrong answer you gave when you were young. Are you sure you didn't give him that answer? Because if you did I may have to expel the boy."

"I didn't. But I thought that for a young boy, that was a fairly insightful answer, won't you say?"

Master Quainoo had straightened his gait. "I never said anything in the lesson about a fine example of anything, or about great losses—and what is this nonsense about ultimately destabilizing whatever? What rubbish is that? The correct answer is that 'Ivan the terrible was bad because he sought complete power, blood was spilt, lives were lost, and it was terrible.'"

On that day, Kwame recalled, he had been stunned stiff, and he kept expecting someone to jump up from behind Master Quainoo's desk in uncontrollable peals of laughter over Kwame's reaction to the headmaster's wonderful performance, as though all of this was nothing more than a bad joke. And he waited. And all he saw was the fury on Master Quainoo's face, taut and unbending.

"Instead of coming here to waste my time maybe you should teach your son to pay attention in class. I have taught this lesson over and over, and everyone else gets it right except your family: 'Ivan the terrible was bad because he sought complete power, blood was spilt, lives were lost, and it was terrible.' In fact that's how he got his sobriquet. That's right, I see you're surprised. You obviously don't know that word, 'Mr. I want to teach my son big words'. Go look it up. It's s-o-b-r...anyway, sobriquet. Now, if you don't have anything more important to talk about, go away."

Neither Akosua nor Edom could control themselves when Kwame shared that story with them. Kofi could only manage a chuckle. He did not find it nearly as funny because he had missed that question himself as a Form One student. Like Kwame's son, he had tried to be creative, and received a few lashes on the bottom for his trouble.

Kwame had said, "I don't think it's funny at all."

"What the hell is a sobriquet?"

"Who knows?"

"Just tell your boy to answer Quainoo's questions verbatim," had proposed Akosua.

"Rote memorization instead of creative problem solving skills. Great."

"Yeah," had said Edom, still laughing. "But at least he was not a hypocrite."

Akosua went back to the floor in another fit of uproarious laughter. What Edom had said was another of Master Quainoo's strongest trademarks—an irreverent, self-serving sense of honesty. Hypocrisy was, he loved to say, Mankraso's greatest sin. In perhaps his single most daring act, Master Quainoo got up in church one Sunday, right after the sermon, when church members are given a chance to publicly request prayer. He got up, cleared his throat loudly to preempt the possibility of interruption, and asked to be heard. A curious silence filled the church, as the pastor nodded to give Master Quainoo the floor. Then the headmaster spoke, very calmly.

"Actually I have a question to ask of you, pastor," he'd said.

"All prayer requests are taken," had said the pastor gregariously.

"This past Friday, when you went on a prayer visit with the widow Agnes Amenfi, who is sitting piously over there, you got naked and did some unbiblical things with her. Why?" Just like that. Then he sat down.

The priest would try to fire Master Quainoo as headmaster after that, but he failed, and instead requested a transfer out of Mankraso. It was of more than passing interest to Kwame that the hostile municipal council director and Master Quainoo both believed hypocrisy to be Mankraso's worst sin. They were probably right. Priests committed fornication with widows and preached on with great piety, while sanctifying the rich in the presence of the poor; spouse abusers spent glorious afternoons with their friends bemoaning the plight of the nation; young boys were caught by strong hands and raped in the brutal quiet of the dark without another soul knowing; and always, the poor envied the rich without knowing what to do about not having. And everyone smiled a happy smile all the time. Mankraso was such a town.

CHAPTER 7

$\mathcal{K}$wame walked towards the sharp bend on the path, edging closer to the spot all the time, even as his apprehension began to well up. Thirty-five years had gone by, and this spot still made him shake—this spot where his nascent understanding of his own essence had taken the first fall, back when he was too young to have possibly understood that there was such ugliness in the world. In the course of time this awful fate had befallen his friends, too, but not in the same way, and certainly not in the deep, immutable way it had happened to him. Maybe what happened to him had been a simple premonition of everything that would happen in their collective lives. A moment in time, strengthened by the inability to share, had presaged their collective fate. Was it all that simple?

Three months after Kofi and Akosua went to the university, a student-led protest over the poor conditions at the school forced the government to close down the school. His two friends came home for six months, during which time they sat around doing nothing, because they were always supposed to be getting back to school the following week. Kwame noticed the panic set in on Kofi, who was plagued by the guilt of not being of any use to his family, or to anyone for that matter. At the time Kwame had felt somewhat better about not making it into the university. He was at least free from the stifling sentiments of pity flowing towards his friends over their arrested march to great futures. Kofi, in particular, had been in a perpetual state of depression and irritability.

"This is exactly why Ghana is going nowhere."

Kwame listened, but never offered any thoughts on the matter, mostly because he was not swayed by Kofi's desperate metaphorical reach, equating the downfall of the nation with his disturbed educational pursuits.

One afternoon Akosua, sitting with them in the blazing heat of the early afternoon, had jolted them out of their lazy silence. "Do you feel yourselves drying up within?"

Kofi had thrown her a look of deep concern, reflecting what Kwame himself was feeling. "What do you mean?"

Akosua shrugged, thinking hard. "I have not found a damn thing in years to make me wet."

"Good grief, Akosua!" A cough forced its way out of Kwame.

Kofi smiled, but he had been hurt, and it showed, right through his thinly disguised smile. He said nothing.

"I don't mean it like that, Kwame. It's just that..." The way she spoke, it was as if someone had wounded her in a way that she hadn't thought possible. Kwame considered for a moment that unless she took great pains to express the source of that pain to them, neither he nor Kofi could possibly begin to appreciate what she was going through.

"It's just that we've had these funny aspirations for some time now. I think that in my thoughts about the ideal life, I always envisioned that we were going to be joined on the way by similarly committed trailblazers, and together we were going to reclaim the best of Ghana for our own people. And along the way I was going to find a suitable husband, from the group of committed gentry, preferably a trailblazer among trailblazers, to stand by me while I blazed my trail. Then, at some point, I could have him give me the children I want. Could you imagine the children from such a union? Well, I could, and I did—a most beautiful feast for the imagination, I tell you."

In that moment, Kwame could tell that she had not been there with them at all. He recalled too, that he and Kofi had reacted very differently to her effort to share her frustration. To that point, Kwame had often wondered about whether he and Kofi might be headed for some moments of tension for the chance to win Akosua for a life partner. But on that day Kwame lost all such interest in Akosua, right with the issuance of her felt emptiness. He'd felt deeply insulted by her suggestion of a desired union with a trailblazer among trailblazers, presumably a man greater than either he or Kofi. So much for the ties that bind. He might not have been sure then about what Kofi's own private ambitions were, but Akosua's offering had not warmed him to optimistic departures from Kofi. Did Kofi also dream of a trailblazing woman who was something far better than his friends? Just three months at the university and they were already this conceited. He could have said something about his own emotional reaction to Akosua's professed private dream. He might have related his disappointment to hearing her reduce them to this status of unsuitability to her bold ambitions, but he did not, choosing instead the quiet patience of a trusted friend. In Kofi's eyes, he had observed a discernible look of felt betrayal, but Kofi had not said anything either.

"You are only a couple of years into your twenties, Akosua," Kwame had said. "What would ever make you think there are no sources of inspiration anywhere?"

"I just spent three months at the university. Nothing I heard from speaking to all these promising leaders of the future, or to the faculty, had the power of inspiration. I still wonder why we Africans continue to be taught that the only way to govern and manage our lives is by borrowing the ways of our former oppressors."

Kwame had taken a moment to stare intently at the young woman whose beauty had always been the most ardent reminder to them of all that is possible in the pursuit of nobility. He had not been sure what she wanted to hear, so he decided to cast out a feeler. "There's nothing wrong with assimilating a mode of governance that works."

"For whom, exactly? We've always had our own forms of democracy, Kwame. You are an Ashanti, yet you sit there saying such silly things, without shame. Do you know how sad that is?"

"What is your problem, Akosua?"

"My problem is that our land is going to hell, and the first thing to go is the culture in which our very essence is rooted. Rumors are spreading right now that the C.I.A. is trying to do away with Nkrumah. Then they will do away with Lumumba and then Sekou Toure, and pretty soon every one of the independence fighters who would push for Africans regaining our rightful place among the world's races would have been done away with before you know it. The future of Africa is staring us in the face right now. It will be the same fragmented mess we have now, with the world powers playing us for the fools we are, using us to serve their needs. East and West, the eagle and the bear, banners still used to manipulate and victimize us. Why do we even care for political ideologies that do not spring from our own experiences? This is what they call democracy. Nobody is thinking about the bigger picture, and there is going to be some serious suffering for our people because of this apathy. So where is the leadership that will set things aright?"

"You still haven't said what your real anger is about, Akos."

And that's when she broke down. As Kwame recalled, it was the first time either of them saw Akosua cry for reasons not related to the passing of a soul. Puzzled by her tears, they stood there in uncertain silence and watched her cry.

"I'm scared."

In all the time they'd known each other, this was the closest Kwame felt towards Akosua. He had wanted to jump up and say yes, he understood, because he was scared too. He didn't feel that it mattered what Akosua was scared of; it mattered simply that she felt boxed in, threatened by the force of so many unknowns, perhaps by secrets so powerful they could shatter a community if shared, and shatter individuals if unshared.

"Why?" It was Kofi who asked the question, and Kwame thought it came out as if Kofi wanted to know whether Akosua was frightened by the same things that frightened him.

For a while it seemed as though she was not entirely certain what the source of her fear was, or whether she really wanted to share it. "Nothing. Never mind. I'm just not inspired by anything anymore and I don't know where I'm going to find the strength to continue living like this."

There was more confused silence from the two men. "I still don't understand why you are looking for inspiration from others in the first place."

Kwame had turned his attention back to Akosua after Kofi had spoken.

"I think that even the inspiration that springs from inside us must still come from a source outside us, a reflective beauty, if you will, that serves to guide the best in us. I see no beauty around me, no sign of promise of something that liberates us from the essential brutality of the unhealthy selfishness enchaining us now. None whatsoever. I almost feel as if there is no such beauty anywhere in this God-forsaken country."

Just then, Kofi snapped. The weight of all the misunderstandings and her veiled insults must have gotten to him. "Then get the hell out and find the great beauty missing from your life elsewhere why don't you? Perhaps it beckons for you in distant lands. You won't be the first African who used the excuse of not seeing any hope around her to flee in search of hope from others. Go find your paradise, just as long as you understand what it says about you that you couldn't find it among your own. And when those whose paradise you seek look at you with pity and disdain, smile the smile of a slave and shut your mouth. You would have forfeited your right to complain."

Kofi had walked out. On a different day, perhaps one filled with less confusion and more openness from Akosua, he might have taken the time to remind Akosua that it was possible for her to be the reflection of beauty in herself, and to spread that to the world around her. They had debated this in times past. What constitutes beauty is obviously not static, they had agreed. But it is possible to say that beautiful things are always those things that elevate the collective welfare, and make it possible for the human spirit to appreciate the balance of its place in relation to the environment, near and far, and to things small and large. Beautiful things, whatever form they take, inspire possibilities and enable this perspective. They enable the opening of the mind and heart to possibilities of redemption from all things that depress the spirit. They had spent some wonderful hours in these discussions, debating what constituted a depression of the spirit and if there were tangible measures of this and so on and so forth. But apparently Akosua had decided this did not ring true to her anymore, or that such a possibility was truly absent in all of Ghana. And Kofi was in no mood to soothe her felt emptiness. If she had decided that she was living a life without beauty and dying for it, then so be it.

On a different day—no doubt—Kofi might have taken the time to remind her of her needless blindness. On a different day Kwame himself might have taken the time to remind Akosua of her needless blindness. This was something they did for each other, and Akosua herself had peeled away the veil of distorted perception blinding her friends to more optimistic possibilities on different occasions. But on this day Kwame watched Kofi walk out angrily, and said nothing to stop him. Akosua stood there after Kofi had left, looking at the wall of Kwame's room, without seeming to see anything. She was still crying.

Kwame, finally deciding that he had little reason to hold on to the pain of her words, had said to her, in turn, "I think you should follow Kofi's advice. Get out and find the beauty missing in your life elsewhere. There's nothing here for you."

When his own outburst came, Kwame was angry that Akosua had started what could have been a soul-cleansing dialogue, and then turned the opportunity on its head by spinning off into this concern about her depressed spirit. Actually he had nothing against her depressed spirit, but it was puzzling why she would persist on insulting them with this persistence on the total absence of inspiration around her. It was a wasted opportunity. They were all truly afraid about the future, even about their present, for very different reasons, and Akosua's initial admission was a table well set. But she kicked out the only guests before any cleansing meal could be had.

As he recalled, Akosua had not even seemed surprised by his outburst. She'd just walked out. Another month later, the university reopened and the two of them returned to resume their schooling. He had seen Kofi a couple of times before they left, but they had not met again as a group in all of that time.

❦   ❦   ❦

Kofi dearest,

I hope the coup was a success. By the time you get to this letter, I'll be gone. God, I hope the elephant would have stopped. My dying won't be due to the elephant, however—at least I hope not. I've managed to get my hands on some slow-acting poison to carry me away, and I'll be taking them soon I'm done with this. Still, I wish the elephant would have stopped because, as I sit here writing, I am sickened to my stomach at the thought of my body getting mangled under those massive tires before your watching eyes. There is something utterly saddening about that image to rob a man of his sanity.

I love you, Kofi. It's strangely hollow now, true. I am almost compelled by every force of reason within me not to say anything this trite. But I love you. Always have. You made the journey of my life worthwhile. It was in your eyes

I saw the essence of my being, and the beauty of my best enterprise. It was in your eyes I saw the best of myself, and my sense of the miracle of my being. You should know this.

I think I should have agreed to marry you. Note that I say I think, because even now I'm not entirely sure. Partly, of course, I had to say no to you because there was a different, perverse comfort in not accepting a lesser version of the dream. And the dream, remember, was always that we were going to be actively engaged in a thoroughly liberating struggle. I still hold as the single most poignant moment in my life when you stood me by the black rock on the beach back in our Accra days and begged that we use our lives to ensure that our people are self-determining individuals in a self-determining country on a self-determining continent. You were a bigger man then, in your youth. God, I found such inspiration just listening to you talk. How strange for it all to have come to this, Kofi. When we started out the idea was that in order to be freed from the yoke of colonialism we needed to marshal our resources in an economic and political system that favors Africa and Africans.

Look at us now. We have fallen further back into slavery here in Africa, at the hands of our leaders and the thieves to whom they have given the keys to our resources. We have leaders who do not understand any connotation of the term. But they do understand how to play the role of modern enslavers, and of their own people at that. They have compounded the vile pithy of their pedestrian leadership with the crime of turning over our countries to forces they do not understand and have no intention of understanding. So the outside thieves follow the remarkably inept thievery of the leaders sitting atop our social orders. Everything has been taken over, Kofi—the seeds we grow for our food, the air we breathe, the springs from which we drink, to very genes that make us what we are. Patents are being appropriated over all this, in the name of capitalist enterprise. It's not to say that there's anything wrong with these advancements in science and technology, but what is the stake of the African villager in any of this? Heck, what is the stake of any African in any of this? We are the dogs of our times, forever waiting for the crumb to fall off the master's table, so we can have our sniff. And then bark. Why are we not infuriated about not being part of the front-runners in these pursuits, to the good of humanity? We are so happy to be second-rate citizens on the world stage I swear I could choke at the shame of it all.

Still, I am perhaps more stunned by the inability of any of us to work towards anything redemptive even after our initial road map was destroyed by Nkrumah's overthrow. Whatever happened to us, individually and as a nation?

Would you be surprised to hear, even now, that I believe we were right all along? My life has disintegrated into this mockery of a dance—another HIV patient soon to take her own life. But still I believe in what we cried in our hearts for, even if I can remain astounded that we could not find better ways of showing our disillusionment. And much as Edom tried with such impassioned desire to equate a life of luxury with integrity, surely we know better than to believe this nonsense, don't we, Kofi? Here in Africa we have fallen behind, and unfettered selfishness is not the way to our salvation. You doubt me? Just look at our leaders—that is the path Edom is dying to walk.

We needed to be better than that. This is the great age of globalization, where everything is tradable commodity, our very souls included. All in the name of a free market that would bring happiness to every citizen of the world! Some people, somewhere, are trying real hard to make us believe that the very deliberate decisions they make to enrich themselves at the expense of the rest of us is merely the hand of God at work. And it's funny, too, because it's so very apropos: they are our gods. Goodness Kofi, why couldn't we find a different way? Why couldn't we slow this soul-robbing ideology? I am exhausted. Thanks for allowing me to get this off my chest. I'm not done, however. I do have a request of you—a demand, really. I am placing a demand on you not because I actually think I have the rights of a martyr, whatever these might be. I'm not a martyr, obviously. I'm a small town girl from Nankesedo who also fell victim to the great plague of our time. I am leaving nothing behind either, except perhaps the single hope of a legacy made possible by your love.

Here's what I want of you. Set up a research center. I'm not sure that whatever we set out to rob will be enough for this, but try anyhow, and if you need partners from outside Ghana, so be it. Find them, partner with them and set up a research center that will be the first of its kind here on our shores. I dream of a center with a technological advancement research unit, developing functional technologies for Africa. I dream of a center with a medical research unit, developing cures for the ailments most relevant to Africa. I dream, too, of a center with a psychosocial and cultural research unit, seeking a scientific explanation for our continued killing of our kin, and the ways of bringing an end to the waste. It would be wonderful if the research could extend to uncovering the source of the disease that afflicts our leaders and reduces them to power mad tyrants and shameless, soulless, uninspired puppets catering to the needs of Africa's exploiters, beginning with themselves, but then I suppose social engineering cannot extend that far, so the research on that might be wasted effort. I dream of a center that would explore and reclaim for us our history and culture, and support a viable advancement of our cultures to the changing times.

And here's the piece to the puzzle without which none of this matters: give the center to women. Your soul be damned, Kofi, if you don't grant me this part of my dream. Recruit women. All over this Ghana, there are enough brilliant women to run such a center. Seek women from across Africa and across the diaspora, if you must. They are all around us, waiting to be found. I want the center to be filled with them. Earmark the eventual intake from the research activities to recruit more enterprising young girls and sponsor their education. Okay, fine, you can help one or two boys as well! This is my dream. Because it is a dream, I'm imagining it on a scale that's probably much too grand. But that's okay. Any reasonable scale would be a start. I want you to do your part to put a dent in all the plans intended to keep us perpetual beggars to the world. It is not acceptable that we would have others decide for us what to wear, what to drink, what to think, and when to cry at and laugh, along with what is moral and what is an affront to humanity! Some day, when we've finally risen from our collective stupor, Africans will rise in unity and finally throw away the yoke of neo-colonialism by forming a power base for Black people everywhere right here on our continent. When that day arrives, I'd want this research center to have been instrumental in the fight.

By the time you read this, I'll be gone, of course. I'm shaking now. I'm actually frightened, all of a sudden, but don't despair on my behalf: I wouldn't be doing this if I found myself consumed by a greed for life. Don't you ever forget that I love you. I have always loved you, Kofi, through all those tempestuous years. Your marriage to Efuwa was never a hindrance to that, and I don't say this to suggest that I did not respect the love between you. Still I blame myself for not finding the wisdom to make our story something beyond ordinary. But it is entirely possible that most lives are to be lived in remarkable ordinariness. Of course we presumably hold the power to transform the ordinary, especially where the ordinary is something that dulls the possibility of inspiration.

I like the thought that love can transform the ordinary into something extraordinary. I felt extraordinary in your presence, but this wisdom came to me a little too late along the way. Build my center for me, Kofi. And get on with living. You don't have that much time before we meet again. God have mercy on us all.

—Akos.

✤   ✤   ✤

Down the clay ravine, at the edge of the slope, the soil grew abruptly fertile and threw up some vegetation against the advancement of the clay soil. Over the years it was sadly obvious that the clay was winning the battle, blighting the fertile soil back. It did not seem to be a particular concern for anyone because this was not where the farmlands were. But you had to wonder. So much erosion, so much blighting, all the time. The treaded path continued on the fertile soil, winding its way in the direction of the heavy shrubbery that obscured much of the view to the other side of town, where Mankraso's market stood. The path cut around the shrubbery at a sharp angle, so that it was quite impossible to see anyone coming from around the bend.

Kwame walked up and stood where the path took its sharp turn and the same, nauseating wave swept over him. Before he knew what was happening, he keeled over, his forty-six year old bones creaking from the sudden demand, and heaved a dry cough, unable to throw any food because he had not had much of anything to eat that day. But the wave of nausea was persistent and strong. A heavy morsel of bitter mucous accompanied his third heave, and in his keeled-over position, he coughed out the bitter taste in his mouth, overwhelmed by the extent of his self-hatred. He stayed bent for some five minutes or so, then gathered himself off his knee, joint bones creaking. By the time he finished the motions of wiping the dirt from his trouser and the unsavory moistness from his lips, he felt some of his composure return to him.

Then he began to laugh. It began with such startling suddenness he thought at first that perhaps it was another cough forcing itself out of him. But then there he was, the next instant, laughing so uncontrollably he could barely keep himself upright. This was seriously funny stuff, the fact that thirty-something years or so ago, shortly after they all moved to Mankraso, someone hid behind these same bushes and reached out for him as he walked innocently by, and sodomized him mercilessly in an act he had not known human beings to be capable of. Or that many years later, when he was almost thirteen years removed from that event, he hid himself in these bushes and reached out for some young girl walking innocently by and did the same to her, and heard himself utter the same sickening guttural sounds that had scared him forever. Or that just when he thought he had done everything to escape this hell, he would be turned away from the university and forced to come back here to live out his life.

And what was funnier than the fact that he, Kwame, became a police officer in this town for a while, and spent the better part of those years redefining revolving door justice? The district court had stopped functioning. The whole situation was comical. There was the young boy from the Gyan family who was caught stealing a wristwatch. Kwame had to put him in the cell at the police station pending his trial. Three weeks after his arrest he was still in the cell, and everyone knew he was not going to get his day in court any day soon, since there was a moratorium on the courts. Meanwhile the kid needed to eat, and Kwame found himself feeding the criminal out of his own pocket. What could be funnier? So he collected a bribe from the boy's father and set him free. And thus began the revolving door justice. His laughter crackled, agony sweeping through his ribs from the pressure. The funniest part of it all, of course, was that for five full years, his brand of revolving door justice was not a sin in anyone's eyes, until he crossed the fat cat Agyei. He could hardly stand the irony, because he actually arrested Agyei on a charge of defilement, when the thirteen year-old daughter of one of Agyei's own girlfriends walked into Kwame's office with her clothes in tatters and reported that Agyei had defiled her. Shattered out of her innocence, the girl did not seem to understand too much about the situation. She felt dirty, and said there was a lot of pain. So much to laugh about in this funny world. Kwame's ribs were groaning by now.

He had made a great spectacle out of his arrest of Agyei that day. What had been his motive? That he could eliminate all the pain and wipe out all injustice by making a poignant example of Agyei perhaps? For all the times he had resorted to the easy way of corruption for offers that were mere pittance, this would have been the one occasion to actually make out with something substantive. He could have just gone in, told Agyei that he knew what he had done, and could make it go away, quietly. Agyei would have been appreciative, for saints need great help to keep their saintliness. Agyei could have endowed Kwame with considerable favor to keep his honorable status. But Kwame refused to hush the matter in exchange for a generous offering. He took Agyei in with aplomb, cuffing his hands behind his back, and shoved him the length of the distance from the big man's home to the station, drawing a large, appreciative and entertained crowd along the way. He kept Agyei in jail overnight, on the threat of taking him all the way to Kumasi to stand trial. He had felt more potent during that episode than he had ever felt in all of his life. Still the greatest comment on that episode came from the Catholic priest, who came to plead, along with a handful of others, for Agyei's release. The priest said that Kwame had dragged Agyei like Christ on the way to his own Calvary. A man falsely accused. Did he not see the mistake he'd made, the way everyone else could see, that you don't do such a thing to a decent human being on the words of a deluded girl? Agyei took his humiliation to heart, and within a few months, Kwame was a police officer no more.

A higher official came all the way from Kumasi to humiliate Kwame in return, firing him on sins real and imagined. A select few of the town's people, mostly the extended family of the girl raped by Agyei, expressed admiration for Kwame, and he continued to go home to his wife and rape her at the end of each day. He did wonder at times how it would be like to see his wife actually appear to enjoy having sex with him, but that would have required, at the minimum, some communication on the issue and God knows what demons he would have had to face from such an enterprise. It was agonizing enough having to deal with the stupid urge that made him ever need sexual release. Compounding such agony with attempts to communicate about it appeared downright sadistic. The silence was much better. And the wife understood her duty, thank God, which was all the more reason for avoiding further complications with attempts at self-examination. Who could withstand such comical ironies, really?

At some point the laughter stopped. There was too much pain in his ribs to contain the mirth of the recollection. Then it started all over again, only now there were tears to accompany his laughter. He had tried, as often as he could, to avoid the path that led past Master Quainoo's home to the other side of town. It seemed particularly eerie, too, that this particular shrubbery hadn't essentially disappeared over so many years. It had remained a mysterious constant in an ever-changing landscape. If he could not laugh at all this, what could he ever hope to laugh at? Through all of its hyped importance, this was how funny life was.

But of all the things that were so funny to him in this moment, the foremost was the realization that when a hand reaches out in the quiet of the night to destroy a young innocent life, effectively engendering a new monster to perpetuate the initial monstrosity, it bespeaks a frightening imbalance in the whole community. And for such heights of imbalance, the restoration needed required efforts that might well lie beyond the ability of mere mortals. You had to wonder when and where such a process could begin. And unlike his friends, Kwame was at no point convinced that the sickness of their lives, and the sickness surrounding them, could ever be cured by mere wealth. There was not enough of that in the whole world. Of course an exhausted generation could always look to its children and smile a hopeful smile with blinders on to help overlook the stark reality awaiting them, but Kwame despaired. It was too much blind hope to thrust on the shoulders of an unknowing generation coming up in a world forever being stilted against them. The imbalance was too great, in individual lives and in the greater society. Perhaps that was why, even with aching ribs, he could hardly contain himself. It just didn't get much funnier than this.

CHAPTER 8

$\mathcal{E}$ dom's first task on the robbery attempt was to keep watch by the hill on the side opposite from where the elephant would be coming. This was possibly the most difficult aspect of the whole undertaking—the fact that they had no control over the flow of traffic. If a car were to come into the stretch of their ambush from the opposite direction, or for that matter if a car were to come in tow of the elephant, it could be the death knell for the whole enterprise. The potential for mass confusion would be too great, and Kofi, for one, seemed to think that the entire operation would have to be aborted to spare the innocent. Edom had almost laughed to Kofi's face when he raised that possibility and suggested that unless someone had a better idea, his proposal was for the operation to be aborted in the event any car happened to come into the stretch of the ambush. Here they were plotting to take the elephant, and Kofi's concern was over the sparing of lives, as though the entire enterprise was a morality play. You had to hand it to the guy—he was an uncommon idiot.

Edom had offered that none of that would be necessary if one of them was positioned on the other end of the stretch. He would gladly be the one, and his position would serve two purposes. Firstly, it would allow him to stop any traffic approaching from that end while the elephant was in their line of fire. Secondly, if the elephant happened to escape their initial rush, he would serve as the last resort for stopping it. If that *happened, all bets would be off, for Akosua would have been crushed to her death. And in some small way Edom wondered if that wouldn't be for the best, since the notion of conscientious theft was so improbably contradictory. Over forty years of living, and Kofi still thought there was honor among thieves. Even if that were so, the fact is that when you set out to rob your country of this much wealth, a ruthless detachment was the absolute, minimal necessity. The only morality worth having was the morality of the theft itself. One had to believe that the theft was the only righteous act of the moment, having its own sanctity; otherwise the whole enterprise would be doomed to failure.*

So he offered to keep watch at the other end, and knew he would stop any traffic from that end at any cost. But he was certain that that was not going to be necessary. The traffic was light around here, and no driver was ever stupid enough to follow the elephant at close range. The greater likelihood was that he was going to be the one who stopped the elephant, amidst the sorrowful mayhem of Akosua's death. He had the additional motivation of having had too many occasions to make it rich go begging, due in large measure to this very pull of the conscience at the worst possible time, and also to his own stupidity, as had happened, for instance, when he went with Chris to try and deal in narcotics so he could come help them all. He had vowed never again to allow such a thing to happen to him.

In the eerie silence of the final moments of their wait, he saw the elephant shoot into view from the direction of Mankraso. It was a welcome sight for him, and he watched for a few seconds as it blazed down the road towards Akosua. But then, startlingly, a passenger van shot into view from the opposite end of the stretch, right where he lay in wait. The surprise froze him for a moment, but he was not about to renege on his vow. That was simply not an option for him. For salvation or for hell, he was not going to lie here in frozen inaction.

✤   ✤   ✤

The message had come as a peculiar surprise to Kofi. It was in the early evening, just past the stretch of noisemaking that accompanies women coming home from the market day, full of the comforting banter of acquaintances rocking together in a boat devoid of sails, with only each other to lean on. Akosua had not come to join them at *Lonely Hearts* that afternoon. Kwame had been there when Kofi arrived. They sat together after they had ordered their drinks, and drank in somber silence. Out of the music speakers in the bar, Jimmy Cliff sang plaintively about many rivers to cross.

At the end of the song, Kofi, with a heavy heart, had risen. "Charley, I for go."

Kwame nodded, rising. "Make I walk plus you," he said. "I hear say Chris no make well."

"Yeah, I see am yesterday. E make sick, but e no make serious. You for stop by?"

"Yeah."

"Say hello from me."

"I will."

At home Kofi ate very little of the dinner served him, his appetite chronically dwarfed by a lingering sadness that he had stopped fighting to shed. Since his wife Efuwa passed on, he had been living with his elder sister, who moved in with her four sons, ostensibly to help Kofi care for his own children. He had no words for the irony, since his sister brought him additional mouths to feed. But his own children were appreciative of the company of their aunt and cousins, perhaps more so in face of the withdrawn father they were left with after their mother's passing.

One of Akosua's nieces had come bearing the request: "My aunt wonders if you'd be so kind; she would like to discuss something important."

Kofi put on some decent clothing and stepped outside. The sight that met him when he got to Akosua's home did nothing to lift his spirits. Akosua had built this house for her parents and some of the extended family, keeping a self-contained apartment in the back for herself. But having done this, she had only whetted the appetites of her loved ones for much more. And of the many things she succumbed to reason and bought to appease voracious appetites, the television had to be the most poisonous. What is to be said for the society in which structure and roles are dismantled in a consciousness vacuum? What is to be said for the people who choose to strip themselves naked of their culture, so they may acquire hand-me-down cultures from yesterday's oppressors? What is to be said for the erosion of the values of Africa, couched in MTV pyrotechnics and the culture of globalization spawning it? Whatever is to be said for the souls caught up in this maddening reduction of all things to a dollar value, and the inevitable dawning of one's worthlessness for lacking, and thus for making its pursuit the be all and end all of living?

It was just an amazing thing to see Akosua's family in the evening. They gathered around the television set and sat transfixed by the images. The token offering of local programming was not high on anyone's agenda. It was the American soap operas, those platforms of great social advancement—those were the shows that beguiled them. They sat nightly like zombies in front of the set, losing themselves in this senseless fantasy, and from their catatonic, distorted frame of reference, could they harbor any greater emotion than hatred for their own lives? And what was feeding their dreams, exactly? Did they truly believe that it was possible for all of them to one day live like those people on the screen? Did they understand that for a few people to live in such decadence multitudes had to abide misery and that they were the first in line for that misery? Could they ever appreciate that the very purpose of those programming was to reduce them to moronic wretches seeking after what they could not attain, and desiring to do anything to acquire them, thereby feeding the cycle of their own wretchedness? Kofi had thrown all these questions at Akosua after seeing her family one evening, until Akosua told him to shut up. The television watchers barely returned his proffered greeting, but two of Akosua's aunts, who were enjoying the breeze in the front verandah, had mentioned that Akosua was in her apartment. They asked of the health of his family, and he responded that they were well, God so good. He wished them a good evening and excused himself. He had to walk through the large living room, past the television watchers into a small compound contained by knee-high walls. Akosua's flat was right across the compound. It had a door linking it to the main house, but Akosua actually preferred to come and go from a back door.

He heard the soft music as he approached her door, and went in when she failed to answer his knock. There was no light on in the living room, but there was a fluid glow of light in the bedroom, where the music was playing. A plaintive voice, tender and optimistic, sang of the sweet pain of the wait for the loved one who left:

> "I hang off this precipice, of loneliness
> Since you've been gone
> The very memory of me
> At the mercy of a chasm without end
> And I hold on
> To the rope of memories you left me
> My only lifeblood
> Since you've been gone
> You will appear again, and bid the chasm close
> You will appear again…"

Kofi recognized the tune. It had been playing with some frequency on the airwaves, but he did not know the artist. He appeared in the doorway to the bedroom, mildly intrigued, and met her eyes. A steady stream of tears flowed down her face. She was standing in the middle of her bedroom, surrounded by forty burning candles, the source of the fluid dance of lights he'd seeing from the living room. When she caught his eye, Akosua smiled, but she did not stop. He stood and watched her dance, gentle tears flowing down her cheeks.

Akosua had never been much of a dancer. But this dance was the easiest of dances, because she was merely moving to the beat of her own heart, not in its mechanical thrust but the smoother undercurrents where her truest essence made home. She was so gentle in her sway that at times she did not seem to be moving at all. The song drifted to its end:

> *"You will appear again, to relieve*
> *This burden of loneliness*
> *Crushing my soul*
> *So I hold on*
> *You will appear again…"*

Past the last riff of the song she continued dancing, cradling herself, releasing herself, sometimes accepting, sometimes rejecting, sometimes ambivalent. She rocked herself like a mother her child, and slept in her own arms, and smiled from the immediate gratification of a happy, fleeting dream. Then the song in her heart must have ceased, ushering in a wondrous silence. And she turned to him, smiling. He was standing there in a sort of lost stillness, observing, not understanding. If this was merely the revelation of a different side of herself, then he was at a loss as to what the purpose of the revelation was. But something in her eyes said that she had far more to offer than a mere revelation of a different dimension of her being.

She did not seek any buffer for her news. "I am dying," she said.

A gaping silence swept in smoothly behind her announcement, arresting time. It took the small space of her bedroom and began stretching it, straining the seams of the walls, bursting through them, then pushing, expanding. Her own ears began to ring with the stillness of the expanding void, as death began to impress its true weight on her. It was a startling perspective, the sharp realization that she did not want to be gone from his presence. The silent beckoning of death was at its strongest now because, for all her angst—all along her adult life to this very day, when the breath of life was an afterthought—she suddenly felt like she was leaving the party. This was curious, this sudden inkling, in the emptiness of the void, that the breath of life was a worthwhile enough gift onto itself. That it was its own light in this deep emptiness that was forever stretching. In time the silence stopped expanding, took a moment to gather itself, then rushed her. For the umpteenth time since she learned of her fate, her legs gave beneath her, and the silence, cradling her from within and without, dropped her on the lip of a motionless vortex, a funnel composed of no substance at all, sinking deeply into an eternal blackness.

Her eyes opened. Kofi Mensah stood in the dark void beyond, watching. He did not have his easy smile, but the probing of his stare was gentle, and it remained gentle even as the void blew him to bits and flushed him away in a thousand particles of dust, swallowing him. In that moment the depth of the darkness shut not only her vision of the world outside completely—it seemed to lock access to the soul itself. Time raced past her, then came to meet her, but refused contact, spinning her instead, filling every void of her being with loneliness beyond her grimmest imagination. She lost her sense of the light of her being. Where was the light in this deep darkness? Where was the love to anchor her to a time, to a place, perhaps to another soul? For a brief moment she caught a wisp of understanding for one mystery that had troubled her always: the human soul preserves itself with faith. But is faith a calculated leap of the imagination intended to shut out an alternative leap of imagination that would make us too insignificant to justify our own continuation? A tear fell off her face, and she followed it down, to where a blood river of her own tears flowed. She sank further. There was so much to cry over that not even a river of tears, she was sure, could make up for. In this space of timelessness, in this space without any substance but the smallest hint of her own presence, bereft of corporal composition, perhaps this was the only time to cry and cry well.

For knowledge unattained, and for tears unshed. For hatred nurtured and harbored too long, and for love forfeited, mostly for love forfeited. And for the lives that could have been touched, or even created, but weren't. And for the daily suffering of the child born at the wrong place, in the wrong time, devoid of the love that would have averted her suffering. She cried, too, for joy. For each tear ever shed, and for the love that had been encountered. For the gift of the self, given from the heart, and for the gifts received. But mostly, it seemed, for the astounding relief from expectations freed. The void expected nothing; it took nothing, gave nothing. It was an expanding, contracting chasm, of all things and one. It was neither adversarial nor friendly, it simply was. And she was herself a part of it, a unique contributor to this simple chaos that was far beyond the reach of cycles of life occupying short intervals on the continuum. Akosua began to laugh at so much void, so much nothing.

At the end of her long laugh her eyes opened again, and this time there was awareness of the physical world. Where she fell down Kofi had taken seat and was supporting her upper body with his own. She thought she had a great deal to say, but somehow her mouth wouldn't open, so she lay in his arms, grateful for the intimacy, and allowed herself to be held.

✤   ✤   ✤

Kofi had barely arrived on time to prevent her from falling completely onto the floor. Her news effectively and immediately stole his speech. He could only remember wishing that time could stop, if only for a moment, to validate the first wave of searing, improbable pain, along with all the pain that was yet to come.

Efuwa, his deceased wife, came to him, even as he held Akosua. He looked up in his search to find her eyes, and shortly after that his tears flowed. He had managed to hide this memory, but those had been his wife's words as well, also without ceremony.

"I am dying," she'd said. It had taken too long for her to save enough just to go see a doctor in Kumasi. She had taken the opportunity to visit with some relatives in Kumasi, and ended up staying with them for a few more days so she could get some tests done. To Kofi's initial surprise, and ultimate annoyance, he had started to miss his wife. When she finally returned, six whole days had gone by. She arrived in the evening, after dinnertime, and their children and some of the nieces and nephews staying with them made a great commotion. He had been happy and relieved that she was back, although he was going to have to get past being cross with her to express any of the happiness and relief. She came into the bedroom after she had given the children some token gifts sent by the relatives in Kumasi.

He sat on the bed, refusing to look up from the book he was reading. "You didn't say you were going to be gone for an entire week."

Usually she would humor him with some silly joke, but she hadn't responded at all that night, forcing him to look up from the book he wasn't reading. There were tears in her eyes already.

"Is everything all right?" He had thought that perhaps one of the relatives in Kumasi had passed.

"I am dying," she'd said.

A painful year followed. He thought he became a husband in that her final year—but how much can one wish to make up for in a year when so much time had gone begging? He begged and groveled to potential helpers, but there were simply not enough givers to have made it possible for Akosua to begin any real therapy. She was in such pain towards the end that he prayed she would be taken away and spared further agony.

"I am so sorry, Efuwa. I didn't intend to fail you so badly."

Even her speech was labored. "What was your failing?"

"I thought I needed to make you matter by becoming someone of consequence myself."

"In the eyes of society, you mean?"

He nodded.

She nodded, too. "I think that's what I expected myself at the beginning." She'd sighed upon reflection. "Such misplaced priorities. And all I really needed was a good man who cared for me. Here, give me your hand."

She had grown so weak by then that the air she breathed in seemed to tear through her. He had taken her right hand in both of his.

"Look at me. I don't need you to spend any more time berating yourself. It was always going to take both of us to make our relationship what we wanted it to be. Taking all the blame would make it seem as if I was never here. Besides, you've been a dream of a partner since…" Her voice had broken off.

"I feel like you're paying for my sins. I deserve this suffering, not you."

Efuwa had smiled, and through her pain, he thought it was the happiest smile he'd seen on her face in a long, long while. "I doubt you have the strength for this. Besides, what ever would I do if you left me behind?"

"Oh please, Efuwa. Please…" He broke down and cried freely. He had done his best to make her last year pleasant, but he never forgave himself for the time lost—for what could have been. He had intended to apologize again, and not allow her to share the blame this time. But he left for Kumasi on another hopeful expedition to seek help from some friends and relatives in the city, and never saw Efuwa alive again.

❧   ❧   ❧

Edom shut his eyes for a second. No matter the extent of his determination, this was never going to be easy to execute, and the rush of adrenaline had his nerves on edge. He aimed his gun. Relax, Edom, just relax. He drew a deep breath, exhaled slowly, cleared his mind, and locked his aim on one of the front tires of the passenger van. A sacrifice needed to be made.

❧   ❧   ❧

The taxi sped along the dusty road, cutting past slower cars on a mad drive to the hospital. The taxi driver was only partly concerned for the life of the sick patient in the back. More to the point, he wanted the presence of the sick patient in his car for the shortest time possible. But for the difficulties of the times he would never have agreed to transport the HIV-positive patient to the hospital in Kumasi. It was probably not worth the trouble, but this was his livelihood. What was he to do? He cut another dangerous line around another car, took the noisy protestation from the driver he was passing with a disdainful blast from his own horn and continued his dramatic drive.

Three years on, Akosua's opportunistic infections had become more frequent, due almost entirely to the fact that she had lost much of her appetite and was showing very little desire to live. Three suicide attempts along the way had compounded the stress her illness was having on her friends. She was completely imbalanced, which, from a physical standpoint, was entirely understandable. But her imbalance went further, and that was disturbing to Kofi, even though he did not feel that any of them could claim the requisite empathy to fully understand the sense of imbalance in her soul. What none of them expected was that in time she would begin to unbalance them, too.

It was just like his grandfather had once said, when he intimated that the whole extended family was sick beyond repair, because no one, least of all the elders of the family, maintained any sense of balance anymore. His grandfather had said that they all had a task, the next generation and the ones after them, to adjust perceptions, and restore balance. But the mirrors of perception had never offered anything straight and narrow. There was a simpler time in Kofi's own life when good and evil came in black and white, respectively. But that was in the time before the assault of alternative perception grew strong with each passing acceptance of relative morality. Distortions are easier in mirrors of perception without a standard, when the common good is said to be far less important than the good of each individual. On such playing field one morality is worth another, and the weak will always falter. Civilized man loses the grain of civilization, and the distortion in the direction against the collective is forever magnified, and desperate measures tapped for quick restoration. His grandfather, bitter in his last days, had expressed the belief that it only takes a single unbalanced soul to unbalance the entire family.

Kofi listened closely that day, years ago, on what turned out to be his last visit with his grandfather. On that occasion his grandfather had seemed surprisingly angered by his pending mortality. He was embittered because he had sent word out that he was dying and few in the extended family had made the effort to come pay their last respects. He deduced that it was because he was not dying a rich man with much to give, and wept for what it said of the newer values being swallowed by Africa. An utter distortion of perception—of what matters and what is of little worth. It had been easy to agree with his sentiment that day. But if it was a loss of culture and sense of self that was killing Africa, or even just their extended family, it still did nothing to alleviate the pain of the living who recognized it. His grandfather died surrounded by few of the extended family. A distortion of values, perhaps, but it was reinforced by a reality of dire poverty that kept relatives who knew of his dying away. Perception, under these circumstances, *is* reality. Which explained why, for him, personally, his perceived need for balance had done little to correct the harsh realities he was living. Akosua had called for him to tell him that she was dying. What perception is there to bring levity to such news? Kofi had lost his wife a few months before Akosua's announcement, long before he could find the mirror of perception that made that passing in any way bearable. That his mother's death came only a few months ahead of his wife's death was all the more shattering. How to view this?

He told Akosua that night the only thing he could offer, the trite assurance that he would be there for her, and they kept quiet about her infection for three years, until the opportunistic infections began, and the truth needed to surface. Their stunned friends nonetheless came with them on every emergency trip to the hospital in Kumasi, with the shared fear, each time, that they would lose her. She began to waste away, and the anticipated rumors about her condition materialized and spread with the wind. Soon passengers on *tro-tros* heading to Kumasi would refuse to ride with her, and taxi drivers had to be coaxed into the task. Kofi exhausted all perceptions through this, and, throwing in the towel, dragged himself to church, an unrecognizable landscape to him in his older years. The pastor, reluctant to welcome him, had said, with reproach, "I'd like you to join the Lord's army on a more permanent basis."

Kofi cringed inside. Over forty years of living buys a man no distinction these days, no respect at all. Wise souls must learn to take the condescension and breathe past it. He had smiled past the priests' visible reproach and said casually, "I'm already in the Lord's army."

The pastor's voice turned belligerent. "Then why don't I ever see you in church?"

Kofi's smile had broadened. The priest had walked right into this one—a common joke among the children. "That's because," he'd said, "I'm in the secret service."

The priest had not been amused. During the open request for prayers, Kofi had asked for prayers, for the trying times besieging him, and for his friend Akosua. An offended church body held its breath. This was so very offensive, asking prayers for a woman whose decadence had forced the Lord to visit her with the plague. The Christian God abiding in the minds of righteous Christians is cruel beyond measure. Kofi also said he welcomed any help, financial or otherwise. That was him at his most painful defeat—admitting his nakedness before a congregated church. He'd fallen that far. The priest prayed that God would provide, visibly angry that Kofi had blatantly chosen the first Sunday after payday to come and make this request. And payday Sunday was the only Sunday there was for generating decent money.

The flow of life is filled with so much that is mundane, frequently forgotten in the fast pace of still lives. But twisted memories return, on the strength of the faintest, true stimuli. The twisted memory returning here was of the competition that took place every payday Sunday to see who raised the most money for the church. Seven teams, generated on the basis of the day of the week one was born, were pitted against each other to see which team truly loved the Lord. Twisted memory. Here the pastor began proceedings with a severe admonition of those who, contrary to the teachings of the good book, refused to dig deep into their pockets to give back a tenth to the God who had given them their very lives in the first place. This might have actually been funny—this idea of God as the ultimate slave master, giving or sparing lives so economic rewards might be reaped. But no one was laughing. Reverend Father Andrews was not done. Don't think God isn't watching, he'd pointed out to the congregation. Some of you have more to give than others, which is understandable.

"But none of you can claim not to have anything to give."

Rapt silence, as always, met this message from God, the baffled faces of worshipers not sure why God wanted their small money, but the message had been heard, and the competition was underway.

The master of ceremonies: "We begin with those born on Sunday. You know yourselves: Kwesi, Esi, Akosua—all of you born on Sunday, come on up!"

The choir, as was the case always, began belting a fantastically danceable tune.

"Show onto your God your gratitude!"

The few rich and the many poor dug deep and rose, dancing. As soon as the last Sunday-born had cast his token, the receptacles were cleared for immediate tabulation.

"It is now the turn of those of you born on Monday. All you Kojos, Jojos and Adjoas—you know who you are." Eerie anticipation rose with each dancing contributor. The real competition, for as long as anyone could remember, was always between those born on Wednesday, Friday and Saturday. Agyei, a Friday-born like Kofi himself, had won enough of these contests for his day, but he was not the only rich Catholic in town, though he was decidedly the loudest and most obnoxious. The impossibly reserved Mr. Kweku Boahene, a Wednesday born, was believed to have more money than Agyei, but lived so quietly and modestly with his family no one was ever really certain. Then there was Mr. Kwame Akoto, a Saturday-born, who was wealthy enough to have embarrassed the flamboyant Agyei on some of these monthly rituals.

On the Sunday Kofi showed up at church, Agyei brought home the glory; he donated the most money that Sunday. He was decidedly understated, on this particular occasion, about winning it for the day of his birth, for reasons no one could seem to understand. But his supporters, the other church-members sharing Friday as their day of birth, derived great pride from the win, and gave each other congratulatory high-fives, presumably for the blessing of sharing with Agyei the great privilege of having been born on a Friday. Kofi sat through it all from his seat in the last pew, and was probably the only one in the building to notice that the trustworthy Edmund, who was charged with tallying the intake from each team, managed to skim a little off each team's giving, and into his pocket. When it was over, the good Reverend arose and opened the Bible.

"Ecclesiastes ten, verses nineteen to twenty: 'A feast is made for laughter, and wine makes merry: but money answers all things. Curse not the king, no not in your thought; and curse not the rich in your bedchamber: for a bird of the air shall carry the voice, and that which has wings shall tell the matter.' The word of God, for the edification of the soul. Go in the peace and grace of the Lord."

"Amen."

Kofi had left the church in stunned silence. Changing times had left him so far behind, for back in his youth, the gospel, if he was not completely mistaken, spoke of rich men having a hard time getting to heaven. Something about camels having an easier time of it getting through the eye of the needle. But now that God had apparently changed with the times, and become best friends with the rich, what refuge did the poor have anymore?

CHAPTER 9

*C*hris abandoned his cover and ran towards Akosua on the fear that the very worst was about to happen, but that this would happen only if none of them did anything. So merely by acting, he hoped that it was possible to avert the madness before any real harm came of it. A small part of his mind allowed for the fantasy that the elephant would stop, and with the relief from the near miss, the impossible folly of their decision would dawn on them. The soldiers would shake their heads and tell them how stupid they all were, to have courted this potential disaster. They would help Akosua up and walk her back to the car they had borrowed for the drive over here to the ambush site, and drive back to Mankraso. They would all laugh on the journey back, relieved that they had not paid the ultimate price for stupidity this immense. And Akosua would live out the rest of her life in dignity. They would rally around her, and put the smile of life on her face again, so she could cherish her final years of life and, when it came time to die, she would die a dignified death, surrounded by loved ones.

There would be no repetition of the perverse thinking that had come to consume them over the past several years, culminating in the sudden and bizarre decision of a couple of months ago to commit this theft. Heaven knows, they had committed enough foolishness over this idea to last a lifetime.

Once he had had to talk Edom out of journeying to Obuasi to buy someone's excrement. Imagine that. Edom had apparently heard from somewhere that some of the diamond miners would swallow prize diamonds to get past security and pass the diamond much later, right along with the rest of the waste within them. So if you bought a diamond miner's shit, then the shit was yours and you could dig through it for all the diamonds it was worth. Because of the menial labor required of the buyer for extraction and cleaning, the passed diamonds came much cheaper. The rumor Edom had heard further suggested that there was this man whose size was of legendary proportions, able to swallow enormously sized diamonds and pass them like wind in his backyard. Once you bought it though, you had to take the whole shit elsewhere to dig through it, lest his whole backyard became one stinking mess. Edom had wanted to go make a shit purchase, and Chris had adamantly refused to accompany him. How could intelligent people be blinded by misguided priorities to such madness? Edom, perhaps aware that the others would chastise him, kept coming to Chris for some support for every inane idea he got to make money. At no point would Chris have considered helping with any of the ideas Edom came up with, but eventually their preoccupation with money began to tell on him, too.

It was true that Akosua's illnesses had intensified, in frequency and severity. True, too, that her many attempts to kill herself had burdened the rest enormously, throwing them in great disarray, and Kofi had, on at least one occasion, cursed their poverty in Chris' presence. Chris had been particularly moved by that turn in Kofi, but he was not entirely sure that all this meant that they give in to this insanity. But they always told him he did not have the capacity to completely understand the full extent of their problems. He thought he did, but no one was interested in hearing his thoughts on anything. Four or five successive inane ideas later, when Edom came up with yet another scheme to make some substantive money that he claimed would be of great help to their own cause, Chris finally succumbed and went along. By then, as he belatedly came to acknowledge, he had become infected by the madness.

❧   ❧   ❧

He followed Edom on that journey, quietly suppressing the awareness that it represented another in the string of defeats for their acclaimed alternatives to a different ideal. He suspected that Edom, while claiming to be driven by the possibility of being of genuine help to their friends, was mostly undertaking the trip for personal gain. But even then this idea was baffling. Edom had managed to get his hands on some five hundred thousand cedis. Granted this was not much in the grand scheme of their need. Efuwa's cancer was their main preoccupation then, and that Chris understood, the cost of the procedure to remove the cancerous cells alone was supposed to be in the range of six to ten million cedis, and that was after an arrangement that made it more affordable, and did not account for the prolonged treatment needed after the procedure.

So the need of their friend was enormous, and in this light Edom's proposed scheme of using the five hundred thousand to earn "about five million in a matter of weeks" seemed, on the surface, like a good idea. Chris could just imagine the look on Kofi's face when they brought him the answer to his prayers and said, "Here, go get Efuwa some healing." Tears of joy would flow down his face, no doubt. And what's more, Kofi might even invoke the name of God again, maybe even start going to church, where he could at least hope for the power of joint prayer. But they were going to Nkwasiafokrom for this great moneymaking scheme. Nkwasiafokrom, people! And everyone knew Nkwasiafokrom was—well, fool's town. Did not droves of humanity find their way to this famed town in search of the meaning of life, according to the legend of the seer from time immemorial, only to perish without the slightest gain in understanding because they were blinded by the promise of gold and the potent intrusion of unhealthy selfishness from seeing that life's meaning dwelt right within them? Then again, what do the breezy legends of yester-year and their easy cautionary decrees have in way of edible food for our sophisticated times? So for the love of a friend they were on their way to Nkwasiafokrom, where these days the only fools to be found were said to be the visitors. They sat in a crunch of humanity in the small passenger van that served as their transport to the place. Over two hours of traveling in this shaky *tro-tro*, creaking at an unnecessary high speed, no one said a word.

The tro-tro slowed down near the roadside market at the edge of the town of Nkwasiafokrom. The market was a startling bustle of activity. Chris was surprised; Mankraso was a bigger town than Nkwasiafokrom, without having a market anywhere this lively. It was an encouraging sign, actually. Chris had imagined a forgotten town, littered with the ghosts of the young, and sustained on the frail life-blood of the very old, with mere sprinkles of children, the way a town like Akyemfo turned into in the short years leading to its total demise. Here a rousing cacophony of voices filled the light air, spiced with the laugh and cry of children and the incessant blaring of horns of passenger cars struggling to remind the crowd that it was still standing in what was a major highway. The driver of the *tro-tro* they were traveling in, amused by the traffic of humanity, cattle, poultry and vehicles that they were up against, belatedly advised his passengers that they might find the going easier on foot. His last stop was just past the market anyway. Most everyone acquiesced. In short order the passenger load spilled out past the tout.

Edom seemed to know just what direction to take. But as they stepped out, he, like everyone else, was engulfed by the exhaust fume from the *tro-tro*. Mixed in with the hanging dust, the concoction elicited a new chorus from the crowd, this one a chorus of coughs and sneezes from those with lungs still unaccustomed, despite years of habituation, to the demands of the deadly combination. One of the passengers sneezed into the space before him and sent a wad of mucous flush onto the back of Edom's neck. The fellow apologized profusely as Edom turned, and willfully reached out with a sweaty palm to swipe the snot from Edom's nape, leaving a trail that might have been worse than the original sin. Chris racked his brain. Somewhere, he was sure he had heard that snot on the nape is, in terms of predictive capacity, akin to a black cat crossing your path—either was a foreboding sign.

He followed Edom across the crowded street and up the rocky strip next to a gutter that appeared to have been created by erosion. Ever resourceful, those who lived up the hill had decided to put the running groove to good use, emptying most of their waste liquid into it. The smell from it was nauseating, reminding Chris of the walkway behind the burned down building that was formerly the local branch of the national savings bank in Mankraso. Past an isolated hut by the gutter, Chris followed Edom—who was still using his collar to wipe away the final trace of the accidental snot—through the soft, moist soil of someone's back yard, until finally they came to a home that looked somewhat cleaner than most of the rest. Chris took a second to notice that the relative cleanliness of the house derived from a recent paint job. He found it a very good omen that they were here to consult with someone who seemed to have some visible trapping of wealth. Much later he would revise that apparent wisdom with the greater truth that the wealthy do not get to their wealth by being honest, altruistic people in their dealings.

There was little time wasted in the transaction, and from the speed of it all, Chris wondered how Edom could have possibly believed that they were going to come out of the deal the better for their trouble. In the first instance two fellows, who seemed to do this sort of thing all day long, ushered them into the house, down a short corridor into a spacious room. There were four men in the room when they entered, and so help him God, Chris almost swallowed his tongue at the sight: these were scary looking men. Chris did not even know that there were Ghanaians in all of the land who looked that scary. Chris stood by the door while Edom sat at the low table with the fellow they had traveled all this way to do business with. The latter came in from an inner room and sat across from Edom. He was wearing sunglasses in an already dark room, which was completely puzzling to Chris, but perhaps that was the point—nothing here was supposed to be comprehensible to him. One of the businessman's henchmen brought a plastic bag after a brief exchange between Edom and his boss. The plastic bag contained what looked like talcum powder. The businessman opened the bag and took out a little bit of the powder on a knife. Edom, surprising Chris, took the knife and tasted the powder. He seemed to enjoy the powder, and he confirmed this with a thoughtful nod of appreciation. The businessman smiled smugly, seemingly glad to be doing business with someone who knew his talcum powder well.

Edom then reached into his bag and counted all the money he had brought with him on the table: one half of a million cedis. The businessman looked at the sum of money before him, blew smoke across his face from the cigarette he'd just lighted and sneered. Nervousness crept into Edom's eyes, or at least so Chris thought, but it could have been the falling shadow. However, in the uneasy silence provoked by the businessman's sneer, one of the scary looking men walked to the corner of the room, where a glistening-sharp machete leaned against the wall. He picked up the machete, felt the sharp edge with his left thumb and began a slow walk towards Edom.

"You are trying to take advantage of my generosity," said the businessman.

To Chris' surprise, Edom spoke without the slightest sign of being intimidated.

"Hardly," he'd said back. "Imagine the cost of getting this to the proper market."

The businessman, showing a hint of admiration for Edom's coolness, brought some levity to his grim face with a small smirk. Chris decided they were both idiots—Edom for dispensing with half a million cedis for three packets of talcum powder, and this supposedly savvy businessman for believing that Edom's trip to the market in Mankraso involved any cost at all.

Edom tucked the packets deep into the bag he had been holding over his left shoulder, and shook hands with the businessman. They appeared to have enjoyed doing business with each other, and Chris, not once forgetting about the machete in the thug's hand, kept his tongue and slipped out the door ahead of Edom.

❦   ❦   ❦

He would have allowed the sheer folly of the transaction to pass without protest if Edom had not, in his final act of utter foolishness, nearly stranded them in Nkwasiafokrom. They had made their way back to the main road in silence, and once there Edom realized he did not have nearly enough left on him to get them back to Mankraso. Thankfully Chris did have some money on him to cover their return trip, but it was all too much for him.

"You are a stupid man," he'd said, fully aware that this was sacrilegious territory he was treading.

Edom had looked at him in speechless surprise. For a moment, it appeared he was willing to accept what he must have interpreted as mere frustration on Chris' part. He seemed to sigh the moment away over a short stretch of patient hubris. "I'll pay you back the cost of the trip and a whole lot more in a week. So spare me."

Chris was livid. "Spare you? Spare you?" The force of his excitement almost choked him. In past times his friends, and his mother before them, had advised him to always take a deep breath whenever he caught an excitement of indignation, lest he swallow his own tongue and choke to death on it. He performed the exercise rather quickly: three deep breaths, separated by a wail of a call to "Jeeesus!" on each exhalation.

When he felt calmer, he said, "Where did you steal that money from?"

"I didn't steal it."

"Oh, so God dropped it down from the sky, that five, five, you know, all the money that you just used to buy the talcum powder."

Infuriating Chris further, Edom had started to laugh, although he did not hold the laugh for very long. "I didn't steal the money," he'd said with a subtle, but stern ring of finality. "I borrowed it. And it isn't talcum powder."

"Yes, it is. You can't fool me. I saw it with my own two eyes. And that's why I think you're stupid, because people are already selling powder in Mankraso, and it hasn't made anyone rich. In fact, yours is not even in the proper container. So how can you expect anyone to buy it? I may be dumb, but that powder is not worth even two hundred cedis, let alone five, five, you know, all the money you paid for it. You are so stupid, Edom. You are so stupid I can't even talk to you."

The last insult changed Edom's mood. "That's the last time you called me stupid, you understand? A fucking retard like you shouldn't be calling anyone stupid."

The sting of his retaliation hovered between them, capturing the heavy hostility of the moment. Chris was hoping he detected remorse in Edom's eyes, but it was not accompanied by an apology.

"I've told you it's not talcum powder I bought. It's a different kind of powder—a very powerful kind of powder. People pay lots of money just to get a little bit of it. In fact, few people in Mankraso can afford it. That's why I'm not going to be selling it in the market at Mankraso. In fact, I'm going to have to travel to Kumasi just to find those who can afford it."

In the lapsed moment allowed for rising tempers to settle, Chris breathed in deeply again, thrice in succession. He could appreciate the explanation that there was a special kind of powder that was very powerful, and for which people were apparently willing to pay a lot of money for. He wondered, if only for the briefest instant, whether this was the sort of powder famed witchdoctors used to cast their magic spells. This was plausible, since Edom had just said he needed to get to Kumasi to sell the powder he'd bought and Kumasi was filled with renowned witchdoctors. Chris shook his head violently to try and clear the line of thought holding his imagination in that moment. One of the things he didn't like about his mind was how it couldn't seem to leave a thought alone even when the thought was merely incidental and entirely useless for the moment.

He said finally, "Remember the other day, when I was the only one who could smell the dead mouse behind the cooler at *Lonely Hearts*?"

An incredulous look swamped Edom's face. "Chris, there was no dead rat found behind the cooler."

"Clearly you have a very bad memory, too."

"I don't ever recall that there was ever a dead rat behind the cooler."

"That's because it was a mouse, not a rat, like I just said."

"Rat or mouse, I don't remember any such occasion."

"Like I said, your memory is clearly not very good either."

"Fine. So there was a dead rat."

"Mouse."

"Fine, mouse. What the hell has that got to do with anything?"

"My nose is really good. It's better than yours. Even Kofi said the other day that my nose is the best one of all our noses, and that was just one example of it. I was the first one to smell the dead mouse. Well, let me tell you, I smelled talcum powder as soon as they brought those plastic bags out. And if you had a better nose, you would know that you just bought talcum powder for a lot of money. And you would know you are the stupid person and not stand there calling me the fucking retard. If you are so sure this thing just bought is the special powder, why don't you just check it and see. Go ahead, check it and see for yourself."

❦   ❦   ❦

Chris had been right, of course. Edom had been playing well out of his league. Each one of the packets he had paid for was filled partly with talcum powder, but the packaging contained a clever disguise involving some of the potent powder Edom had thought he was buying. Such sheer idiocy! Imagine paying all that money for talcum powder—and talcum powder that was in the wrong container at that. Even with all the tragedy that had befallen all of them—and Kofi's tragedies were only the latest—Chris did not understand why they felt compelled to regard life as such a gloomy experience, and litter theirs with such regrettable choices.

At various times over the years, Kofi, or Kwame, or Akosua had gone to great lengths to explain to him that life was a bit more complicated than he seemed to appreciate, and no doubt this was probably true. But he had always felt that for all the difficulties they faced, they had reason to feel blessed. He, for one, had always felt blessed for the life he'd lived. There was never any real justification for stooping, for example, to the lows that Edom had sunk under the pretext of wanting to help Kofi.

On the day of the talcum powder purchase, Edom had actually stormed back up the hill to the businessman's home. By the time Chris got up there, his friend was a bloody mess. They had almost killed him. One thrust of the machete had come down on his left thigh. Somehow he escaped with a flesh wound on that thrust, but he had sustained broken bones in both arms and in his rib cage, and had needed the kindness of strangers to save his life. And for what, all this? So much unjustifiable insanity over how life is supposed to be lived, as if none of them could understand that there was enough to appreciate about the gift itself.

He ran towards Akosua with resolute determination, waving wildly to get the driver's attention. It wasn't too late to stop the insanity. He had to believe that, until he could call everyone to silence. Losing his balance, Chris fell down heavily, picked himself up, and fell again. He picked himself up again. Beads of sweat rolled off his forehead as he forged ahead, confident that there was still a chance he could save the woman he loved. He fell again. The third fall was infinitely more awkward and painful. He was sufficiently occupied with the futile task of regaining his balance that he did not notice the tree stump that sat awaiting his third fall. The contact dazed him. He heard someone yell his name, and it angered him, even in his painful disorientation. No doubt one of them was trying to prevent him from doing what was right. He had to press on. He needed to deliver them all from this madness.

❦   ❦   ❦

Edom zeroed his aim on the left front tire of the passenger van, surprised to realize that his nerves were utterly calm again. In the tense couple of hours before they left Mankraso in the car borrowed from Kwame's uncle to come lay siege, Chris, looking perpetually perturbed, had asked him if he was truly capable of the task. The issue had been discussed before, but it was as if nothing Edom had said had gotten through.

"You might have to kill whomever is coming from the other direction."

Edom had stared coldly into Chris' eyes until he had detected fear, then he laughed, but said nothing.

Kwame, apparently listening in, had said, "It beggars belief."

"What does?"

"Your claim that you'll do it. I just hope Kofi is right and we can pull this off without a gun being fired."

Edom threw away the cigarette he'd been massaging. He was the only smoker of the lot, and had a tendency to take a considerable amount of his resentment against them by forcefully lighting up when he suspected that it particularly bothered them.

"This is not an elementary school game, Kwame, do you understand that?"

The anger in his voice had quelled any possible rejoinder, and the trip from Mankraso to the site of the siege had proceeded in utter silence. Kofi had driven. Next to him, in the front seat, Akosua, terribly weak, had sat holding herself in a tight embrace. Kwame and Chris had traveled with Edom in the back. They took the car off the road at about a five-minute walk from the ambush site, and walked the distance. All along, everything was very clear to Edom: you don't go to this trouble to falter on account of misplaced ethics.

Holding his aim, he calmly fired the first shot into the pregnant space, shattering the womb of silence encircling them. He had meant to hit the front tire, but at the register, the driver of the passenger van keeled. The passenger van had been traveling fast anyway, barely making it around the sharp curve that brought it into view with all tires grounded. The driver's lifeless body slumped onto the steering wheel and slipped off to the side, turning the wheel. He must have pressed simultaneously on the gas in yet another inadvertent act. The van veered sharply off the street and accelerated onto the embankment, with all of thirty feet of space of level ground to cover. From his position behind the cover of a small tree, Edom watched the van shoot in his direction and swallowed his tongue. If the beeline had been right at him, he probably wouldn't have safely gotten away—it was all so fast. But the van, surprisingly throwing no passengers on the sharp turn, missed Edom, and the tree providing him cover altogether, and sped off the cliff at the edge of the embankment.

Three seconds were about as much time as had passed between his firing of the gun and the flight of the van off the cliff. Edom rose and ran up to the edge of the cliff, and was engulfed by an unholy fire as he watched the work of his hands. The speed of the van had taken it on a trajectory far from immediate contact with the slanted descent. It was on its way to make first contact at the bottom of the cliff, a quarter-mile below. Edom turned away from the unfinished spectacle. His immediate sense, strangely enough, was that he wanted desperately to live. He could not recall that he had ever felt this agonizingly desperate for any-

thing. His thirst for life was almost overwhelming. He broke into a ran towards the elephant, his heart thumping as though he had just inherited the souls of each of the travelers he had just sent over the cliff on the trip without return. For all his transient agonizing, his choice had been decisive and immediate. He had to live now.

❦   ❦   ❦

It was on the occasion of Akosua's third attempt at suicide. Following the frantic negotiations to get a taxi driver to take them to the hospital, and the forceful pleading at the hospital to get her some attention, they sat on a concrete ledge outside the hospital, drained of far more than physical energy. Kwame had felt the first inkling of anger begin a slow boil deep inside of him even as they waited for word on Akosua's well being.

"At some point we're going to have to respect her wish," he'd said. "This cannot continue. Even pulling our resources together, we can't afford this nonsense."

He was certain that Edom was in full agreement with him, and that Kofi and Chris would be justifiably offended. But no one said a word in reply. Later on, assured that Akosua was stabilized, but in need of some rest, they strode down the way in search of a place to buy something to drink. A kiosk would have done just fine, but they walked on for ten minutes in the oppressive humidity under the glare of a merciless sun without finding a kiosk, and so they entered into what was to all intents and purposes a modest-looking restaurant-bar. Much as they all would have appreciated some beer, they were not sure they could afford beer just then, and ordered soft drinks that they drank in troubled silence. Then came the bill and Kofi blew his top.

"What's this nonsense?"

The waiter, a congenial fellow with a ready smile, had actually said, "It's the bill, sir."

"I know it's the bill. Why are you charging us three times the usual price?"

The young waiter, not entirely sure how to handle the situation, went to fetch the manager.

"How do you justify charging us three times the price of a soft drink?"

The manager, completely serious, had said, "It's the ambiance, sir."

The comment pulled Kofi to his feet. Frustrations long buried for being without easy answers or targets came barreling to the fore of his suddenly uninhibited tongue. He just about exploded.

"Who ordered ambiance?"

The manager was taken aback. He had clearly not heard this one before.

"Did you order ambiance, Kwame? What about you, Edom? Chris, did you order ambiance when we sat down?"

Not that Kofi was waiting for any of them to answer his pointed question.

"So who ordered ambiance?"

The manager, completely flustered by Kofi's volatility, accepted the going price for the soft drinks, without ambiance, and appeared only too glad to see them leave. Right outside the restaurant, a beggarly fellow who was not there on their way in had taken a spot, hoping for the generosity of the emerging clientele. He begged of them. Would they be kind enough, being so much more fortunate, to give a little something so that he, too, could buy something to eat? At the time, coming out of the ambiance-ridden restaurant-bar, they were trying to find enough change to get themselves back to Mankraso.

Chris stopped and started searching in his pocket for money. When Kwame looked back, Chris was apologizing to the fellow.

It was Kofi who had said, "What do you think you're doing, Chris?"

Chris caught up with them.

"You're going to have to start growing up, Chris. Otherwise we won't be inviting you to accompany us anywhere."

The comment had wounded Chris to complete silence. Later that night, back at Mankraso, Kwame had gone to see him.

"He didn't mean anything by it, you know?"

"That's not why I'm crying. I just feel so bad about life in general. That man who was begging was so much worse off than us. At least we had had something to drink. But then Akosua is dying and we can't afford to care for her, and it just seems like nothing is fair about life. And I wonder why everything is so bad."

Kwame sat in silence with him for a while. "Do you know why we call the armored trucks that come barreling by elephants?"

Chris shook his head. "I've been wanting to ask you about that."

"There is a story told about a young, idealistic auditor who came up around when our country became independent."

He told the story of the government official who likened independence to the killing of an elephant. Kwame had not been sure that Chris would fully understand, but Chris had surprised him.

"When Nkrumah led us to independence, it was supposed to be the start of something truly special for Ghana and for Africa. But you're saying that most of the people who could make a difference think that independence was just the slaying of a big elephant. So everybody should just think about getting their piece."

Kwame said nothing.

"That explains Edom's bitterness, I guess."

They were silent for yet another spell.

"Would you say that's the bigger reason why things are so bad for us here in Africa? I hear a lot of confusing things about the economic system we are supposed to follow and how if only we will follow the system in America or England then everything will be fine and we would all be living well. What is this great system? And why is it not saving us here in Africa?"

"That's because at the end of the day, it is just as you said. It is less about stringent adherence to one system or the other, especially systems that are not even based on our experiences. It is more important, I believe, that we agree first on a wholesome vision about who we are as a people, where've we've been and where we're going. In terms of how we get there, we only need to take our best ideas, and combine it with other good ideas, so that all those confusing economic systems you hear about are put to the service of a more wholesome ideal, not the reverse. It's not much more complicated than that."

Chris had nodded. "And here we are."

"And here we are."

    🍁   🍁   🍁

Kwame was jolted back to the moment by Chris' pre-emptive act to stop the current madness. For a moment or two, before he could do anything else, he watched Chris with detached admiration, and felt the flow of yet another tear down his left cheek. Faced with the fullness of the action he had until now condoned, and therefore with the fullness of the extent of the evil within himself, he felt his will abandon him completely. What was particularly disappointing, now that he thought of it, was that the generosity of Chris' spirit had always been with them. He was God's gift to guide them to through the cruelties of life. He had to be, to so consistently find the hopeful seed in every situation. And in the end, he had more peace than all of them combined, so who was the simpleton?

He clearly should not have been the first out of hiding, yet there he was, struggling against the forest, intent on averting a disaster that never should have been courted. And here, in this moment of reckoning, with Chris bravely doing his part to restore some sanity to the proceedings, the mindlessness of their exploit stood in mocking relief, staring at them, and Kwame just felt like laughing right back at it. It was a funny blessing, this simple perception Chris had, that the breath of life was its own reward, even on a hot, humid day fraught with dangerous, moral decay. Life as its own reward, free of ambiance—what novel idea.

Kwame leapt into action after the first shot had been fired into the hypnotic prattle of the siege. A second shot followed some moments later, from the elephant, which was when it first occurred to Kwame that the first shot had come neither from them nor from the elephant. Had Edom fired it in his impatience? He began a trot towards the road, but already he was without illusion. With some luck, he could perhaps save Chris' life. For now it was all he could hope for. He had no illusions beyond that.

CHAPTER 10

Over a lifetime of endless disappointments, the moment of the most important decision of their lives came almost as a non-event. As they sat idling at *Lonely Hearts,* shortly following another one of Akosua's close calls with an opportunistic infection, the elephant appeared in the horizon. Kofi was thinking then that in the reality of his life, little had gone right, and there was no better indication of this than the utter lack of validation of his life. It might well have been the death of his soul to abandon virtues he had cultivated over his life, but then again what did any of this matter when he could not even recall the last time he felt inspired by the run of his life? In the here and now, what did it matter?

He had simple, immediate desires, like wanting to keep Akosua around for a while longer, like wanting his own life validated in the eyes of his children and yes, the damn community! Isn't that, too, a liberation in its own right? He'd sat by and watched as cancer wrested the life out of his wife. He'd sat by and watched his children grow with little understanding or respect for him, for what he had once envisioned for the country on their behalf. And all along, he'd been drowning in this growing sense of inadequacy—and irretrievable impotence. So what did it all matter anyway? Kofi was the first to see the vehicle of theft materialize on the horizon. In the time it took for the speeding armored truck to be fully past them, the revelation hit him. The sight of the elephant had always anguished him, by what it said about the leaders of the land, who robbed with impunity, and by what it said of the citizenry, himself the first of the lot, who sat by idly and watched it happen. But on this occasion he did not feel anguish at the theft—not the smallest sense of being played for the fool. His only sense was that this could be the answer to their problems, and if the acquisition was dangerous, and it signified a disintegration of his own soul, then so be it.

Kofi had stared intently at the armored truck as it sped by on its merry journey. "Do you remember that time when we were in secondary school, Kwame, speculating about what we'd do if life didn't quite turn out the way we were hoping it would turn out?"

Kwame smiled a casual smile. "You mean when we spoke of taking the elephant?" For a moment the glaze of remembrance clouded his eyes. Then he shook himself back to the moment and regained his smile. "Our retirement plan. Ah, the folly of youth, huh?"

Kofi thought Edom's eyes lighted up immediately, but if they did, he quickly tamed them and kept quiet. Kofi held his own silence a bit longer, looking at their small group, and observed that Akosua had began shaking her head, although she did not offer a word.

Following a prolonged pause, when the festering silence began to tell its sinister intent, Kwame had said, "You can't be serious."

Kofi did not immediately respond. Instead he kept his probing stare on Akosua, as though he were waging a telepathic battle with the woman. He did not once waver with that stare. "What exactly have we got to lose now?"

Chris appeared to have an objection, but he couldn't quite process it fast enough to raise it. Kofi thought he saw relief—the emotion was puzzling—on Edom's face, but Edom still remained silent, and Kwame sat in complicit silence, his face shadowed by a bit of disbelief. It was as if they were all realizing just then that they had actually crossed the line long before, without having ever acknowledged it. The cat out of the bag, Kofi suddenly found himself sitting in startled silence, fighting against the validity of his own question. Maybe they truly had nothing to lose.

"But the elephant stops for no one, Kofi. What you're suggesting is suicide."

Kofi had looked at Kwame and offered this sinister smile. "There is always a way, you know that."

Again the ominous, startled silence. Even at that point, had any of them tried hard enough to ask why, the spell might have been broken. Kofi sat there awaiting the question, knowing he couldn't very well supply the full interest of corrupted reasoning to justify his proposition. But the question never arrived, and as the monster he had proposed began taking form in his mind's eye, a chill bathed over his heart—a cold, utterly invigorating chill.

❦   ❦   ❦

Akosua sat there that day with the heaviest heart. It had jolted her to hear Kofi propose taking the elephant as though this was something normal human beings did as a last resort to unfulfilled living. Quite a few citizens had tried their hand at this, true. But there were no stories of success, and besides it spoke to the very moral decay they were so concerned about. So naturally, it couldn't ever be a way for them, for then would they not have lost every little bit of integrity they had left? She might have been the one to ask Kofi to defend his own rusted principle in wanting to stoop to thievery, and probably should have. But the moment, though it lost its trance-like currency in retrospect, had been disarmingly captivating when it took life, in a way none of them could very easily explain.

Three times she had tried to kill herself, and all she'd succeeded in doing was to create a bloody mess and impose an obligatory emergency on them. Combined with the numerous emergency trips to save her from opportunistic infections, she had already exhausted her reserves, and was wholly dependent on their graces. She could have argued again to be let go, except that such a peculiar argument cannot be conjured on a day when one is not necessarily under any heavy cloud of depression. Moreover, arguing that they let her die did not exactly put them in any better financial place. They would still be burdened by their utter lack of reserves, along with the debts they had incurred trying to keep her around. For all that, she still felt, at the first expression of intent, an instant revulsion, and a need to ask why, perhaps because she liked to think that they still had shreds of dignity left.

But on second thought she chose not to put Kofi on the spot. She remembered the words of her cousin Owusu, who used to say that it is not wise for the rat spat out by a snake to return to inquire about why it had been spared. Better to accept the favors accorded you with gratitude, and leave it at that. It had become increasingly obvious that they were all very desperate. Their collective desperation had grown feverish, with Kofi confiding in her, only a few weeks before, that he had actually gone to pay a visit to Agyei, to place a personal request for help. Agyei had said no, of course. He had said he didn't have nearly as much as most people in Mankraso seemed to believe he had, but that appearances needed to be kept. What do you say to the friend who would endure the ultimate humiliation to save your life? Even from the loved one of whom this might be expected, the way to expressing gratitude is not to wonder aloud about his motivations for seeking riches.

But the conflict within was never going to dissipate on any easy argument such as this. She had chosen not to put him on the spot just then, but it was still worth asking why they insisted on saving her when she felt she'd made her peace. Kofi's alternative perceptions, however well intentioned, were always very ambitious, and they never convinced her. That she stopped trying to take her life was not so much because she grew to appreciate Kofi's great wisdom. It was due more to the unsettling feeling that she was leaving nothing worthwhile behind, to mark her passage through this cycle. Talk about wanting children at the wrong time. Perhaps that was the real reason why, no matter the corruption of Kofi's proposition, right behind her initial repulsion, she felt a quickening, based on the possibility of committing one final act of great love: she would give her life so they could live. Surely even a single theft of the elephant would set them up for the rest of their lives. Perhaps they could even do some good with the intake, and she would have been an integral part of what made it all possible. It wouldn't be the greatest act of love ever committed, but it would be her act of love.

So instead of being the one who put Kofi to task, she'd said instead, "Do you think the elephant would stop at the sight of a potentially hurt woman lying in the middle of the road in the middle of nowhere? Maybe a farmer in need of medical attention?"

She'd felt sick to her stomach. This was insanity, this deliberate destruction of self, especially since the desperate urge to leave a legacy was itself so vain. But another voice within bid her yet another pause. This wouldn't be the first time a woman laid down her life so loved ones might live. Here in Africa, it happens every day, if in less dramatic form. But it happens every day—exhausted mothers and wives drawing on unnatural strength to keep children and households thriving, under the heavy toll of restricted opportunities. So much sacrifice, so little gratitude. This would be her final gesture of love, and of gratitude felt, even if the life she was giving up was decidedly diminished in value by the anticipated, inglorious ending that awaited her.

"I can't imagine that it would run over a human body, no matter the rumors." Edom offered that rejoinder as his first contribution that late afternoon.

Akosua turned in the direction of the fast disappearing armored truck. It was too soon for her to imagine the possibility of being run over, but she was contemplating an alternative, more attractive way to pass on. "Then that's how we'll stop it."

Kofi began to shake his head immediately, and Akosua felt a strong sense of relief, not because she did not want to be the sacrifice but because she desperately needed at least one voice to tell her that even the risk was unacceptable.

Smiling sadly, she'd said, "You have a better way of stopping the elephant then?"

Kofi had seemed frustrated. "I'm surprised that no one has even objected to the idea. I was expecting a lengthy debate. Why isn't anyone objecting?"

"I object," had said Chris.

Kofi glared right through him, obviously awaiting objection from the other three, but none of them wanted any part of the bait as yet. Looking at them in that moment, Akosua's heart sank. She had never quite considered them so dead as in that very moment, and clearly neither had Kofi. But his simple suggestion seemed to have brought to him a clear, brutal image of themselves: they were truly dead, all of them, with the possible exception of Chris. To be saddled with cynicism so deep that a thoroughly corrupt proposition fails to elicit any moral objection was frightening; it was a sort of a demoralizing, complete death.

Akosua had said, eventually, "You must have voiced the exact feeling of everyone at this table, Chris excepted. Am I right, Kwame?"

Kwame had mulled over the question for only a moment. "If by that you mean I don't believe I have much to lose at this stage of my life, you're probably right."

"Does the thought of stealing repulse you particularly?"

"Well, it's morally objectionable, I agree. But I think my hesitation is more a matter of lacking the courage. I think you're right—Kofi voiced an opinion that I would have never voiced, but not because I consider it so morally reprehensible I couldn't even bring myself to think it. I think it is more likely that I lack the courage to have ever bluntly said let's do this and get on with living."

"What about you, Edom?"

They were not prepared for him. "I know that Kofi and Kwame and you, Akosua, have all sought after the better being in our souls.

Or is it the better soul in our beings? I admire the principles you've held on to so nobly. But those principles have failed us. I think that especially for three people of your intelligence, you should have found a way to adjust your principles to the changing times. We no longer live in a world where the noble and poor are honored. I don't know that we ever lived in such a world.

"What I know is that a stomach growling from hunger does not need principle; it needs food. It seems to me that all our lives we've been living with growling stomachs, our own and that of loved ones all around us. But instead of going out there and getting our hands dirty like everyone else to find the food that would calm the growling, we've been sitting back trying to keep our hands clean while feeding people principles. Look at us now. Which one of us has any respectable standing in this community?

"I hate to tell you this, Kofi, but the other day I sat in your living room and overheard your children fantasize about how they wished they could be Agyei's children for just one day. It is clear that your great principles have done nothing for their nascent appetites. How much are you willing to bet that if we were suddenly to come into enough money to be in position to feed the whimsy of our loved ones, we won't have our entire existence validated and glorified?

"And I don't even mean that we suddenly start living an exorbitant lifestyle. I simply mean that we put ourselves in position to be able to give our loved ones the things they ask for, without meeting them with a rebuke and a reprimand for daring to ask, as a way of masking our felt impotence. Tell me you won't feel good about yourself to be in that position, to know that you can put a happy smile on your children's faces when they come with a request, and have the means to surprise your wife every now and then with something a little extra, apologies to you, Kofi, and to you, Chris.

"To top it all, we would be able to pay for their education, and ensure that they can move on to better things. So you ask me if the thought of stealing from the elephant repulses me. The answer is no, not one bit. Everybody who can get away with it is stealing anyway, so why not us? Sainthood with poverty is the worst sin of them all—we all know this. It has brought no one any validation. As to whether or not we have anything to lose, at last check we were grasping on to the last shreds of our battered pride. At least I think the rest of you were. Personally I haven't been burdened by that particular annoyance for a long, long time. So I say to hell with all of that cowardice. We need to take the elephant and get on with living. And I'm rather convinced we can pull it off with proper planning."

Edom finished airing his grievance and sat back with a dour look about him. That Akosua could tell, he did not appear to be relieved to have finally had the chance to let them know how he felt. It was clearly not about a simple, inconsequential moral victory for him, or about the happy release of an oppressive burden too long harbored in silence. He was unequivocally telling Kofi that his casual remark about taking the elephant was nothing short of an absolute surrender to the forces he'd railed against—foolishly, apparently—over his whole lifetime. His own children, according to Edom, provided the most compelling proof of his worthlessness, or at least the worthlessness of his ways, wishing to have been sired by Agyei. Akosua was stunned that Edom would say something that hurtful to his friend just to make a point.

She could feel Kofi's emotions as though they were her own. He was resigned, even though he certainly must have had reservations about Edom's cut and dried wisdom. But Akosua was thinking, somewhat sheepishly, that Edom's growling stomach, at least for just then, was a reasonably potent argument to ignore. The question now was whether any of them cared to reconsider their position, given Edom's strident simplification of the issue. To do so would have required a sudden hypocritical turn-about, particularly from Kofi himself, combined with a renewed attempt to feed more principles to a man who had heard them all and was done digesting them. No one took the bait.

❦   ❦   ❦

She had figured that before they actually got around to the day of reckoning, he would try to offer her a more reasonable explanation, if such a thing was possible. But it was always going to be a tricky matter, given that he was going to need a much more refined argument than the casual one he had thrown at them that afternoon, ahead of Edom's proselytizing about their misguided principles. The moment came only three days later. Kofi had come to visit with her, as he did virtually every evening now that she was getting more and more sick. In the itchy uneasiness that had now come to characterize the silence between them since Kofi made his covetous proposition, Akosua found herself immensely conflicted. She was at great pains to avoid making him feel guilty, while still wanting to understand, in the most desperate way, why it had become all of a sudden so necessary for them to sell their souls.

She was not going to say anything as yet, but Kofi looked up from reading the newspaper and found her gaze on him, and he must have sensed that this was perhaps as good a time as any other, because he said, without prompting, "He was just being honest."

"I know." Akosua had gathered herself to a sitting position so she could rest her gaze more squarely on him. "But was he right? Were you right?"

"I wasn't thinking."

"Yes, you were. You knew exactly what you were offering. That's why you never said a word back to Edom's bold insult. The man told you that your children are ashamed to have you for a father, and you said nothing. So was he right?"

A cold sadness clouded his eyes. "I don't think he was lying about what I heard my children say. Besides, I couldn't very well argue against his growling stomach."

Kofi said this with a quick, uneasy chuckle, then fell into a prolonged silence. Akosua thought he looked utterly defeated. Still uneasy about pushing him, she kept silent.

"What do you expect me to say, Akos? This has not been a happy existence. So maybe we were wrong. We won't be the last people who were deluded in their thinking about the world around them. We could have been very wrong."

"About what, exactly?"

He thought over this for a moment, then threw her a surprise: "Human nature," he said. For a moment he looked to be pondering his own answer. "I don't think we ever wanted to face just how selfishly brutish it truly is. We thought it was something better, I don't know why. People, even the poor and destitute, do not crave a more equitable world. They simply want to have more for themselves."

"That's vicious news to one waiting to die," had said Akosua, dabbing at the fresh tear that immediately met Kofi's comment. "But I never quite thought that we talked and acted in pursuit of a particular belief in human nature. I thought we were appealing to something more ennobling. The brutish character of human nature has not altered the fact that humans have found ways across history to collaborate in founding great societies. Nor has it altered the fact that the ultimate definition of integrity is more often than not based on group identity. I don't find that the shortsightedness we've displayed as a people provides ultimate validation to your argument. I'm asking you to be honest with me."

He thought on this for a moment. "You know I can't very well sit here and say to you that I've found a moral plane on which this is acceptable. We thought we could find validation by living honestly and telling the world around us that there is a better way. A better way to redeem ourselves, a better way to redeem Africa—all this nonsense. There may be a better way, but it clearly sounds more acceptable coming from the lips of the man with a pot of gold, don't you think?"

"You're saying then that we were the wrong messengers?"

"Deluded idiots, is more like it."

"Tell me the message was right."

Kofi appeared to struggle with whether he wanted to dignify the dialogue. "The message was right," he said, almost fuming. He took Akosua's reproving stare, "No really, I mean it. Who truly believes that the sham we've been caught in since independence will ever lead to our true liberation? Independence, we've now found out, was simply the best strategy of our former colonizers to continue managing our affairs without accountability. As a people, we Africans are going to remain a mockery to the rest of humanity so long we refuse the uncompromising imperative to unite and set the agenda for our own destiny, free from the meddling of others. This is not a lie, Akosua, much less one that bears repetition."

"So how do you envision this, exactly? That you will come into some money from having robbed the elephant and say to people: 'follow me for I have money to give'?"

Kofi shrugged. "The money will propel the message. It is not the message, but the public is so gullible to the lure of money."

"And you say this with a straight face, Kofi."

"That's how it works everywhere. The right of governance to those who can afford it. It is the great secret of America, the champions of democracy, don't you know?"

"Fuck you, Kofi! I am sitting here talking to you, one African to another, about the fact that our whole land is going to hell and you're telling me that your new ideology of theft is sanctioned by America? What ever happened to your integrity, Kofi? What ever happened your spiritual essence, to the kernel that bids you to stand responsibly for a principle?"

"Like having unprotected sex with someone you hardly know?"

It was as though he took a bamboo stick and smacked her in the face with it. Frost covered the space between them, perhaps even crawled into his heart, for his face looked to have shut her off completely. It was her first and, it turned out, only taste of the bit of disdain he felt for her.

"Maybe you should learn to get off your high horse, Akosua," he'd said, rising. "You talk as if you live a different reality. It's time you woke up."

The chill lasted two full weeks, thawing only because her condition dictated it. In that time, she mourned the ultimate severance of all the ties that bound them.

❀   ❀   ❀

About a month and a half later, a week to the day they had set to take the elephant, Kofi found Akosua dancing in her bedroom when he went to see her. He had noticed that in the last few weeks leading up to the theft, she would gather herself as frequently as possible when she had the strength to do so, and dance these small, gentle dances. The very first time he found her dancing by herself, back on that harrowing night a few years back when she shared the soul wrenching, deflating news of her pending mortality, she'd been crying during the dance. Since then, Kofi noticed, she had never cried while dancing. The dancing had become her soothing balm for all occasions, and while she still bore the burden of self-blame, and dreaded a prolonged death, she had come to the wistful acceptance that each day remained a new gift—at least until she decided she no longer wanted the gift.

Earlier in the day of this latest visit, Kofi had traveled out of town to meet someone who was supposed to have some small role in making the ambush a success. He was gone for most of the day, and came back with an easy, assured smile that he could not seem to shake. Kofi was feeling very good about things. Approaching Akosua's home, he went around the back to her bedroom window and found it open. She was clearly not very concerned about mosquito bites this evening. He parted the curtain on a quick, delinquent impulse, and saw her dancing. Quickly, he made his way to the front entrance and walked into the family compound, past the obligatory greetings and stood once again in the doorway to watch her.

A broad smile graced her face when she met his eyes, and she reached out a hand to him. It was the first time she had ever asked him to dance. He moved forward in a giddy trance and took the offered hand, and together they danced.

Near the end of the song, Kofi said, "I have some good news to share."

Akosua smiled. Her head shaking, she raised her index finger to his lips, but never offered a word back. The next song came on, and she picked up her pace to match the faster rhythm. He followed her bidding. A third song came on, a mellow number that slowed them both down from the racing pulse of the previous song, the racing pulse within. By now their bodies were beginning to move with a better understanding of each other, but he was in every way unprepared for the sudden warmth that touched and spread up his arms from the tips of her fingers. That moment of sudden awareness was quickly followed by another, and in short order, every pore facing her was flooded by her warmth. A soft sigh escaped him, while his mind clouded, against all wisdom, to the question of his tickled desire. He had already forgotten the good news he came to share in this sudden maelstrom of a primal urge long denied, but he came to his senses in time to realize that they had suddenly stopped dancing.

He either took her or she took him. It did not matter much here, where each giving and taking formed part of a special gift they had now decided to share together. In this revival of their dormant desire for one another, it did not matter much who was doing the taking. The giving was all that mattered. It had come to this, but the circumstance of their first ever exchange of the ultimate physical affection should never have been so unnecessarily burdensome. True, he had made love to her many times in the tender throes of his imagination, where he had willfully kept an inviolable temple for her. He had also made love to her many times over through the fierce loyalty he'd kept for her, and through the silent pain over her rejection, that he actively fought to suppress.

He had dreamt of this before, back when their eventual getting together was a possibility merely waiting to happen, and the wait itself was the sweetest pain of them all. Neither of them had, in those years, had any doubt that it was worth the wait. What would have been the need to rush into the meeting of their bodies when they had a lifetime for each other, and the meeting of their minds had barely began enabling them to open up to all the beauty and possibilities within? What would have been the need? And since this particular, physical expression of everything they meant to each other had a tendency to belittle those expressions of affection that were not as intensely overwhelming and short-lived, there had been the reasonable belief that it was better to wait. It should never have come to this.

He held her face in both hands and looked down into a soul that he had always known in the fullest way one could hope to know another soul. Then he reached down and rolled the salt of her tears gently on the tip of his tongue, his heart pounding. It's all right, he said to her, whispering. It's all right. We have this time, don't you see? We have this time.

He felt a strong shudder grip her body, squeeze her spine and numb her nerves waist-down, causing her to lean against him for support. Holding her in a gentle hug, he offered a kiss, bearing the best of his psychic energy to lighten the burden on hers', and applied just enough pressure to feel the hurried beat of her heart against his' through the thin fabric of their clothes. He held her there, comforting her with soft reassuring squeezes until the tension holding her in the chronic shudder had spent itself and released her. She reached out then, opening herself, and welcomed him into her grasp. Her head dropped sideways into the groove of his chest. The tension seemed to have ebbed away, but she never stopped crying.

The pace of his heartbeat quickened further when she touched the tips of her fingers on the back of his hands and breathed gently on his left shoulder. This was quaintly familiar, the gentleness of her breath, the softness of her touch. It revived the single memory of a happier time, when they had touched just like this, and breathed in the fullness of their bodies, before deciding together to arrest the ferocious force of their unleashed passions before it pounced on them without let up. It was a happier time, of the sort that glued the distant years together and smoothed the turbulence of the times when understanding was not as easy to come by.

He closed his eyes in the warmth of her arms and waged a silent battle to allow his own tensions to ebb out of his body. He felt her pull back and kiss him on the forehead. Suppressing the immediate urge to kiss her back, he allowed himself to be kissed, and felt a tear of his own flow through the wall of his protective shield.

Twenty odd years ago, under the shade of a mango tree, deep beyond the retreat of the Franciscan brothers in the shallow forest retreat in Koforidua, they had sat and talked, pondering the meaning of life. He'd said it was right here before him, the meaning of life. She was flattered but chided him for being childish. She'd always been so serious in her thinking. But he mocked down her serious demeanor then, and insisted that this *was* the meaning of life. It was exactly what he felt in that moment—this overwhelming joy that made his heart feel as though it was soaring with every breath he took, and made him want to scream a happy cry to the world and tell one and sundry that the possibilities for redemption were without limit. It was this love he felt in him, so strong he believed it could cure the afflictions of the heartbroken and assuage the pains of those who suffered from the hardships of living, and bring peace into the hearts of men. A feeling powerful enough it made him believe that redemption from any ill of the spirit, body and mind was within his grasp.

You make me feel like that, he had said to her. He had stunned her into tears that day, under the wide shade of the mango tree deep beyond the retreat of the Franciscan brothers, and she had kissed him on the cheek and turned her head away quickly in embarrassment.

He kissed her fingers again, searching her eyes, and blew on the thin layer of hair covering her hands. She smiled. This simple gesture always felt so good to her. Taking his hand in hers', she put it on her face and asked him to close his eyes so he could memorize her face again. Every touch between them was purposefully gentle and soft. In that way the touches lingered, so that after a while the sensation produced was that of a gentle breeze touching the hair of the skin in a continuous flow, covering every inch of her simultaneously. There was this motion he made, where he wove his fingers through her hair and began to massage her scalp—that felt so good she was completely taken aback. For a moment her tears froze from the pleasure, then resumed with surprising intensity. He could not have known why, but she looked delighted and surprised at once, as though she had just discovered something new about her body.

His hands moved down the contour of her frame and idled about her thighs, where he brushed her soft skin. The next memory, far less pleasant, swept into focus as he brushed his fingers on her thighs and then her breasts with just enough lightness to allow him feel her nipples rise. It was a memory drawn from the occasion of their graduation from the university, a particularly trying time for the health of their bond. Things had not mended well between them after that unpleasant episode at Kwame's place, when Akosua had spoken of the lack of beauty in her life.

The pace of her arousal quickened. Still, she seemed to manage to fight the urge that threatened to disrupt the serene beauty of their easy exploration. She took Kofi's fingers and sucked on them in turn, nibbling softly at the tips.

The memory shadowing him now was of the time around graduation, when more men than Kofi cared to know were seeking after
Akosua. Two of them in particular, Ebow Fameyeh and Kwesi Ansah,
were so completely taken by her that they spent the better part of
their years at the university sparring over her, forever inventing new
ways to woo her. Akosua had allowed them to do so when she could
have told them that she was spoken for. At least that was Kofi's perception, and when he once saw her on a date with Kwesi, holding
hands with him and looking perfectly content, Kofi dismissed Akosua in a private funeral of the heart, held in the dark of midnight at
an isolated spot on Labadi beach on a festive weekend. He swore her
off until a couple of years later, when, incapable of the level of denial
required, he finally gave in to the greatest yearning he'd ever had and
asked her hand in marriage.

Would Akosua's life have been much happier if she'd accepted to
marry Kwesi Ansah, or Ebow Fameyeh for that matter? Certainly
they had done well for themselves, those two. They stayed in Accra
and figured out how to play the games well enough to acquire some
wealth for themselves. Ebow passed on at a relatively young age, but
Kwesi was around still, and last Kofi heard the man was doing well.
Why had he despaired so heavily over her when he had never been
sure he had the fortitude to risk it all for her material well being?
Why so much jealousy when, for the sake of his love for her, he
should have gladly pushed her away to bigger things? The memory
was painful even now. In its sheer power, it was second only to the
memory of her saying no to him when he asked her hand in marriage. And they all stood before him in this moment—all these God-
awful, unpleasant memories—because only the strongest emotions
could possibly find expression in this space, and in the process free
his mind. There was no better time to feel the strength of the pain,
and to release them.

Still, the conflict within was strong enough that they froze the
flow of his actions momentarily. She took his hands in hers' in

response, and passed them up and down her torso, hips and thighs until her own breathing had grown shallower, and then she led them back to her chest, to the buttons of her blouse, and asked him to undress her. He obliged her, and did so without rush, allowing her magnificence to rise and meet his desire without overwhelming him.

Travelers of the Serengeti talk of the spellbinding beauty of the landscape that is the habitat of the wild life. So do travelers of the desert, for whom there's nothing to match the rolling rivers of sand on their dormant journey into the distant horizon where, in their meeting with the sky, it is not possible to tell whether the sky is swallowing the sand or the sand the sky. Here and now, Kofi understood something about all that. In its full splendor, the majesty of the human form does match, with relative ease, the most majestic landscapes nature has yet carved out. He saw this now. And so wars have been waged, kingdoms brought to the ground, and kings to their knees! Aha! He was on his knees before her when her underpants came off. He looked up at her, at the soft petals of curves that rounded the edges of her form. For the first time he took full notice of the wasting of her body under the assault of the little creatures. They had yet to waste her enough to leave an indelible mark on her form, but their chipping away was visible nonetheless. And still she was the most beautiful sight he'd ever seen.

He kissed her navel, traced his tongue down the slope of her stomach and kissed the hair of her mound. Then he breathed her in. Not yet, she said. She took her own time disrobing him, nibbling at his ears the whole time. The sensation was ticklish, he said, but it still made him feel drowsy. Time spun again, taking him out of his shirt and trousers under soft, feathery touches that left him with a permanent tingling itch on every inch of him. She kissed his erection and danced him on the tip of her tongue for just a breath, swallowed him and released him, all in one motion so well executed he did not seem to have any control whatsoever of the low moan that escaped him. Gently her lips climbed up his frame, and brought her needling, teasing breath back up to his neck, and up to his face. Kiss me, she said, as softly as you've never before kissed. He smiled a light smile, reached down and blew a soft breath across her lips. How's that, he asked. Soft enough, she said. Now kiss me as though I were the most delicate flower, depending on you for my life breath. Tears had returned to her eyes as she spoke, but they failed to break. He met their lips and offered her a complete kiss.

This sense of lovemaking that rested somewhat uncomfortably between the purely physical and the intensely ethereal was how he had always imagined it would be like, being with her. But he had not imagined this level of sadness at the front end, and suddenly he began to shake uncontrollably. Akosua pulled back again to look into his eyes, and smiled at his tear. We don't have to do this, was what she offered for comfort. It's quite all right.

He'd said, "The feeling inside me is cheapened by this easy erection. That's why I'm hesitant. But I want to, Akos. God help me, I want to."

After that there was this continuous spinning sensation, shortening his breath as wave after wave of overwhelming pleasure bathed over him, and he would have willingly died in that state, but there was an interruption somewhere, when, producing a condom, she'd uttered that she could not very well allow him to risk his life for the moment. It was a brief interruption, followed by a few efficient strokes to cover him, swallowed by the next wave, and an improbable lift beyond his senses.

At the end, lying back in repose, she experienced the touch of a sweet, warm exhilaration that managed to send endless currents of pure electricity on random searches through her whole being, twitching her muscles. She had imagined that they would be good together, since their love for each other had never been in doubt, and their spiritual connection had always worked so well. But this was startling in the most troubling way, and for the next full half hour after it was over, she struggled to find her voice.

All the while, the thought kept crossing her mind, filling her with doses of suppressed laughter each time, until finally it begged for release, and she said, "I'm sorry, Kofi, but no one should have so much creative energy contained in the head of his penis."

The laughter that rocked him was so forceful he coughed uncontrollably at the start, straining for his breath in the physical attack of her wit, and then, when the strain had passed, he must have laughed for another half hour or so. He kissed her at the end, and breathed her in. The cassette player, running out of songs, had snapped shut to summon a deep silence that was breached initially by their breathing alone. Moments later the wall fell, and a flood of sounds from without barreled into their private space. The awareness of the world outside was wholly unwelcome, but they did well to avoid it altogether.

"That was no doing of mine, you know that. It was our creation." He paused for a moment, unable to find the voice to tender the depths of what he felt, which made him feel terribly silly. "I have always loved you, Akosua."

She cupped his face, nodding. "I know, Kofi. I know. Can you ever forgive me for saying no? I just did not know. I had no idea at all what I was doing."

Kofi smiled. "There is nothing to forgive, Akos. I was blessed in my marriage to Efuwa. And you never ceased being my inspiration."

CHAPTER 11

"We're going to need some guns and ammunition for this." Edom had said this with his eyes fixated on Kwame.

"And you are looking at me because?"

"Are you with us or not, Kwame? As far as I can tell you're the only one with the necessary connection to get us the weapons we need. You were a police officer once, were you not? I thought you told us once that you still have a gun."

All eyes shifted back to Kwame.

Kofi shared a quick look with Akosua, took a swig from his beer bottle and set it down, clearing his throat to cull attention. "Kwame can get us the weapons."

"I don't appreciate your tone."

Only Akosua and Chris seemed visibly delighted with the heavy, unpleasant silence that rolled in behind Kwame's remark.

Edom, not particularly keen on hostilities that might derail the entire enterprise, said, simply, "People, please."

Kwame smiled wryly. "I don't mind getting us the guns, really. I'm just not sure that you understand the weight of this undertaking. Are you absolutely sure you have what it would take to carry this through?"

Edom, feeling more resolute all the time, had said, "I think we've argued the point already. Whether or not we have what it takes depends, I believe, on whether we believe we have anything to lose."

"Not entirely. You may be willing to sacrifice your very life for this. We all may…"

Chris, hearing that, began to raise his hand in protestation, but Edom shot him a look so frightful Chris aborted the attempt and returned to his silence.

Kwame continued, "…But are you able to look at another man in the eyes and kill him, who has done you no wrong?"

Edom stared deeply into Kwame's eyes. He had no hostility, but his stare was morbidly grave. "Like I said," he pointed out, "what do I have to lose? Better still let me ask you this, what do you think it could cost me? My life?"

"It could cost you your soul."

Edom began to laugh. "How many children have you lost in your lifetime, Kwame? Two, right? What about you, Kofi? How many of your children did you lose before you lost your beloved wife and your mother? As the providers of your homes, having failed to provide them the cure they needed to get well, are their deaths on your hands? If so, you are already damned. But if their deaths were acts of God, as we continuously deceive ourselves to believe, then so will the death of anyone who falls while we take the elephant. It would be an act of God—we'd be merely the instruments, nothing more. Besides, like all rich people, we would be able to buy our forgiveness in time. Count me the number of rich people you know who are not saints just for being rich. Wasn't it you, Kwame, who brought me that article in the newspaper about the pope giving some high honor to some rich media mogul whose only real virtue is that he is wealthy?"

"Normal people don't do this, Edom."

"Do what, Kwame? Normal people don't steal? Are you serious?"

Kofi had intervened, "No one would have to die if we do this right. And Edom, I don't want you to ever again cite any of us as examples of your morality tales, do you understand? Kwame, will you please get us the guns we'd need for the task? We'll also need some training, obviously."

Kwame had nodded. "Sure thing. Do you have a timeline?"

🍁   🍁   🍁

"What's the plan, exactly?"

They were huddled around a table in Kofi's room. Kofi had sketched a diagram of the stretch where the ambush was to take place; it was a very simple sketch, but it did have the detail of the trees along the stretch, foremost among them the baobab tree, and it also detailed the breadth of the embankment leading to the precipice that bordered the road on either side.

At a spot on the map just past the baobab tree, Kofi marked a small 'x' in the middle of the road. Akosua, he indicated, would lie down at that spot; it was about a distance of one and a quarter mile from the sharp curve in the road that the elephant would take to enter the stretch of the ambush. The distance, Kofi explained, was necessary to allow the driver to see the body and make the humane decision to stop. Kofi marked a spot in the secondary forest embankment at the end of the stretch, in the direction the elephant would be headed if it were to leave the site of the ambush. "You'll be here, Edom, to prevent another car from entering the stretch. The chances are quite small that any vehicle would be coming from that direction, but like we said, just in case."

"Of course."

He marked two spots on either side of the road from where he had marked the 'x' but a little distance closer to the direction from which the elephant would be traveling. He wrote Kwame's name over one of the newly marked spots and his own over the other.

"There's nothing elaborate about how this would all happen. It really should be quite simple. We wait, the elephant stops, we pounce. The most critical part of the operation is the timing of our attack. We need to have our guns to the heads of the driver and first guard before they can react. It is our only chance of averting any bloodshed. We'll use the two riding in the front to secure the surrender of the two guards in the back, and that's it."

Edom nodded approval, but Kwame was shaking his head, clearly less accepting of the ease of the plan. "What do we do with the guards?"

"We will disarm them."

"And then?"

Chris looked intently at Kofi. He seemed happy that Kofi appeared a bit thrown by the question.

Kofi said, "I don't understand."

"If we simply disarm them, steal the loot and leave, they'll just radio in the theft. I think we'll need a much, much, longer lead time than it would take them to set the search dogs after us if the guards radio in the theft."

"So we'll destroy their radio equipment. And put them out for a while."

"What do you mean by that?"

"We'll knock them unconscious, Kwame."

Kwame was silent for a while, before he said, "Do you know how?"

Edom, sounding frustrated, had intervened by saying, "I think we've all seen enough films to know that you just knock the person over the back of the head."

"You're kidding." There was an incredulous look on Kwame's face. "You think you can do something just from seeing it in a film? How old are you, Edom? Tell me you're more intelligent than that." He turned his puzzlement to Kofi, "Is that what you had in mind?"

Kofi, looking more and more uncertain, had said, "Haven't you knocked anyone unconscious before?"

"When would I have had the occasion?"

"They didn't provide any training for when you joined the police force?"

"Not on how to knock someone unconscious, no."

By now Kofi was visibly worried, but it was Edom who rejoined the conversation, "What's wrong with just hitting them at the back of the head with the butt of our guns?"

"You could kill them. I think there's a fine line between hitting someone with just enough force to knock them unconscious but not with enough force to kill them."

"Are you saying that we're going to have to practice that, too?"

"I am not making any suggestions at all. I'm simply wondering whether we know what we're getting into. Until we've actually successfully done this, I think we have to wonder about all these details. Surely you'll agree with me, Kofi, that it's going to be a terrible mess if we're trying to knock the guards unconscious and all we end up doing is creating a bloody mess, or worse killing them."

Looking at Kofi, Edom seemed quickly alarmed by the discouraged expression on his face, and offered this, "I volunteer to be a test case."

All eyes turned to him. There was profound perplexity on the faces of the others.

"I am volunteering myself as a test case" repeated Edom, almost as if he was trying to convince himself of the wisdom of his sacrifice. "It allows you to get the chance to learn how to knock a man unconscious."

Kwame said, "You've lost your mind, Edom. You've completely lost your mind."

And, finding one opportunity to say something, Chris had asked, "Do we all get to try, and knock you unconscious one, two, three times? I'd like to go first. Trust me, I'll knock you out cold. And how much time do we give you to recover from each knock out?"

This caused Edom to pause, as Kwame snickered. Several seconds of indecisive silence followed, then Kofi said, "We ought to bring some ropes with us. We'll tie them up and gag them, and leave them some ways off the road. Having said that, the most important phase of the whole operation is still the speed with which we pounce on them. We have to be fast enough to surprise them before they can fire even a single shot. That makes it the responsibility of you Kwame, and I, to see to it that there is no bloodshed. You understand? Chris, you'll be with either Kwame or me. You'll have the ropes. All you have to do is watch us, and bring the ropes after we've obtained the surrender of the guards. We'll call you out. Can you do that?"

Chris nodded. "May I ask a question?"

"Sure go ahead."

"What will we do with the elephant when it's all over?"

"We'll push it over the precipice. I wish every question was that easy to answer."

🍁   🍁   🍁

The two friends walked in solemn silence for a long while, taking in the cool evening breeze with detached appreciation. Kwame had his eyes trained on the dark horizon beyond. They had been walking for about an hour without saying very much that was substantive. But it had been a long time between meaningful conversations for just the two of them, and Kwame felt a keen need for a revival of the bond they had always shared. Several months had gone by since the last time they'd really talked to each other. Such was the mayhem of the times that it had robbed them of the desire to reconnect, until they decided on this walk, two weeks or so before the intended crime.

The walk had already served them well. It was a pleasantly cool evening, and while they had not said too much to each other, the long stretches of silence had progressed from the uncertain discomfort of the early walk to a more settled and comfortable silence—the old silence of yester-year, with its organic feel, generating its aura of gentle love to link them. It took Kwame back to their days in elementary school, when they used to meet sometimes, just the two of them, and talk about everything, from girls to who was the better football player, to who was the smartest kid in school, and then, most importantly, to how their preferred teams were doing in the football league table. They would share a snack, usually a stick of sugarcane, and frequently end up at the gutted ruins of the old Methodist mission, which had grown so much vegetation the ruin had merged into the forest, a structural chameleon hiding so many secrets, the sins of a missionary past. There, amidst those ruins, they would hunt for green snakes and keep at the hunt until they finally caught one, which they promptly released. Typically the fun would stop just then, and they would head back to their meeting point, and bid each other goodbye before heading to their adjacent villages through the green forest, while the sun raced ahead to grace others with its joy.

"So what happened?"

It was time to talk, although Kwame did not particularly enjoy breaking into the sweet silence guiding them. Kofi sighed a sigh of defeat. Looking at him, Kwame felt the deepest sense of grief in his own heart.

"What did you think of Edom's growling stomach speech?"

Kwame shrugged. "He's a desperate man. He seems to truly believe that money will solve all his problems."

"You spoke yourself of not caring for the morality that's kept you honest and poor."

"You know I actually did mean that when I said it? I was surprised by it a bit after the fact, but I actually did mean that. The timing had something to do with it, I suppose. My wife and kids were playing on my mind. I have sinned against them, Kofi. I have sinned against them in more ways than I ever dare to remember if I'm to keep my sanity."

Kofi said, "Speaking of sins, I was telling Akosua when she tried to put me to task about my proposition that she had better grow up and face reality. I threw her mistake in her face as an example of her own moral depravity. I don't remember feeling that low in a long, long time."

Kwame shook his head and reached out to give his friend a calming pat on the back. "Remember to apologize to her for that."

"I will."

The silence between grew gentler still, touching them with a rhythm that was easy and unobtrusive. Kwame listened for a moment to the easy taps of their walk, and had the faintest hint of happiness brush by him.

"I think I'll be happy to die during the robbery and have you take care of my family for me. They are better off without me, but they could use the help, obviously."

Kofi shook his head without showing any alarm. "We've both failed our families. But it seems to me that our failings reflect a failing in the direction we've chosen as a people. How did the acquisition of wealth become a value in and of itself, and the only value at that?" He stopped for a moment to think, then said, "I think I'd have been quite content not to have played any role in the politics of the country if I'd felt any real sense of validation in teaching. That's probably what has hurt the most, the fact that I have felt no appreciation in being a teacher. It was once a noble profession, and even when I realized that we weren't exactly going to shake the world on some grand scale, I entertained dreams that I could still mold minds in the right direction. But that didn't quite happen, and teaching does not make anyone wealthy, and so I blink one day and I am this nobody teacher, the butt of children's jokes, and I'm trying to figure out how this happened. It's been hard to live so insignificantly. Even then, I don't like hearing you talk about your family being better off without you. What we are going to do is morally debased, and bad for the nation, but I suspect that we will do some good with it anyhow. And I also hope that, personal comforts aside, we will turn out better people for all this."

Kwame nodded, but he was conflicted. "I still wonder what happened to us. And I wonder who finally sets Africa on the right course. I mean, we all make excuses, Kofi. One way or another, every one of us is making excuses while others run our continent for us. We are belittled, we are disrespected, raped by family and foe, and we are self-destroying idiots. This is shameful stuff, Kofi. This is not a station any self-respecting people should be smiling about. I know we've said this time and again, but how do we keep quiet about it?"

Kofi smiled. "Nobility has always suited you, Kwame, whatever else your sins. You remain your brother's keeper. I like that in you."

Kwame spoke gently. "Me? My brother's keeper? I'm not so sure. That instinct died in me long ago. I'm being vainly proud and selfish, ready to yell at the world of Africans and to say, 'where is our place alongside the big nations of the world?' I remain puzzled by the extent of our passivity and preoccupation with pettiness. But these days I also realize that I know next to nothing, Kofi. The world's passed me by. I couldn't be more honest than that."

"You and I both."

They came up together behind the grounds of the Methodist Church, up the small hill in the direction of the hospital, and Kwame felt a sudden and deep sadness over the inevitable end of the conversation.

He had a final thought for them to consider. "Is it too late for us to back out of it?"

Kofi did not seem surprised by the question. "It's never too late. But would you want to?"

"I wonder what happens if we back out now."

"Well, Akosua will die much faster. We will still have all the debt we've accumulated from trying to keep her around a little longer, and from all the deaths of loved ones of recent times, and from trying to just keep our families together. And we'll continue to mark time. If we find all that acceptable, then we can definitely back out."

A wan smile touched Kwame's face, but he did not say anything back, and they continued to walk in silence.

Kofi said, "What do you propose to do with your take?"

"I'll take care of the children's education. I think we've forfeited the right to public service by doing this. But I don't see why we can't learn about ways to do some worthwhile things anyway. I can imagine starting some enterprise and giving a few people work opportunities. Or making anonymous contributions to select causes." He paused for a longer stretch. "I am not about to suggest that charity is the answer to anything, but we're going to end up with more than we need. We might as well give some back."

Kofi nodded, smiling faintly, and continued walking.

"And you? Do you still intend to pursue that dream of starting a newspaper?"

"You remember. I don't even know the first thing about it, but yes, I think I'd like to do that. I do presume we'd get enough money for me to try my hand at that, to see if I can't channel some of the debate about the direction of our people. It will allow me, too, to teach some useful skills to some of the youth and give them a source of livelihood. But I'm a bit leery about getting too excited about what I intend to do with the take. It is interesting though, isn't it? I've been deriving this guilty pleasure from the hope of using the money to do some things that contribute to the betterment of our society, and I feel surprisingly rejuvenated in those moments. You know what I mean?"

"As a matter of fact I do, Kofi. I really do."

There was deep appreciation and gratitude in Kwame's voice. Even in his immediate happiness, his fondest thought was that he was going to ask his wife for forgiveness, and, if his wish were to come true, die during the robbery attempt, with a modicum of peace. He was immensely grateful for this wonderful feeling.

❧   ❧   ❧

Towards the end, Chris thought that perhaps all this could lead to some good. He figured that since Kofi was so very entrenched in the idea, it might serve as a good omen that he, too, accept the necessity of the intended action. He sat down with Akosua one lonely afternoon to discuss some of his troubles over with her.

Akosua suggested that things have been falling apart around them for some time, and that, while the theft was nothing to applaud, it had indeed come to a point where it was conceivably the only option left. The justification sounded too contrived and easy, and utterly unconvincing, but Chris figured that Akosua, too, wanted to bless the mission with good fortune. It was either that, or, as Chris feared, Akosua was feeling guilty at the time of the conversation over the amount of money she'd cost her friends. By then he was beginning to understand that the money they provided him for drinks and other amenities did not spring from a bottomless well, a realization which caused him no small amount of fear. He was beginning to understand.

He told Akosua that he felt like crying whenever he observed the sobriety of Kofi's face, which had deepened so ominously since—God, since so long ago he couldn't quite accurately recall. Akosua had nodded agreement, and said something like, "He has none of his bellicose laughter anymore. I think his wife's death shattered him."

Chris nodded agreement. "It did. But he was quite sad when he told us about his Easter pain. Remember that?"

Again Akosua nodded. Five or six years back, Kofi woke up on Easter Sunday at the nadir of his felt impotence, conflicted over whether the church would approve of his use of the erection that had teased the sleep out of him. Chris thought it was strange that Kofi had ever had that struggle, since he hardly went to church anymore, but Akosua had suggested that she understood something about how a man would lose his sense of relevance in a society that had either lost its essence or was losing it all the time, with little understanding of the fullest repercussions of such loss. The Wednesday following the Easter Sunday of Kofi's expressed inner turmoil, his wife Efuwa started to feel unwell, and was in such sudden, severe pain that Kofi took a day from school to enable her to go to Kumasi.

The way Chris saw it, God was not exactly fair in the way *he* pulled the surprise on Kofi. Chris could understand that Kofi did not go to church often anymore, which was obviously a very sinful thing, but God decided to punish Efuwa instead. That lovely woman came from the trip to Kumasi with the diagnosis of something Kofi called cancer of the breast. She looked fine, but apparently Efuwa had been suffering in silence for some six months, and within another year after their trip to Kumasi, she was dead, just like that. In one hurried year, Efuwa was gone, and that wasn't even the worst of it. The doctors had said that they needed to cut her open and try to remove as much of this thing that was killing her as soon as possible. Their house of collective morality, carefully built and silently abided, came crumbling down around them. Contrary to what anyone thought, Chris saw it happen, and the process was as painful to him as to everyone else caught in the mess. Kofi, having spent every little dime he'd earned as a teacher on his family and on a hundred comers from all corners, came to realize, admittedly too late to matter, that the unselfish are not a loved group. Favors given did not return in the time of need, perhaps because those to whom the favors had been conferred were not necessarily in standing to return them. But even then it could have been much different. Prior to the death of Efuwa, just after she had been diagnosed with the thing Kofi called cancer, Kofi set about trying to reclaim earned favors by soliciting some much needed funds for the procedure that would save her. He received no help, not from family, not from friends, not from the church, certainly not from the wealthy Agyei that he stooped low enough to beg from.

The times were not without their ironies. One humiliating denial after another later, Efuwa died. But then, blessed twisted tradition, Kofi sat beside the corpse of Efuwa during wake-keeping and watched as friends and well wishers poured nearly as much money into the consolation basket as he'd needed to save his wife. Are Africans caught in a perpetual, symbolic celebration of their own death over the promise of their lives? So much giving in festivities for the dead, so little giving for the preservation of life. It wasn't necessarily that the amount given would have bought his departed wife the operation she needed, but no one had extended a helping hand when it might have mattered. And who knows if he could have convinced the doctors with something a little less than the full rate of payment required? Not that it mattered anyway, the proffered money was taken from him and divided between the sister—who would move in with her husband to help Kofi care for his children—and the family of his departed wife.

Kofi had sat quietly and sadly by the bed next to his deceased wife, not saying much. Snide comments about incapable providers driving their loved ones to their graves too soon accompanied the presents offered. Then, too, he sat in silence and soaked up the disdain with a brave face. Agyei helped by inviting the mourners to his place to show them films from America with rich men driving rich cars and firing glistening guns to kill in beautiful orchestration. People came out of the screening with awe in their eyes, as ones who had seeing paradise itself, and found Agyei their closest link to it. Efuwa was forgotten before the day was over, and much later on, people spoke of the wonderful thing Agyei had done to make her passing bearable for everyone. Combined with the sorrow from his mother's death—which had preceded Efuwa's by mere weeks—Kofi shut down for months.

So Chris did have some appreciation for the desperation that had pushed them this far, even if he did not fully agree with the proposed solution. There was just this matter that he could not escape: who loved whom in this polluted mess? Who was sacrificing for whom? For in the absence of love, how could they truly justify any of this?

"I just want to let you know that I love you more than any of them."

Akosua had raised her eyebrows.

"I am the only one who wouldn't stoop to using you to stop the elephant. I just want you to know that. I may not understand as much as everyone else, but I won't ever have you lie down to stop the elephant. And I think that's because I'm the only one who truly loves you. And that's what bothers me. Nothing we're doing is truly inspired by genuine love."

CHAPTER 12

A small detail about the elephant, that the people of Mankraso did not appear to have noticed, was that there were times when it came barreling by with a modicum of restraint. It was always speeding, true, but for one of the drivers, the speeding was done with great caution, especially through the town of Mankraso.

Recruitment for the driving and guarding of the elephant occurred exclusively in the military, and was further restricted to those soldiers who did not hail from the region of the elephant's operation. Past those two requirements, those who would ride the elephant had to meet a host of additional requirements. But the first cut was predicated entirely on military service, preferably but not necessarily active, and on region of origin.

David Ofosu, the driver on the day of the robbery, had enlisted in the military several years after his family had moved out of Mankraso all the way to Accra, initially, and then to Swedru. He got employed to drive the elephant obviously because, his former military experience aside, he never made any mention of having been born and raised in the region of the elephant's operation, nor of still having extended families in a town on one of the preferred paths of the elephant. The opportunity had come his way a few years after he had been booted from the service for a sin he did not commit, and it would have been foolhardy to jeopardize a job that was to pay him far more than he was earning as a useless security guard. David, who had always admired Kofi growing up, had sent a letter to Kofi to let him know that he was now on the elephant, and that if Kofi paid attention, he could catch a glimpse of him when he was driving. Several years later the two of them ran into each other in Accra. On that surprise meeting, they had both changed their respective plans so they could have lunch together. They reminisced, David reminding Kofi of the inspiration he used to draw from him.

"You're one of the main reasons I joined the army," had revealed David, to Kofi's bafflement.

"I don't understand."

David had explained. "You guys were so smart, you and Akosua and Kwame. And you were so dedicated. When you'd talk about what needed to happen for Africa to get somewhere, I felt so proud to have you for a cousin, and I would think that everything was possible for all of us. My friends and I, we used to call you 'little Nkrumah'. I was so certain that you guys would get into politics and become part of the leaders of the country, maybe even run the country yourself. When I enrolled in the military, I was hoping all the time that eventually you'd become President or another really important person in the government, and I could have become your personal bodyguard. That was my biggest dream, and I would have protected you with my life, I swear."

A dramatic, uneasy silence followed his words, and the two sat before a spell of nervous shifting and eye-contact avoidance. Kofi kept his attention on his food, chewing slowly and purposefully on the morsel in his mouth.

Came the inevitable question, "So what happened?"

Kofi chuckled, but it was entirely bitter. "The West didn't bless our ideas."

Confusion clouded David's face. "I don't understand."

"Oh, it's nothing, just an inside joke. We say that Africans are the only people who need the blessing of the West to feel we're doing something right. If others, the West especially, decide that something we've thought of for our own liberation is not a good idea, we accept it and watch them replace it for us. For our own good, mind you. As soon as they frowned on Nkrumah's ideas for a union of African states, it became a terrible idea for Africa, and has since been regarded as such. And what have the nation states left behind by our former colonizers wrought for our people? That's why I say the West didn't bless our ideas. If they don't agree—which means if it does not serve them—they stamp it out, whether by aggression, seduction or cajoling. And small-minded Africans jump to take up the mantle. It's quite funny, when you come to think of it."

Again his chuckle had been uneasy, and David, saddened to visible distress, had said, "I don't find it funny at all."

They continued their lunch in relative silence after that, until, at the very end, David had said, "So does that mean that you have completely given up?"

It was perhaps the closest Kofi had come to offering the truth about himself, but he faltered. He should have admitted that he was never a doer—that for all the rhetoric they'd spewed back when, he had never really known what concrete steps to take towards it. Or, better still, he could have taken refuge behind the convenient excuse that the currents of history simply hadn't favored them. There was, after all, the very good likelihood that he could get away with telling David that history makes the man, and not face any real debate on the matter.

He'd said instead, "As long as we have our lives, there's no need to give up on anything."

David had said, "It's just amazing to see what goes on. It's sickening. We drive the armored car carrying wealth that goes into the coffers of politicians or to pay for some debts we had no hand in creating, so others can continue fattening themselves on our resources. I drive that car week after week, and my only hope is that the thievery would stop one day, because if it continues, and everything just goes on like this, I swear I'll take my chances one day and try to hijack it. I mean, what would I have to lose if I failed? My freedom? I don't feel free anyway, with all this poverty hanging around my neck. I have all kinds of illnesses, cousin, most of them probably caused by stress, but most of them having to do with things just not functioning right with my body. And I can't ever go to see any doctor for any of it because I simply can't afford it. I've been trying really hard, for so long, to just get by, but this life is really hard, cousin. I mean, I just took this little time to have lunch with you, but truth be told, I wouldn't have sat to eat lunch if I hadn't run into you. I can't afford this sort of thing, you know? I can't afford to eat lunch every day I please."

Kofi, seeking to ameliorate the sacrifice, had said, "I'll pay for lunch, don't worry."

"Thank you, cousin."

"But your point is well taken. We shouldn't have to be reduced to making choices between starvation and everything else. It bespeaks a terrible atrophying of our communal values when even those with jobs still have an impossible time trying to meet the most basic of needs."

David, who Kofi thought was visibly more delighted with his meal after he learned that his cousin would pay for it, had stopped eating for a moment. "That's exactly what I was talking about. Whenever you start talking about what's wrong with Ghana I get the goose bumps. That's exactly what I was talking about."

They had fallen back into silence after that, and concentrated on their food a bit longer. Taking the moments between bites to study his cousin, Kofi was impressed to sheer sadness by the absence, in David's general disposition, of the quiet joy that used to be his trait in his youth. He had grown into bitterness.

Just before they were to part company, David had said, "You have only to say the word."

Confused, Kofi had said, "I don't understand."

"You know, taking the elephant. If you could think up a plan for taking it—and I don't think it's too difficult—I'll be with you all the way."

"That would make us every bit as bad as the bad leaders we say are ruining our country."

"I don't think so at all. First of all we are not public officials yet. But more importantly, one of the things I learned when I was in the army is that you don't have to be a saint through and through to lead a country. In fact, you can't really be a saint and run a country, because as soon as you come into power, you find yourself surrounded by multitudes constantly scheming to bring you down, either because of jealousy or the simple desire to have that power you have. It's true, I tell you. And you have to strike back at them with ruthlessness. It's really the only way to keep your power. What really differentiates a good leader from a bad one is not what you do to stay in power and avoid being overrun by the power mongers surrounding you. It's the policies you push, and whether it improves the situation for the poor or those who are already powerful."

Surprised by the brand of wisdom coming to him, and by the source of it, Kofi had said, "Why don't you kill the elephant yourself and run for office?"

"Oh I'm not a leader, cousin. I know that of myself. I may know something about the ruthlessness required to get into power and stay there, but I don't know much about economics or politics or foreign relations and all that stuff a political leader must know."

Kofi sighed, and they took in another stretch of silence as he shook his head.

"All I'm saying is that if you decided that we should take the elephant, I'm with you. You may or may not choose to rise through the political ranks with the money. If you did, your security would be ensured, because I would protect you with my life, and make sure you had the proper corps of guards.

"But if you chose not to run for office, that would be fine, too. We'll at least have the ability to live well, you know, and provide for our families. Just between you and I, cousin, I'm tired of living like this. I have this heartburn all the time because I'm always having to think up more innovative ways of saying no to my children, and fearing that any second they're going to hurt themselves or contract some serious illness and completely expose me for the incompetent provider I am. And then my parents and all those fucking relatives—excuse my French—always hanging around your neck like leeches, as if I don't have enough problems trying to take care of my wife and children.

"I don't know about your teachers' salary, but my salary is usually completely exhausted with only two weeks gone in a month. And that's in a good month, when none of us is catching malaria or any other sickness. And my wife, bless her heart, she works so hard to try and fill the gap. And it's just really humiliating and depressing, you know?"

Kofi nodded. "I know what you mean."

"Anyway, it's just a thought. If you ever should need to get hold of me, send word to Kumasi. There's a barbershop at *Okomfo Anokye* Circle called *Beautiful Cuts*…"

"I know *Beautiful Cuts*."

"Good. I pass through there at least twice a week. They know me really well there, so you can send a message to me through that place."

"I'll remember that. It was good to see you, little cousin. You're all grown now."

"Good to see you, too, big cousin. Please give my greetings to sister Akosua and brother Kwame and brother Chris."

"I will."

❦   ❦   ❦

The message came eight years later, when David might well have given up on the twisted hope for it. *Beautiful Cuts* was still operational, and David still passed through at least twice a week, to socialize. The message came a full week ahead of Kofi's intended visit to Kumasi. The cousins hugged when they saw each other the second time. As it was lunchtime, David had gladly recommended a canteen they could retire to for lunch. His choice was a very modest canteen, perched behind the *Reggae King* record store, right off a main drag through town. The modesty notwithstanding, the place was very clean, with floors that looked to be frequently swept, and even for Ghanaians, the staff was extraordinarily friendly.

In the very first purposeful silence between them, coming after they had placed their orders for food and drinks, the two cousins looked at each other and had a mutual understanding pass between them, that this was to be the conclusion of their unfinished conversation from eight years ago, and there was no other direction for the conversation than an agreement on time and plan.

As if to confirm just that thought, David had said, "I take it you summoned this meeting eight years after our last conversation to tell me that you think it is a bad idea to take the elephant."

This drew the expected, if nervous and awkward laugh.

"This is not something to take lightly, cousin."

David's face closed. "I know," he said. "It's precisely because it is so unnerving that I have to try to make light of it. Otherwise I couldn't possibly go ahead with it."

Kofi said, "How much time would we need to set it up?"

"That depends entirely on us. We could do it on my next drive, which is only two days away."

The suggestion drew a smirk from Kofi. "We've waited this long. We can wait a little longer than that, just to make sure we do it right. But I need to know from you the logistics of your operation, what your standard response to threat is, what the elephant actually carries, in terms of bounty and security, who is the first in the chain of command and so on."

Lunch arrived, along with a bowl of water for the washing of hands.

"We travel four to a car, two up front, two in the back. The elephant actually has safe deposit boxes welded into it, but that can always be cut through once it's in our possession. There is not a standard chain of command among the riders, which is to say, it is not always the driver or the guard next to the driver, although it's always one of the two. Most of the time when I drive I am the one in charge.

"In terms of operational procedures, these are also relatively simple. We take any attempt to stop the elephant as a potential robbery, and our instructions are to shoot to kill, simple as that. We don't ask questions, we don't seek surrender. But as to what happens if we are taken by surprise, the response is situation-specific. There is obviously no point in all of us dying, for then the elephant would be in the hands of the perpetrators completely, so there is a provision for trying to stay alive long enough to alert home base of what has happened. Because of that, the possibility of using the element of surprise to secure surrender is there, and that's the crutch we must use."

"Would you run over a prone woman on the street?"

David did not hesitate with his answer. "No. I won't run over any human being, especially when we pass through towns, or even out of the boundaries of a town. But as soon as we saw it, we would be on alert to a possible robbery attempt. You'll have to move very fast to surprise the two of us in the front before we can open fire. Once we surrender under the threat of death, we'll have to convince the two in the back that there is no way out except to surrender. Offer them a three-second reprieve and then you'll have to open fire to open the door if they hesitate."

Kofi took a moment to mull over the information given. "What do we do with you?"

"Oh you absolutely have to treat me exactly the same way you treat the others. You'll have to knock us all out, with a powerful blow to the back of the head, but obviously not powerful enough to kill us. It's that simple. What will happen to us—the very worst thing that can happen to us when we finally report in, is be fired on the spot for incompetence. And that's most likely what they would do to us."

Still contemplating, Kofi took down a morsel of his *fufu*. "So location is as important as anything in this undertaking, to ensure the surprise element. What do you think of that stretch between the two hills on the way here from Mankraso?"

"You mean where the road narrows to almost a single lane? That's an excellent spot. Excellent spot."

"Good."

"There is one thing."

"Yes."

"It's the only thing I worry about."

"What is it?"

"One of the real deterrents against a hijack from those of us who drive the elephant, quite apart from the fact that we are soldiers bound by some dubious honor, is the fact that the elephant sometimes travels with absolutely nothing on it."

Kofi's face squeezed.

"Well it probably doesn't happen often. It would be a waste of resources if it did. But it still serves its purpose. On any particular drive, none of us, the riders, know exactly what we are transporting. Our trips are not from the source of wealth or to their final destination. We fit in the middle somewhere. We drive one elephant from point A to point B. When we get to point B, there's another elephant to be driven, either back to point A or to a different point altogether. But, as you know, we don't have alternative ways of getting to most of the other places we must drive to. We still come right through Mankraso. It is usually from here in Kumasi that we take alternative paths to get to our other destinations.

"Still, the point is that on any one trip, we could be transporting a lot of raw cash, gold, diamonds, all three, or some combination of the three. Or we could be carrying nothing at all. It is that particular possibility, that we're not carrying anything, that I think is most responsible for keeping us the riders somewhat honest. I mean, imagine risking it all to try and steal something, and you come up with nothing, and not only would you not have the means of fleeing the country to save your skin, but now you've put your whole family in danger. They hold that threat over our heads, and as you can see, it is a very effective deterrent, because you'd be hard pressed to find any driver who would risk laying siege to the elephant."

Kofi's heart sank. There was something so harrowing about the prospect of selling their souls for no apparent benefit that his food lost all of its taste. He sat in deep thought for a while. Then he said, "That does bid one pause. I can see why the riders would be discouraged. But it's not a likely scenario, since, like you said, it would be a silly waste of resource. I'll bet that the elephant doesn't travel empty but once every hundred trips or so, if that. I suspect that they probably only did it once to plant the doubt, and have not done it much since then. There's no reason to believe that we can be so unlucky as to kill it on one of those rare instances when it is not loaded with anything other than its human cargo. So let's just concentrate on getting the job done. Do you know what your driving schedule is over the next week?"

"Yes, I do."

❦   ❦   ❦

The sun blazed with ruthless intent that afternoon. High up above, a couple of hawks hovered in still flight, gliding silently against a white sky that was full of the promise of ghastly, brutish death.

Kofi watched Chris come out from where he was hiding, some distance behind Kwame at the opposite side of the road, and start towards the road, his right arm flailing wildly at the elephant. The development jolted Kofi out of his dreamy trance, but however quickly he hoped he had regained his wits to attempt a remedy to this unfolding disaster, he was already too late. Why had they brought Chris along in the first instance? Edom had been dead set against it. "Pure silliness," he'd said. "We don't need to bring a child on something this serious."

Kofi had looked right past him. He'd said Chris won't be armed—he would be there just to be part of the experience—and in that same moment, the foolishness of bringing Chris along had crystallized in his mind. He had turned to Akosua and Kwame for comment, but neither of them offered any. Perhaps then their walk on the broad path to damnation had already begun. Here reasoning ceases, common sense disintegrates, and a maddening silence fills the void that ought to have been filled by a final thrust of reasonable communication. The walk on the broad path to damnation had begun, and the child among them panicked first. Kofi's senses came to him, but still the emergence of the stark unfolding was blurred.

A first shot went off, and all at once the illusion was all over. The second shot came from the elephant, but it caused no harm to anyone, that Kofi could see. Chris continued his struggle towards the road, and Kwame, emerging from hiding, took off after him. Chris took a heavy fall, but collected himself with unusual determination. He was moving like a man possessed. Following the second shot, the elephant lurched forward, covering the final stretch to the prone body of Akosua in a blink of an eye. Kofi saw this, and, with a start, aimed his gun at Akosua. But before he could squeeze the trigger, the elephant rolled over her. Her brittle bones offered little resistance to the massive front tires, and the back tires summarily completed the task.

Kofi froze. Up above, past the witnessing hawks, the white sky opened up initially to reveal a void so deep and immense his mind shrunk before it. Then the void closed at the source, and caved in on him. He stood as he stood. From the heights beyond, one of the witnessing hawks issued a cry. Carnage below, humans at work. Chris continued his run towards Akosua, and Kwame, steely in his determination, stayed after *him. He was calling after Chris to come back. That observation was Kofi's last coherent thought.*

He became aware, suddenly, of the gun in his hand, because it had grown a ton, and on reflex, he turned it on himself. But in the brief moment before he could act, he forgot what exactly he needed to do, what the consequence of his action would be, or why it had to be done at all. The gun felt suddenly very strange to him, an object so foreign even the feel of it was beyond his comprehension. He dropped the gun, his vision blurred by a thousand needle pricks, and began walking. He had taken only a few steps when he swiveled around abruptly to catch a glimpse of the multitude shouting at him. It was utterly infuriating to him that so many people could be screaming at him without any of them being even remotely coherent. He tensed for flight when, upon turning to face them, he saw a throng of thousands coming after him, but he would have never escaped them if he'd tried. So he covered his face and braced for the assault. At that precise moment, they all disappeared, every single one of them, into thin air, leaving the hum of their teasing laugh ringing in his ears.

He resumed walking, picking up his pace. With some luck, perhaps he could outpace the maddening cacophony of their incoherent drone. A better idea occurred to him: squeeze out the sound. He cupped his ears and pressed hard. The effect was startling: the voices actually grew louder, and caused his ears to begin ringing, although he still could not make out a single utterance. He released his ears, and spun again, ducking simultaneously. His attacker, the one with the glistening machete, aimed for his ear, missed him and disappeared. Up stepped a woman, a half angel. Nothing about her was recognizable except the smile. The smile was Akosua's smile. She reached out a hand to him, and sighed the gentle sigh of a lover, and immediately a ball of fire shot out from her open mouth, barely missing his face. Her hands grabbed him and pushed into the skin of his arms, smashing his bones, and two serpents dove out of her eyes, recoiled for a moment, and shot out at him. Issuing a wailing cry, Kofi spun again, beating a hasty retreat that sent him stumbling at first, and began to run, surprised that the arms he thought were broken were swinging strongly and ably.

❦   ❦   ❦

Sylvester Preko wasn't entirely sure what he intended to do when he first aimed his gun. He hadn't been thinking at all. He had an initial feeling, caught somewhere between fear and hope, that since this was obviously an attempted robbery, great would be his personal reward if, in the telling of the foiled attempt, it was said that his swift and impeccable reaction had much to do with turning the perpetrators on their heels. So he had somewhat instinctively wanted to play the hero, under the watchful gaze of David Ofosu, the driver, who would have to tell the truth in his report, that it was to him, Sylvester, that all the accolades were due.

He should have reconsidered. For one they were jumping in and out of too many potholes for him to have imagined that he could possibly pick the target that was his focus. And that was not accounting for the fact that the target wasn't stationary, and that at his best he wasn't that good a shot. More importantly, he had to reach across David in order to fire his gun at the man coming towards them from the forest. When the first shot tore into the space of the attempted robbery, all thoughts left him. He lost interest in anything but the frightening awareness that the robbers were serious enough to be armed, and therefore prepared to kill or be killed. Panic swallowed him. Leaning back against the door on his side of the elephant, he aimed his gun, trying to pick out the man waving at them, and fired his first shot, just when it appeared that David was about to warn him about not firing his gun.

As soon as he fired the shot, Sylvester Preko recoiled in horror. At the moment of squeezing, the armored car hit another pothole. Neither he nor David had been expecting the jolt, their full attention distracted by the emerging figure from the bushes and the initial shot whose source they could not discern. The sudden jerk from the car hitting the latest pothole threw David slightly further away from Preko against the win-

dow on his own side, while also swerving David's arm inwards, so that just before the bullet flew off the mouth of the rifle, the opening was pointing directly at David's temple.

The gun cracked, pushing back with recoil against Preko's shoulder. He took the recoil firmly, but was thrown by drops of David's blood falling on him. His mind refused the sight before him at first, and much like everyone else caught in the desperate mayhem, Preko froze.

❈   ❈   ❈

The rest of it must have lasted only a few seconds, stretched out into a painful eternity. The surprise to Preko, beyond the shock of his unintended murderous act, was that when David took the unintended bullet, his head jerked away, spun half-way and fell with the rest of his lifeless body onto the steering wheel, while the deadweight of his feet sank into the gas pedal.

The car shot forward. Much as his mind screamed at him to do something, the pace of the drama was beyond the reach of his ability to react. He'd effectively gone limp, and sat frozen before the sight of his unintended act. Strangely, his first thought was that David had died without knowing that Preko admired him greatly, even though he was always giving the impression that he despised him. What was he going to tell his superiors about this? Would he go to jail for the act, even though it was an accident? Who would care for his wife and young child if he ended up in jail? Who would care for the family of David? Dear God, who would announce this tragedy to the family of David? Did David's family know that he was a noble man to the last? Did they care that he was a noble man to the last?

Before the avalanche of assaulting questions could release their grip on him, Preko caught another motion that drew his attention back to the road. The woman on the street appeared to have stirred. Preko's eyes bulged initially, as his mouth fell agape. Then, unable to stomach what was about to happen, he squeezed his eyes shut. Without knowing it, he began to scream. The contact came immediately after the woman had disappeared behind his squeezed eyes. There was simply nothing he could have done. Even then his mind opened a new assault on him with such fury he was not sure he would ever recover from it. He heard the sickening strike of the front iron bar against the woman's body, followed by what could have only been the breaking of bones as the massive front tires rolled over her.

Preko shot up. Now the new warning in his mind was that they were all going to die, every one of them, unless he did something, and did that something within the next breath. Shaking off the grip of paralysis, he stretched out a leg to step on the brake and straighten the course of the car. To do so, he grabbed the body of David without looking directly at his head and hauled the body off the steering wheel. The action spun the wheel, and threw the elephant off its previous course.

The car veered sharply, and was now heading in the direction of the secondary forest. That was only partly alarming, since the elephant certainly had the legs to navigate the secondary forest. Except that as the destination of their new course shot up to meet him, Preko noticed that the embankment was not only very short, it led to what looked to be a sudden and precipitous drop.

The order begun to ring in his head: "Stop the car, Sylvester! Stop the car! Stop the car, son of Preko!"

There was no apparent end to the nightmare in sight.

CHAPTER 13

*C*hris finally made it to Akosua, and had a simple wish for death. What he saw was the absence of love in its absolute starkest form, and it superseded the grimmest imagination contained in his mind. Akosua had been passed over by the four massive legs of the elephant while they stood watch. Something inside of him gave, and while he was aware that he was crying, Chris Agyekum could not hear himself, or for that matter feel anything about him at all. The only sense working was the eye beholding their judgment, and the faintest hint, from somewhere deep within, of the last remnant of the love they had shared.

On the day he told Akosua of his love for her, a potent love that he said was evidenced by the fact that he was the only one who wouldn't volunteer her to stop the elephant, he had wanted to know if she loved him. She had smiled kindly and affirmed that she did indeed love him. It had warmed his heart to hear that. Then he had sought clarity about this matter of her rejection of Kofi, which had always puzzled him.

"Why was he not good enough for you?"

"Oh it wasn't that," she'd said. "Love is a complicated matter sometimes."

"My mother used to say that it is only as complicated as we make it to be."

Akosua had hesitated for a while longer before she agreed, saying, "Sometimes the ugliness in the world around us blinds us to the possibility of beauty in front of us. I think I could have done my part to nurture something exceptionally beautiful with him. I think we could have transcended the ordinariness around us by creating something inspiring together, but I never understood that until it was too late. And all that time, while he waited, I kept waiting for the world to give me its approval, so I could live a dream. I kept waiting for the world to tell me that it had seen what I had with him and recognized it as beautiful. You're right, it never should have been very complicated."

He'd reiterated his point, that for all their professed wisdom, this was the one thing they weren't wise about, because they only understood love as a concept. The love for a nation, he said, was a different kind of love. It was love as an object. And none of them understood anything about love as an experience. He knew that, because his mother had constantly told him about it. He recalled—in what was the proudest moment of his whole life—that Akosua had looked at him with genuine surprise in her eyes when he said that.

"I know that I'm not as smart as you guys. And I don't really think that you should listen to everything I have to say. But I have learned some things in this life, you know? I am a bit slow, but I've lived for a long time. You learn some things. I have seeing all of you do some things that weren't smart at all. But I think that's a part of life, you know? And I don't think it means you're not smart. For example look at this idea to steal from the elephant. I think it's pretty dumb, to be quite frank. I see you're looking at me with surprise on your face, but I am smart enough to know that. I know it's dumb. I also know that it is worse than that.

"Edom says that Kofi's children expressed an open wish to be Agyei's children. Even if that was true, I think it was just a passing wish. Children have a lot of those. I bet you that Agyei's children, even though they have a father who can provide them with more things, probably have lots of moments when they wish they had a father like Kofi—a decent school teacher who lives a quiet life, surrounded by people who love him. I mean think about it, Akos. You know how people joke that Agyei's penis is one of the most widely distributed commodities in this town? Well, Agyei's children don't even know how many brothers and sisters they really have. Do you think none of this is of any consequence because people give Agyei false respect due to his wealth?

"Now we are going to steal. And that changes everything, Akosua. I know that I'm not too smart. Kofi was telling me the other day that the reality of life bites, and bites really hard. I won't argue that it doesn't. But does that mean that we have to become thieves? I mean, I hear you talk all the time about what's wrong with our town, with Ghana, with Africa. Okay, this stuff is really too high over my head. But how are we supposed to be helping by stealing? And how do we live with ourselves after we become thieves? I just don't understand it."

Tears had gathered in Akosua's eyes.

"So now we are going to steal all this money, and you have offered to put yourself in the way of the elephant. And nobody said no when you offered to do that. I mean, Akosua, isn't that really sad? I think I should have just left that day. I was so angry when Edom won't let me say what I had to say. He wanted the stage to himself, so he could say all those things about his growling stomach and everything. I mean, if your stomach is growling, I say go and eat some *gari* and *kyenam*. Everybody can afford some of that. But I think what he was saying was that people's stomachs are growling for expensive, showy things. That's what I think he meant. And then he's going on and on about how the way you and Kofi and Kwame have lived has been a failure. Why? Just because you don't have people lining up at your door with this faked admiration and respect for you the way they do with Agyei?

"I'm saying all this because I'm just really sad that we are now going to become thieves. We'll have the money, but who are we going to pay to buy our dignity back? And can the elephant carry enough money for that? Anyway, this is all I have to say. I wish they would have let me speak, but no one would listen to me. Well let me tell you something, Akos. I'm going to be there when the ambush takes place. I'm going to be there, and if I see anything I don't like, I'm going to do something about it—I don't care what anybody says or does."

By then he was in tears himself, for reasons he could not readily grasp. In his excitement his heartbeat had shot up several notches higher, and his head felt a bit light. He was furious—and he thought he understood a little bit of the reason why. By resorting to an act that invalidated the best of themselves, his friends were essentially invalidating his trust in them, and with it the very basis of his deeply rooted ties to them. And since his whole life had revolved around his relationship with them, they were practically invalidating his whole existence. He had finished speaking his mind and sat there, his chest heaving to meet his tears.

❧   ❧   ❧

As David had rightly pointed out, two guards rode in the back of the elephant. Shortly after the dual bumps that signaled the elephant passing over Akosua and the sharp turn that came with Preko's belated attempt to regain control of the car, the two guards riding in the back shot their way through the door and spilled out onto the road.

The first one to hit the ground and gather himself looked about in confusion. As his wits returned to him, he made out a man in the short distance, kneeling and crying over what appeared to be a human form. Without another moments' hesitation, the guard began to shoot, just before someone issued a plaintive wail to try and stop him. It was too late.

Three or four of the bullets the guard released found their mark, and Chris, the man kneeling over the human body that had been Akosua, collapsed on top of her, lifeless. Kwame, with a mournful scream, fired at the first guard and felled him. The second guard meanwhile was gathering himself from his own fall, just in time to see Kwame fell his colleague. He looked at once indignant and surprised that the robber appeared to be pleading with him to lay down his weapon. The two exchanged desperate fire from close range, and fell together.

As the force of the inevitable brought the final embrace of death upon them, Sylvester Preko tried, in one final desperate effort, to gain control of the runaway elephant before the circle closed. The lifeless body of David Ofosu, once again, refused cooperation, and then there was no time remaining at all. The armored car covered the final distance of level ground on the embankment and careened off the precipice.

❧   ❧   ❧

He hadn't been running long enough to have his heart squeal in such agonizing protest, but Edom understood just enough to know that this pain was inevitable and demanded the requisite courage from him to overcome it. It was more than mere physical pain. This was the deep hell that comes from tearing one's soul from its moral anchor on the blind hope of future restitution, a most damning experience when the door to tomorrow begins this sort of slow closing before watching eyes. This was a thousand pounds heavier than the worse physical pain he could bear. But in one part of his brain, the pain did not exist at all. This is where the push came from. This is where the command sprang from, to run with the enthusiasm of a child, buoyed by the instinct to save. He needed to live, but it wasn't entirely for selfish ends. He genuinely believed that he was the only one, by virtue of a particular wisdom denied the others, to set things aright.

His friends did not seem to understand him, especially in his harrowing, obsessed zeal to see the theft succeed at all cost. In their hearts, they had probably begun to entertain thoughts of him as a monster.

They did not understand. They did not understand anything at all. It was just as well. It will come to come them later. Here in this daunting time, he stood alone for something far grander than any of them had the imagination to grasp. He was the archangel Michael, descended through Marcus Garvey and Nnamdi Azikiwe—at least back when Zik had his thunder. He was the ghost that shocked back the forces of evil around them by providing them with the power to do all the good they had wanted to do with their lives. They did not understand him, but it was all right. They would understand when the time came. He was the redeemer they had never known, the one among them who first knew, long when none of them had developed the wisdom to even dream it, that they needed to lay claim to a piece of the national pie in order that they may realize the good they always wanted to realize. He would be the final word—Daniel freeing them from the jaws of lions. He was Shadrach, Meshach and Abednego all by himself, here to walk them through the burning flames of poverty and wasted lives. They would understand when the time came.

Surely they had to know, no matter how naïve and unsophisticated their thinking, that the end justifies the means for everyone, and that the rationalizations are simply that, rationalizations by which losers and winners seek comfort. But never has even the most remorseful winner been known to return the spoils. They were naïve now, but soon enough they would understand. They would finally understand that being good was never intended to be such a silly aspiration it precluded the necessity to fight for the just cause one desired. In a society of great suffering, in this land of constant crying, children die in shameful numbers and their mothers right after them, when they've had just enough time to savor the sharpest cut from the misery of their poor state. Who understands their suffering? Who truly cares for them? Infants are left to die the slow, painful death precipitated by their malnourishment, after they've lived just long enough to see the mean-spirited insouciance of human beings. That is the end result. And no matter the hell of the moment, somebody is a winner somehow, living grand and hording more than anyone could need. After that come the rationalizations, but the end result is not changed. So those who would do good must learn the way of ruthlessness for their good cause.

He was the good angel who would smack Lucifer, son of the morning, to oblivion. He would make this operation a success. He would free a lot of money for all of them. And because he knew their hearts, he knew he would have released some forces of good in the process. They would understand him when the time came. They would understand when they started to put their wealth to ends that replaced the tears on the faces of the little ones with broad smiles to lift the spirit. They would understand, because the winners always find ways to reserve sainthood to themselves in the telling of the story that accompanies the battle. So it was quite all right that they thought him obsessed by a terrible spirit in the drive to kill the elephant. They would understand when the time came.

❦   ❦   ❦

The register of gunfire from the direction of the elephant was disturbing. He told his mind not to even consider the possibility that Akosua had been killed. But he saw the elephant turn very sharply and race towards the embankment. He imagined that the sharp turn was the result of the effort by the driver to avoid running over Akosua. There was too much dust for him to see clearly, even though he was getting closer all the time. Then there was the register of more gunfire, much more than was needed if it had just been a warning shot.

Kofi burst onto the scene from the secondary forest out of nowhere at all. As Edom watched, Kofi spun and threw a couple of punches into the air over his head, then spun again and took a heavy fall. So pronounced was his disorientation he hit his face on the road. Without hesitation he jumped up, spun again, and then a sudden calm seemed to descend on him. Edom watched Kofi turn again from the scene of the robbery and come towards him. He was smiling a small, nondescript smile. Edom, utterly confused, waited for Kofi. He saw a frightening blankness in

Kofi's eyes, so unnerving it momentarily wiped away all his thoughts of being their savior. Kofi walked up to him, and looked at him, but did not seem to register any recognition. Edom entered a dream.

In it Kofi and a thousand ghosts walked in a procession, just like he was walking now, incapable of recognition of living souls. Lost ghosts, these ones. They walked the walk of sedation, absent the vibrancy of spirits who have lived and conquered their tests. They walked the walk of spirits no longer capable of claiming validation, and therefore banished to the fate of purposeless nomads. He wanted to call his friend out of the procession, for surely the truest love of even one friend should be enough to free a lost soul from this procession. But the caller would need to have a pure purpose, an understanding beyond material.

This was a lot of responsibility for one man. He could be the brave warrior and conqueror, the liberator. But was he to massage lost souls and play therapist as well, all in this same hot hell? And if he stopped to be one thing, did he not conceivably risk failing at the other task? It would be better to go get the wealth, the source of all this trouble, or at least make sure they were secured, then come massage the souls that needed massaging. Still, this was too much responsibility for one man to take on in one desperate stretch of time between heaven and hell.

The dream faded. Kofi had almost reached him. He was still smiling, and still there was no recognition in his eyes. Edom, more perplexed than before, tried to meet Kofi's smile with one of his own, as though he was afraid Kofi was putting him on even in this impossible moment. Nothing in Kofi's demeanor changed. He didn't seem to see Edom at all, much less recognize him, or his nervous smile. He simply walked on by in his happy sedated state, as Edom watched in dumbfound silence.

❦   ❦   ❦

For a few moments after Kofi walked past him, Edom considered going to him to stop him. He could sympathize. He remembered how it was when he was a youngster himself, back when he used to lose himself in the moments he got to spend with Antobam, who was dead at the time. In retrospect he could recall that he was very happy in those moments for reasons no one could have possibly understood. It was the only space in which he could meet Antobam, the only space his young cousin would come to see him for a visit. And there was so much ground to cover on each visit. They had to go over the good times, the numerous times when small, subtle events linked them in this inspiring love cousins have a way of reserving for one another. They had to play together during every visit, and eventually, towards the end of the visit, they had to replay the football game that would spell Antobam's end. They had to replay it for reasons that were not always very clear to Edom. Sometimes the ending of the game would be different; they would imagine that Antobam saved the back pass from Edom, and continued with his running commentary, and Edom would spend hours laughing over Antobam's increasingly imaginative names for the opposing team players. And then, just before Antobam would leave to end the visit, they would replay the actual ending: the ball bouncing over Antobam's attempted save, his panicked rise and blind pursuit of it, his sudden flight through the air.

Each time Edom would sink to his knees, his laughter seamlessly transformed to tears, and beg Antobam to forgive him. And the visit would end, always before Antobam would have responded one way or another. That Edom could recall, Antobam never forgave him before the end of any of his visits. He would be gone before Edom was done asking for forgiveness. Always. He could not remember that his cousin ever did last long enough on a visit to forgive him, no matter how long or short the visit But eventually he stopped visiting anymore.

All this nightmarish living had started with this awful event. He turned away from Kofi's departing figure and continued his race towards the scene of the ambush. Edom did not pause to cry over the dead bodies of Akosua, Chris, the two guards and Kwame. In his mind, nothing had gone wrong. They were on schedule, the wealth would be acquired, and there would be merry-making in a few months down the line. He followed the trail of the elephant past the embankment and down the steep precipice, careful to pay attention to the likelihood that the elephant might have spilled its cargo on its quarter-mile tumble down the precipice. All the way down the dangerous descent, the elephant had not spilled its cargo.

He found the elephant on its back. The driver had been shot through the temple, but the guard did not have any visible sign of gunshot wound. He was dead all the same. Edom was about to move to the back when something bid him to take a closer look at the driver. It was uncanny. The man looked just like a grown up version of Kofi's cousin, David Ofosu, whose parents had moved out of Mankraso many, many years ago, when David was still quite young. The resemblance was absolutely uncanny. He went to the back of the elephant and peeked inside. Puzzled, he brought his attention back to the environment around him, casting a quick visual net for something resembling a bag or anything that might possibly serve as a bag for transporting wealth. He saw nothing. He looked back into the elephant and saw what appeared to be four safe boxes welded into the body of the elephant.

"Oh!"

He climbed inside for an inspection, and stepped back from the safes. He climbed out of the elephant, checked his gun and aimed it. One after another, he shot open the safes. He took quite a few shots to successfully open each one. Once they were all loose, he climbed back into the elephant to manually open each one of them. Then he stepped back. The puzzlement on his face had not evaporated; it had actually deepened. He looked around him again. He went back to the safes and inspected them closely to ensure that there were no secret compartments around them. He looked inside them again, as though he could cause the materialization of something out of nothing, if only he looked long enough.

He stepped out again. Quite deliberately, he walked all the way around the elephant, and noticed that it had miraculously landed on a branch that had refused to be pushed into the earth, instead allowing a peak under it. He examined the spaces underneath, and having satisfied himself, he arose, his puzzlement intact. Edom began a slow panic.

Holding himself together, he began climbing up the precipice along the path of the elephant's fall. He made it all the way up, then came down again. Then, expanding the radius of his search, he climbed all the way up again, and returned to the elephant. Again he pushed the radius of his search and went all the way up again. On the way back down from the most extensive radius, he accepted that it was quite impossible for the cargo of the elephant to have been thrown that far off.

He went back to the elephant, climbed inside and looked into the empty spaces before him. The touch of heartburn was swift and deep. He felt the rush of blood to his head, and a spinning sensation, and then a rumble in his stomach foretold the beginnings of diarrhea. Edom stepped out of the elephant and looked about him. Picking out a sturdy, reasonably tall tree, he walked over to it and climbed as far as the sturdiest branch that could support his weight, then traced his visual search down the path of the elephant's fall. Finding nothing hopeful, he climbed down and went back to the elephant. He looked inside, very closely, at the empty spaces. His breathing had grown inexorably shallow. A sudden tightness gripped him by the heart and dropped him to his knees. A groundswell of emphatic condemnation, a sort of a closing in of a hostile spirit that had been bidding its time, pressed on him. Edom looked up into the vast skies above, searching for the face of God.

Then the softest whisper escaped him. "Why, dear God? Why?"

❧   ❧   ❧

If you traveled the main road from Mankraso in the direction of Kumasi, one of the small towns you would be sure to come across is Akwahu, known for its buoyant Wednesday and Saturday markets. People traveled from near and far to Akwahu on the market days, and typically doubled the population of the small town. Buyers and sellers bargained and bartered, for economic welfare as for the psychic fulfillment of social interaction with humanity. Along the main road through town, the distance from the chief's compound to the Roman Catholic Church covered a half-mile, littered by eateries and the small shops of small entrepreneurs. The actual town market sat in the plot beyond the Catholic Church, separated from the main church compound by a football field and a high cement wall that served the sole purpose, ostensibly, of keeping some of the boisterous market noise at bay. The peculiar Steve Netteh, a grown man whose devotion to the church verged on the fanatic, tended the church compound. Some thought he was truly insane, a man of great repression trying hard to mask away his deficits in pronounced adherence to Biblical rituals.

Steve Netteh was not insane. But in Akwahu madness was an easy label. Mad men and women did seem to show up out of the blue to mingle about on market days. Often no one paid attention to any of them, although just as frequently one trader or another will offer a mad person something to eat. Over time some of the mad men and women would become regulars, at least for a while, known to the traders by some given moniker. But the insane frequently left, as the insane are wont to do, especially when it would seem the most logical thing for them to stay. Such was the cycle of continuity in Akwahu that even the mad people who disappeared were shortly replaced by the arrival of some new mad man or woman.

No one among the regular traders at Akwahu's market could quite remember when this particular mad man appeared, no doubt because he kept such an uncommonly low profile for a mad man, and also because the sane do not spend their time pondering the appearance of the insane. He was a quiet mad man, this one, so quiet he walked among the sane as a ghost, virtually unnoticed. He did not beg, neither for alms nor for food, was never known to talk, and hardly ever shifted his eyes much when he found a spot somewhere near the market to sit. He was never seeing eating either, nor even drinking, which readily explained his disturbingly emaciated stature. It was as if the mad man was on a mission to starve himself to death.

Once in a while, some of the children of Akwahu, being so much more observant than the adults, would catch the mad man smiling to himself, often in the midst of an extended conversation with himself. Then, all in a second, his face would close, he would appear extremely confused, and tears would flow down his face. He would cry for a long time, but no one, save the observant children, would ever notice that the mad man was crying. There was no ready explanation for why the mad man, clearly a very private man, nonetheless preferred to sit around the market in his invisible space. Once, a child in the town watched as a trader, wanting the spot that the mad man was occupying, kicked the man and told him, in very harsh tones, to get up and away with his filth. She said Ghana had enough useless men as it were. The mad man's bones seemed to creak when he received the swift kicks.

He arose quietly from his perch against the wall and walked off a little way, then sat down. His measured distance did not appease the trader, who went after him once more. A string of expletives preceded her towards the mad man. She was threatening to inflict more punishment if the mad man did not get going. The mad man arose again, always lethargically, and walked away to a much farther distance. But by then he had gotten too close to another trader's space. He received another warning immediately after he had sat on the ground. This time when he arose, he walked casually until he was far separated from the bustle of the market, and found a spot under a lone tree by the winding path that led from the market place to one of the town wells.

The child who had witnessed the mad man's dismissal from the market approached him later on with another child, a close friend obviously. They must have been feeling sorry for him because they brought portions of boiled cassava and smoked herring for him. The sight of the two young girls startled the mad man initially. But he smiled when they stretched out their hands to offer him their token. For all their compassion, the young girls were clearly afraid of the weak man in front of them. The mad man took their offering, and uttered one of three statements anyone in the town of Akwahu ever heard from him. In the first instance he thanked the two girls. The girls backed away and stared at him, waiting for him to begin eating. But he did not appear to be in a hurry to eat.

"What's your name?"

The mad man looked uneasily into the eyes of the young girl, as though the question was by far his greatest source of pain.

"Do you have a name?"

The mad man nodded after careful consideration.

"Well, what is it?"

To that his face clouded. He had either forgotten his name, or perhaps was never sure what it was. His eyes stayed intently on the little girl before him, as he searched with great determination for the answer to the question put to him. Finally, a connection appeared to have been made. The confusion on his face cleared momentarily.

"Kofi Mensah," he said, hesitantly. "I think it's Kofi Mensah." After he'd said that, the previous uncertainty about his identity returned to cloud his face.

His answer was initially confusing to the two young girls, who could not seem to imagine how a man could have doubts about his given name. But they must have recalled that the man was a mad man, which eased their initial confusion. And at any rate they had already lost interest in the mad man, satisfied with their deed of compassion. They waved him goodbye and took off on their way, hopping and skipping playfully, with the mad man watching them with his perpetual, glazed over look.

An early riser walked the path from the market to the town well the next day. She was an elderly woman, but she was not old. Perhaps because it was so early in the day, she was shuffling her feet, and a tad too preoccupied with the two buckets she was holding to have noticed the obstacles as she approached the lone tree on the path, until she stumbled upon them. Her stumble was heavy and almost caused her injury, but for the fortune of experience that allowed her to use the buckets to good advantage. The woman opened her mouth as if to curse, but nothing issued, for she must have been keenly aware that in the dawn of the day, no sane soul curses to wandering spirits. She gathered herself for a moment before turning to investigate the obstacle.

The sight of the legs seemed to take her totally unawares. She leaned closer to be sure, and followed the legs up to the rest of the human form. Then she pulled back, her face a sudden mask of sadness. Setting her buckets aside, the woman went back to the body and, pulling the legs together, she set about shifting the body so that by the end she had straightened the dead man's gait alongside the path, not across it. She did not seem to mind that this was one of the mad men who passed through town. She would have to go to the chief's courtyard to announce the death. She took one of the clothes wrapped around her waist and covered the dead man with it. Then she said a short prayer for the soul departed, proclaiming quietly that, if the soul should return, it return with better fortune than the madness that had marked the end of its time in this particular cycle.

Finally she picked up her buckets and continued towards her original destination, to go get the water that needed fetching, for the cycle had to continue.

New Orleans–Kenya–New Orleans: November, 1998–August, 2000.

0-595-27128-6

Made in the USA
San Bernardino, CA
16 March 2015